SAVIOR

BLACKWINGS MC - DEVIL SPRINGS

BOOK THREE

BY

TEAGAN BROOKS

Copyright © 2019 Teagan Brooks
All Rights Reserved

No part of this book may be reproduced or utilized in any form or by any means, electronic or mechanical, including photocopying, recording, or by any information storage and retrieval system, without permission in writing from the publisher.

This is a work of fiction. Names, characters, businesses, places, events, locales, and incidents are either the products of the author's imagination or used in a fictitious manner. Any resemblance to actual persons, living or dead, or actual events is purely coincidental.

Adult Content Warning: This book is intended for readers 18 years and older. It contains adult language, explicit sex, and violence.

ACKNOWLEDGMENTS

Cover Design: C.T. Cover Creations

Cover Model: Chase Ketron

Cover Photographer: Golden Czermak

Proofreading/Editing: Kathleen Martin

Content/developmental Editing: Rogue Readers

Special thanks to Kathleen Martin, Melissa Rivera, Tina Workman, Jennifer Ritch, Katherine Smith, and Brittany Franks.

Dedication
To my friend.
Love you, mean it.
And to all the good guys who have had bad things happen.
You're still good guys.

CONTENTS

Prologue	1
Chapter One	5
Chapter Two	11
Chapter Three	18
Chapter Four	26
Chapter Five	29
Chapter Six	37
Chapter Seven	42
Chapter Eight	46
Chapter Nine	57
Chapter Ten	65
Chapter Eleven	73
Chapter Twelve	82
Chapter Thirteen	89
Chapter Fourteen	95
Chapter Fifteen	106
Chapter Sixteen	119
Chapter Seventeen	134
Chapter Eighteen	148
Chapter Nineteen	162
Chapter Twenty	172
Chapter Twenty-One	180
Chapter Twenty-Two	185
Chapter Twenty-Three	191
Chapter Twenty-Four	199
Chapter Twenty-Five	209

Chapter Twenty-Six	220
Chapter Twenty-Seven	226
Chapter Twenty-Eight	235
Chapter Twenty-Nine	243
Chapter Thirty	244
Chapter Thirty-One	246
Chapter Thirty-Two	254
Chapter Thirty-Three	261
Chapter Thirty-Four	271
Chapter Thirty-Five	283
Chapter Thirty-Six	296
Chapter Thirty-Seven	303
Chapter Thirty-Eight	311
Chapter Thirty-Nine	317
Chapter Forty	327
Chapter Forty-One	335
Chapter Forty-Two	347
Chapter Forty-Three	356
Chapter Forty-Four	365
Chapter Forty-Five	375
Chapter Forty-Six	385
Chapter Forty-Seven	398
Chapter Forty-Eight	406
Chapter Forty-Nine	417
Epilogue	424

NOTE FROM THE AUTHOR

The Prologue...It's emotional and might be difficult for some of you to read. I assure you, it was hard for me to write. But I did it because things like this really do happen. There's not always a bad guy to blame. Sometimes both parties are victims. Somewhere along the way, with the help of social media, a mob mentality has developed. People attack other people based on something they heard or read without knowing the full story. And they post nasty, hateful words that serve no purpose other than to fuel more hate. Bad things happen to good people. Don't assume. Don't judge. Be helpful, not hateful.

PROLOGUE

SAVIOR

Crash.

The sound of metal crushing metal on impact filled my ears while an unrelenting pressure against my chest held me in place. My neck snapped forward and my vision filled with a flash of white. Before I could make out what was in front of me, my eyes began to sting.

Something was happening, but I didn't know what and I needed to find out. I pushed myself forward only to be stopped by something holding me in place. I was tired. I closed my eyes and started to drift off when another loud noise caused my aching body to jolt.

"Hey! Hey! Are you okay? Can you hear me?" someone was screaming. "Hey! Fuck, man!"

Then another voice, or maybe it was the same one. "It's bad. We need help now! I can't get either one of them out! Please hurry."

My body started to shake. "Come on! Please! I need you to help me."

My eyes shot open, and I tried to take in my surroundings. My vision was blurry, and my eyes stung, but I knew right away I was in my truck. And the airbag had deployed. And I couldn't see anything other than my smashed-up hood through the windshield. What happened?

Fingers snapped in front of my face. "Help me!" a man I didn't recognize insisted and pulled on my door. I undid my seat belt and pushed against the door. It took a bit of force, but we got it open, and I climbed out of my truck.

"This way! We have to get him out," the man said and took off running.

I dazedly followed him, unsure of what we were doing. I looked around and wondered where I was when it hit me like a ton of bricks.

I'd worked late. I was driving home on the interstate. And then, nothing. My vision came back into focus and landed on the car in front of me. Suddenly, my adrenaline kicked in, and my body sprang into motion. I ran over to the car, and together with the man who'd helped me, we wrestled with the mangled car door until we finally pulled it open.

"Hey there! Sir! Can you hear me?" the man screamed.

I pulled out my knife and watched the man's eyes widen in fear. "Here," I said and held it out handle-first. "Cut the airbag and his seat belt so we can get him out."

"Yeah, yeah, that's a good idea," he rambled.

"Did you already call 9-1-1?" I asked.

"Yeah, as soon as I saw the accident. I didn't know if—"

I cut him off. He didn't know if we were dead. I didn't need to hear it. "Good. They should be here soon."

It seemed like hours, though it was only minutes. First, the fire trucks and an ambulance arrived. Then, the highway patrol. And then, at least ten more police cars showed up. Why? Because I'd fallen asleep at the wheel and crashed into a police cruiser.

I was completely sober.

I passed two separate field sobriety tests.

I passed the breathalyzer.

I offered to let them take my blood.

I wasn't speeding.

I was tired.

It was an accident.

But, hours later, none of that mattered. Because, accident or not, I'd killed a police officer.

CHAPTER ONE

Savior

I don't remember much of the first few days after the accident. I was extremely sore, and my chest had a nasty bruise from the seat belt; but, I didn't have any other injuries—not physically anyway.

While I laid on the couch in a complete daze, my grandfather hired an attorney for me, deactivated my social media accounts, and turned my phone off for a few days. But some of his efforts were too late. I'd already seen the comments about me on social media.

"Piece of shit was probably drunk or on drugs."

"I hope he rots in hell."

"Those babies will grow up without their father thanks to this asshole."

"It was intentional. He was targeting a police officer."

"Cop killer."

I refused to see or talk to anyone except Gramps, my lawyer, and the police officers working on the case. I didn't know what to do. How do you continue on with your life after something like that? I knew there was nothing I could do to change it, to make it right, but I needed to do something.

"Gramps," I called from the entryway to the kitchen. He whirled around, surprised to see me off the couch. "I want to go talk to her."

His face fell as he shook his head. "You can't, Kellan, and you know that."

"How can I not say anything to her?" I yelled. "I killed her husband. I should at least fucking say I'm sorry."

"That's not how this works, Kellan. You can't contact her right now, or ever for that matter. And, honestly, how do you think she would react to hearing your apology? Do you think she wants to talk to you? Because I sure as shit don't. No, you need to let her be and focus on dealing with your own issues," Gramps said firmly.

"Can I at least send some fucking flowers to the funeral home?" I asked with unnecessary venom.

"Yes, you can if you do it anonymously. And check your attitude, boy. I'm on your side."

I pinched the bridge of my nose and dropped my head. "I'm sorry, Gramps. I just don't know how to handle any of this. I know what it's like to lose a parent, and it kills me that I did that to those kids," I confessed.

"I wish I had some words of wisdom for you, but the fact of the matter is, there isn't anything you or I can do to make this better. Not right away. Just like when you lost your parents, it's going to take time for the hurt to lessen, but it's never going to go away completely."

***

Six Months Later

"Kellan," my grandfather called. "Come have a seat, boy. We need to have a talk."

I knew what he wanted to talk about. We'd

had the same discussion a number of times in the last few months. But, he was all I had for family, and I loved and respected him. So, I sat down and listened.

"I'll keep this short since we've been down this road several times now. I had lunch with Ranger last week, and we talked about you and your situation. He called today and said you've got an hour to get your ass over to the Blackwings MC clubhouse. You start prospecting for them tonight."

Was he serious? "I'm sorry, Gramps. What was that?"

"Phoenix Black is the President. He's expecting you. When you arrive at the gate, tell them who you are, and they'll direct you to him," he continued.

"Gramps—" I started.

"This isn't an option, Kellan. You're going over there, and you're going to put on that leather vest. I will not sit idly by and watch you guilt yourself into an early grave. I've already buried my wife, my daughter, and my son-in-law much earlier than I should have; I won't add you to that list. Even if I have to strap you to the roof of my truck and drive you over there myself, you will do this," he said vehemently.

I'd never seen Gramps so worked up. He rarely, if ever, got angry or raised his voice. I was so shocked by his outburst that I didn't even attempt to argue with him.

"Yes, sir. I'll get changed and head over there."

***

Gramps was right; joining the MC was the best thing for me. He knew I was spiraling downhill fast. Who wouldn't be? The guilt I felt about the accident was slowly consuming me.

I'd originally planned to get kicked out of the club; but after being thrown into the fray right off the bat, I discovered that I wanted to earn my patch and be a member of the club. I found another family—something I'd only had in Gramps since I lost my parents. The Blackwings quickly became my brothers, my family, and my home. But, there was another reason why I wanted to become a patched member.

After the first thirty days of prospecting for the MC, I started earning money for my assignments. It wasn't close to what the patched members made, and nowhere near what the officers got, but it was more than I was making working as an electrical assistant, which meant it was more money I could spend on Officer Parker's children.

Gramps and my lawyer forbade me from contacting the family, so I found other ways to make sure they were okay—or as okay as they could be. For two years, I gave them as much as I could. And even though everything I did was for them, it ended up helping me, too, by giving me a purpose.

Until the day I found out they were gone.

CHAPTER TWO

SAVIOR

I didn't realize how I'd changed since they disappeared until it was brought to my attention one afternoon.

"Savior, Phoenix wants to see you in his office," Badger said.

Being called to the President's office out of the blue was the adult equivalent of being called to the principal's office in the middle of class.

"Have a seat," Phoenix said from behind his desk. "You've probably heard by now that Coal is transferring to the Devil Springs Chapter.

He's going up at the end of this week, and you're going with him."

"Excuse me?" I asked in complete surprise.

"You heard me," he said and leaned back in his chair. "You're a good brother, and I hate to lose you. You take any assignment I give you, and you do it well, but your heart isn't in anything you do, and I think you need to get out of Croftridge. You're merely existing here. As the President of this club, it's my job to know everything about my members, but I didn't feel the need to share your past with Copper. I'll leave that up to you to decide when the time is right."

I sat in stunned silence for several minutes. "I can't leave Gramps," I blurted.

"Bullshit. Your Gramps is perfectly capable of taking care of himself. You've already moved out once, and he was fine."

I wanted to argue with him, but he was right. After my parents died, I lived with Gramps until I was nineteen. I moved out for a few years before moving back in with him. I didn't intend to stay as long as I did, but it turned out living with him as an adult was very different than it was when I was growing up, and it worked well for both of us.

"Listen, Savior, I'm not going to pretend to know what you're going through right now, but

I think this is the best thing for you, and your grandfather agrees. Go to Devil Springs and give it an honest shot. If you do that and it doesn't work out, you can come back here."

"I just don't see how things will be different there than they are here. My physical location doesn't change anything."

"Well, then, there you have it. Nothing changes. So, Devil Springs shouldn't be an issue," he said, effectively dismissing me.

***

A few days later, Coal and I trailered our bikes, loaded my truck, and headed to Devil Springs. The club had a rental house for us, but it wasn't going to be available for a few weeks. So, Copper worked out a short-term lease agreement with a nearby apartment complex. Thankfully, both the rental house and the apartment were fully furnished. The minimal amount of belongings Coal and I had between the two of us fell somewhere between comical and pathetic.

The club welcomed us with a party, but Copper didn't waste any time putting us to work. He wanted me and Coal to hang around the bar owned by the club to see if we could catch anyone running drugs through there. Not a bad assignment, per se. Just a little odd considering Coal wasn't old enough to drink, and I refused to put any alcohol in my body if I was going to be driving.

"You want to play some pool?" Coal asked.

I shrugged. "Might as well. We gotta be here for a few hours, and it's not like there's anything else to do."

There were three pool tables at the back of the bar, and they were positioned perfectly to give us a view of the entire bar, with the exception of the hall leading to the bathrooms.

As I expected, the bar was dead as hell. Regardless of what they did on the other six days of the week, most people in small southern towns didn't go out drinking on Sunday night.

It was much the same for the next two nights. Things picked up on Wednesday and Thursday, but not enough to make the time pass any faster. But Friday night was a different story.

Precious Metals went from having five customers to being packed in a matter of an hour. It didn't take long for the bartenders to become overwhelmed.

"Think one of us should go help them?" I asked Coal.

"No. Copper doesn't want anyone knowing we're associated with the club."

"I feel like an asshole just sitting here when I could be helping," I grumbled.

"Yeah, I do, too, but we're doing our job."

"Let's go sit at the bar. Between the two of us, we can at least keep the crowd back some," I suggested.

"Lead the way."

There was something about being a biker. Even when we weren't wearing our cuts, people just knew not to fuck with us. Well, most people did. There were always a few idiots who didn't get the memo.

A few hours later, the crowd thinned out to a more manageable size. I was still sitting at the bar when I saw her. She was at the opposite end of the bar staring into the glass in front of her. As people moved all around her, she kept her eyes fixed on her drink. And I kept my eyes fixed on the beautiful woman with long, auburn hair.

After several minutes, she picked up the glass and downed its contents before placing it back on the counter and staring at the bartender with her bright green eyes. Sam made his way over and briefly spoke to her before returning with another glass, which she immediately drained.

The pretty woman with the sad face was clearly on a mission.

Shit. It was none of my business what she was doing. People came to bars to get drunk for whatever reason. But I knew why I was drawn to her. Because she was alone. No one went to bars to drink like that by themselves. Everything inside of me was screaming at me to leave her alone. But I was given the name Savior for a reason, no matter how hard I fought it.

By the time I got my ass off the stool and went over to sit beside her, she'd had three more drinks. I caught Sam's eye and signaled for him to cut her off. I took a sip of my drink and kept my eyes facing forward when I asked, "You wanna talk about it?"

She didn't hesitate. "No," she said firmly.

"You meeting some friends here?"

"No."

"Can't let you keep drinking like that by yourself."

She scoffed. "You gonna drink with me?"

"No."

"Then go away," she said and waved her hand at Sam.

When Sam looked at me, I shook my head. "I told him to cut you off. You've had enough."

I expected an outburst and braced myself for it. What I did not expect was for her to throw some money on the bar, slide off her bar stool, and start attempting to walk to the front door.

"Where are you going?" I asked as I followed closely behind her.

"I'm leaving," she said.

"You can't drive. You're drunk."

"No shit, Captain Obvious. I'm not driving anywhere," she said with a slight slur. "I'm gonna walk."

"You can't walk home."

"You're kind of a buzzkill. You should go away."

"I'll take you home."

"Nope. Nu-uh-uh. Stranger danger. I don't wanna end up on the news. No, siree," she said and shook her finger at me.

"Go ahead and take her home. I'll finish up here," Coal said from my side.

"He's a good guy. Let him take you home," Sam encouraged. I didn't realize he'd followed us to the front door.

Surprisingly, she didn't argue. She nodded once at Sam, followed me to my truck, put on her seat belt, and let me take her home.

But then she came back the next night.

CHAPTER THREE

Avery

I was a mess, and I knew it. My kids had gone to spend most of the summer with their grandparents leaving me all alone. I didn't want to spend the summer without them, but a good friend convinced me that I needed some "me" time. And I wasn't handling it well. I was new in town and hadn't made any friends, but that was probably because I hadn't tried to make any friends. I was a single parent with two small children. I didn't have time for anything that didn't involve them.

After my mother picked up the kids, I spent the first night crying in my closet. Something about being tucked away in a cozy space was comforting to me. However, waking up the next morning with a crick in my neck and a dull ache in my back was not comforting. So, I found a different way to spend my unwanted free time.

Precious Metals was a small, locally owned and operated bar that was in walking distance of my house. All I had to do was walk past the trees lining my backyard, across the open field, and hop over a small creek to be in the lot behind the bar.

I managed to get a seat at the bar and drink in peace until some guy thought it was his duty to rain on my parade. I didn't know where he came from or why he was bothering me, but he wouldn't go away, and he was ruining the little bit of drunkenness I'd achieved. Then, the pain in the ass insisted on taking me home.

When I finally looked at him, I mean really looked at him, I struggled to contain my reaction. He was the most breathtaking man I'd ever seen in person. Tall and muscular with a chiseled jaw and a captivating smile. The bastard even had dark blonde hair and blue eyes. Or maybe they were gray. Either way, those eyes saw more in a few short seconds than I ever wanted anyone to see. And because of my need to get away from his penetrating gaze, and possibly my drunken haze, I allowed him to take me home.

He didn't say a word to me on the ride to my house, and I didn't say a word to him either. I put my address in my phone and let him follow Robot Sally's directions. He gave me a strange look when he pulled into my driveway three minutes later. I smirked and closed the door without so much as a thank you. I went inside and, once again, cried myself to sleep.

I should've just gone to the liquor store and drank at home. But, for whatever reason, I wanted to drink alone with other people around. So, I went back to Precious Metals and started drinking as soon as I got a seat at the bar.

A good two or three hours had passed, and I was well on my way to being drunker than a skunk when someone pulled a stool up next to me and sat down.

"You do this often?" a familiar voice asked.

I dropped my head to the countertop. "Do you harass all the people who drink here or is it just me?"

"Just the ones who drink excessively by themselves. Right now, that's you, sweetness."

My head shot up, and I tried to glare as the room spun. "Suck it, pretty boy."

"Yep, you're done," he said and got to his feet. "Let's go."

"You can fuck right the hell off. I'm not going anywhere with you. And you can't make me," I said and stuck out my tongue.

He grinned, and for a moment, I was captivated by the damn dimple that popped up on his cheek. But, the moment was ruined when he hoisted me over his shoulder and carried me out of the bar. At least he had the decency to use the back door.

"Put me down, you giant assface!" I screamed and did my best to kick him.

"Stop fucking kicking me. I'll put you down in a minute."

I continued to kick him and scream all sorts of profanity at him, but he kept going until he put me down on my front porch. "Open the door and go inside."

"Fuck you," I spat and started to cross my arms over my chest when he snatched the keys from my hand.

Within seconds, he had the door open and shoved me inside. "Sit," he barked and pointed to the sofa. "You need to eat."

Who in the hell did he think he was coming into my house uninvited and telling me what to do? I did not sit. I followed him into the kitchen, raising hell with each step I took. When I caught up to him, I grabbed his shirt and tried to pull him toward the door.

He didn't move an inch. Instead, he whirled around and grabbed me by my wrist. I stared into his fiery gray eyes as he glared at me. And something changed. My anger morphed into need as I became hyperaware of the situation—his big hand encircling my wrist, the way our chests brushed when either one of us inhaled, how much bigger he was than me, the anger in his eyes that matched the anger in mine.

I licked my lips and opened my mouth to speak but couldn't find the words. Frozen in place, I couldn't even make myself pull away from him.

His eyes flicked to my mouth and hardened. "Don't. Because I will fuck you. Drunk or not. And hear me now, sweetness, I won't be gentle."

"Will you hurt me?" I whispered, almost hopefully.

He cocked his head to the side. "Sounds like you want me to."

"Maybe a little."

Those three words unleashed a beast. He fisted my hair, yanked my head back, and crushed his mouth to mine. No one had ever kissed me like that. Not even close. It felt like he was trying to consume me, and I wanted him to.

He kept his mouth on mine as he walked me backward. When the backs of my legs hit the sofa, he reached for the button on my jeans. With sure movements, he had my pants and panties pushed down around my thighs. Using the hold he had on my hair, he turned me around and bent me over the arm of the couch.

There was no foreplay, no gentle caresses, no warning. The moment my hands hit the seat cushion to brace myself, he pushed himself inside of me. "Oh, shit," I breathed and dug my nails into the couch. He was big, and it burned. But I needed it to hurt, to be savage without an ounce of feelings involved.

His fingers dug into my hips as he roughly slammed into me over and over. The only sounds breaking the silence around us were the slap of his skin hitting mine and the involuntary grunts escaping from me. Until he started talking.

"This what you wanted?" he demanded, punctuating each word with a thrust.

"I-I," I gasped, earning a sharp slap to my

ass. "Yes!"

"That pussy was begging for a rough fuck," he said and slapped the other cheek. He leaned over me and lightly bit down on my shoulder. With his mouth still pressed to my skin, he asked, "You want more?"

Did I? I wasn't sure what 'more' entailed, but I was too far into it to care. "Yes," I moaned.

"Beg for it."

I pushed up on my arms and turned my head to tell him he could fuck right off, but the words died in my throat when he wrapped his hand around my neck and started to squeeze, all the while he maintained his rhythm. I began to panic, thinking I'd made the ultimate mistake.

"Please don't," I squeaked.

The hand around my throat moved up to squeeze my jaw and turn my head. He locked eyes with me and, without uttering a single word, I knew he wouldn't really hurt me. Keeping his eyes on mine, he slid his hand from my jaw to my throat and started to squeeze again. He applied more pressure as his hips moved faster. It was too much. I couldn't handle it.

"Come," he ordered and tightened his hold for a brief, terrifying second before sheer ecstasy overtook every sense of my being.

I was still basking in the pleasure coursing through me when he groaned long and low. He stilled after he reached his climax but didn't linger. I heard the sound of his zipper immediately after he pulled himself from my body. Then, he tossed the condom wrapper on the couch in front of my face and said, "Make better choices," as he walked through the front door without a backward glance.

CHAPTER FOUR

SAVIOR

I walked back to the bar with one thought on my mind. What in the hell had I done?

"Where've you been?" Coal asked.

"Took a drunk girl home."

Coal arched an eyebrow and studied me. "You look just like your dad right now."

He sat back and rubbed his chin with his thumb and his forefinger. "How about now?"

I couldn't stifle my laughter. "I've seen Copper do that, too."

He smirked but continued to rub his chin.

"So, you gonna share why it took you over an hour to walk a girl across the field out back and now you smell like sex?"

"Fuck," I exhaled and pinched the bridge of my nose. "Didn't mean to fuck her."

Coal laughed and slapped the table. "You didn't mean to fuck her? What kind of bullshit is that?"

I shrugged. "I meant it's not why I took her home. It just happened."

"You gonna see her again?"

"Nah. It wasn't like that," I said and changed the subject. "I haven't seen shit going on in here, have you?"

"Not a thing. Either nothing's going on, or people know who we are," Coal suggested.

The next morning, I stopped at a gas station to fill up before heading to the clubhouse. I had just stepped out of my truck when I saw Oliver Burgess walking out of the gas station with a pack of cigarettes in his hand.

Pulling the knife from my belt, I took quick steps to the oblivious prick. He looked up when I threw my arm around his shoulders and pressed the blade to his side. "Oliver! Long time, no see!" I shouted, then lowered my voice. "Get in the truck and don't give me any shit or I will gut you like a fish right where we stand."

When he hesitated, I pressed the blade harder against his side. "I'm not fucking playing."

He swallowed audibly. "Y-yeah, okay. I'll cooperate."

I was a little disappointed when he didn't put up a fight. Instead, he let me walk him around to the driver's side and stood perfectly still while I secured his hands behind his back. He didn't even try to kick me when I tossed him into the back seat.

I pulled up to the apartment I shared with Coal and called his cell. "I need you to come down to my truck."

"Be right there."

Coal blinked in surprise when he got in and looked in the back seat. "Nice catch. Where'd you pick him up?"

"Gas station. Didn't even put up a fight."

I didn't have much of a chance to think about Grace with the sad eyes over the next few days while we were dealing with club business. But once all was said and done, I ended up at Precious Metals. Grace was there, but she left as soon as she saw me. I shrugged it off and sat down to throw back a few drinks, because, fuck, it had been a long few days. And the more I drank, the more my resistance crumbled.

CHAPTER FIVE

Avery

I'd been crying since he left me laying ass up over the arm of my sofa. What had I done? It felt like I'd betrayed the memory of my husband, the man who was once the love of my life and my soulmate, even though I knew that wasn't the case. It'd just been so long since I'd experienced anything physical with a man that I was desperate for it. And as soon as I got it, I regretted it.

I ran upstairs to my bathroom and showered immediately, scrubbing my skin until it hurt.

Then, I screamed in frustration and started to hyperventilate. The pain in my chest made it hard to catch my breath, but I knew what was happening, and I let the panic attack have its way with me until the water ran cold. Then, I dried myself off and climbed into bed. I may have gotten a few hours of sleep over the course of the night, but it didn't feel like it when I woke the next morning.

And then I did the stupidest thing I could've possibly done. I went back to Precious Metals, took a seat at the bar, and started drinking. I told myself I was there to drink my troubles away and not to see him, but even I didn't know if that was true.

"We've been seeing a lot of you recently," the bartender observed.

"I'm sorta new in town," I mumbled.

"I'm Sam," he said and extended his hand. "I'm here most nights."

I shook his hand. "Hi, Sam. I'm Avery."

"So, Avery, how are you sorta new in town?" he asked as he made my drink.

"I moved here about ten months ago. My kids are spending the summer with their grandparents, so this is the first time I've been able to check things out."

"Ah, I see. Well, let me tell you something. Obviously, this is a bar, and we've got nothing against people drinking, but the Blackwings want people to be safe while they're partaking at their establishment. So, when you're ready to leave, let me have one of the guys walk you home."

"The Blackwings?"

"The Blackwings MC. You've not heard of them?"

"No."

"Local motorcycle club. They own the bar and a few other businesses around town—nice bunch of fellas. Most of them are ex-military. You keep coming in here every night, then you're bound to run into a few of them. Actually, you've already met the two that just walked in."

It was just like when someone tells you not to look and you automatically look. My head turned toward the door on its own volition and my eyes connected with a familiar pair of angry, gray ones. I quickly turned back to my drink and cursed under my breath.

"That's Savior and Coal. They're good guys," Sam said and patted my hand.

I forced a smile and nodded. "I'm sure they are."

I felt sick. I don't know what I was thinking earlier, but I suddenly knew I no longer wanted to see him. Quickly draining my glass, I kept my eyes on Sam so I could pay my tab and get out of there.

After what seemed like an eternity, Sam turned and brought me my tab. "Thank you," I said quietly and placed some cash on top of the receipt.

"Leaving so soon?" a deep voice rumbled from my side causing shivers to run up my spine.

"Yeah," I said with a nod. I couldn't bring myself to look at him, to see those eyes of his judging me.

"You don't have to leave because of me."

"Yes, I do," I said quietly, although firmly. I kept my head down as my feet carried me to the front door. As soon as I was in the clear, I bolted for my house.

***

Pounding on the front door pulled me from my restless sleep. Muscle memory had me reaching over to the other side of the bed only to find it empty. I sat up and waited to see if whoever it was went away.

Thud.

Thud.

Thud.

Pulling my gun from my nightstand drawer, I checked the chamber and held it by my side as I tip-toed down the stairs. It took a solid two minutes for me to find the courage to peek through the peephole.

When I saw who was on the other side of the door, I was pissed. "What the hell are you doing here?" I shouted.

"Open the door."

"No. Go away."

"I just want to talk to you for a minute," he said, and something in his voice, maybe a hint of a plea, had me slowly cracking the door open.

"This is as open as it's going to get. Talk."

"I'm sorry. About the other night."

"Sorry about what? Carrying me out of the bar? Fucking me? Fucking me like a whore? Walking away while you were still zipping up your pants? What exactly are you sorry for?" I spat and, damn, it felt good to release some of my anger.

He dropped his head and rubbed the back of his neck. "All of it."

I waited for more, but it became clear he

didn't have anything else to add. "Huh, usually excuses follow an apology," I observed.

"I have reasons, not excuses."

"What's the difference?" I asked, genuinely curious.

"A reason is an explanation. An excuse is an attempt to justify."

"Okay, well, um, goodnight," I said, unsure of what else to say.

He snorted. "You're not going to ask what my reasons are?"

I shook my head. "No, because I have reasons too, and I don't want to talk about them."

He gave me a curt nod. "Goodnight." I hadn't noticed how he was leaning against the column on my front porch until he straightened. When he turned to leave, he swayed and reached for the column again to steady himself.

"You're drunk," I said, stating the obvious.

He looked back at me over his shoulder. "I'm fine."

"You're not, and you know it. Come inside, and I'll make you some coffee," I said and opened the door without a second thought.

"You know how to use that thing?" he asked and nodded at the firearm in my hand.

"Yes."

"Is the safety on?"

"Nice try. Glock's don't have that kind of safety," I said and arched an eyebrow. "You coming in or not?"

He slowly blew out a breath. "Yeah, I'll come in for a minute."

"Have a seat. I'll start some coffee," I said and gestured to the sofa. And that's when I noticed the damn condom wrapper still laying in the exact same spot where he'd tossed it.

I felt my cheeks heat, but I didn't acknowledge it as I continued on to the kitchen where I proceeded to fumble, drop, or spill everything I touched. As soon as I pressed the start button, I felt his presence behind me. "Do I make you nervous?"

He was too close to me. I could feel the heat emanating from his body. "Y-yes," I stammered.

"Been thinking about your hot little pussy all day long," he whispered against the shell of my ear.

"Is that why you came over here?"

"No," he said, and trailed kisses down my neck. "I came over to apologize, but then you let me inside."

I pushed away from the counter and stepped to the side so I could turn and face him with a little distance between us. "I let you inside because you're drunk and need to sober up."

He studied me for a moment and smirked. "Nah, you want it. You just don't want to admit that you want it."

He hit the nail on the head with that statement, but I wasn't going to admit that to him.

He took a step forward. "I'll let you hurt me this time. You can dig your nails into my back and sink your teeth into my shoulder while I sink my cock deep inside of you."

My knees weakened, and I braced myself on the counter. I opened my mouth to tell him no, to tell him to leave, but that's not what came out. "I don't even know your name."

"Savior," he said and took another step. "And yours?"

I panicked for some reason and blurted my middle name. "Grace."

He grinned and closed the distance between us. "What's it going to be, Grace?" he asked and captured my lips with his before I could answer.

CHAPTER SIX

Savior

I don't know what it was about her, but I lost all control when we were alone. I managed to stop devouring her lips long enough for her to answer me.

"Yes," she whispered and pulled my mouth back to hers.

After pushing her tiny shorts to the floor along with her panties, I ripped her flimsy tank top from her body completely baring her to me for the first time. I briefly registered how thin she was before I realized she was struggling to push my shirt over my head.

When I reached for my collar, her hands moved down to unbutton my jeans. Her movements were almost frantic, causing her to fumble with what should have been an easy task.

I took over for her and started moving forward, forcing her to walk backward, while I undid my belt and jeans. I pulled a condom from my wallet and rolled it down my shaft just has her back hit the wall. Grinning, I hoisted her up and dropped her down on my dick in one fluid movement.

"Fuck," I breathed and buried my face in the crook of her neck while I started thrusting into her.

She tightened her legs around my waist and dug her fingers into my shoulders. "Harder," she groaned.

I moved my arms under her knees and slid her legs up toward my shoulders. With my hands planted firmly on the wall, she was damn near folded in half while I pounded into her.

"You gonna come? Or do you need me to turn you around and smack that ass again?"

"Yes," she moaned.

I used one hand to reach down and firmly

grip her ass cheek before I drew back and landed a sharp slap that echoed around the room.

And that did it. As soon as my hand landed, her pussy was rippling and pulsating around me.

I continued my rhythm while she rode out her orgasm before I picked up the pace for mine. Sweaty and sated, I carefully lowered her to the floor. After tossing the condom in the trash, I righted my jeans and pulled my shirt over my head.

When I turned back to her, she was already dressed and staring at the floor. "Well, looks like I don't need that coffee now," I said and walked out the front door without another word.

This went on for a couple of weeks. Sometimes she came to the bar, and I took her home and fucked her before I left. Other times, I knocked on her front door late at night, fucked her, and went home. We never said more than a few words to each other, but what we were doing was working for us. I knew it wouldn't last, but I had every intention of enjoying it while it did.

Then, one night, I stopped by Precious Metals on my way back from visiting Gramps and found her sitting at the bar. I was exhausted, but being back in Croftridge had me feeling antsy, and I needed an outlet. So, I took her home, we drank a little, we fucked, and then we fell asleep on her couch.

Crash.

The sound of metal crushing metal on impact filled my ears while an unrelenting pressure against my chest held me in place. My neck snapped forward and my vision filled with a flash of white. Before I could make out what was in front of me, my eyes began to sting.

I bolted upright, breathing heavily and covered in sweat. That fucking nightmare. It happened every night at first, but had lessened over time to once or twice a month. I hadn't actually had one that I could recall since I'd moved to Devil Springs. Wiping the sweat from my brow, I carefully moved Grace so I could wash my face off before I left.

I made my way down the hall looking for the bathroom. I'd never been anywhere in her house other than the living room or the kitchen. Once I found it, I took a piss and then splashed some cool water on my face.

Fuck, I hated that dream. It always messed me up for a day or two afterward. Ready to get the hell out of there, I dried my face off and yanked the bathroom door open only to freeze in horror. The picture hanging on the wall across from the bathroom was of two small children I knew very well. They didn't know me, but I knew everything about them. Because I was the one responsible for ruining their lives.

Oh, fuck! I whirled around and dropped to my knees just in time to vomit into the toilet.

How could I not know it was her?

It was her.

She didn't look the same. She was so thin.

Because I ruined her life.

I'd been dicking down the wife of the man I killed.

And she let me.

Each horrific realization was followed by another burst of vomit until my stomach was actively trying to hurl itself out of my mouth. I had to get out of there. I didn't even bother to rinse my mouth out. I hit the lever on the toilet with so much force I probably broke the damn thing as I got to my feet and bolted for the door.

I didn't give a shit what time it was. I fired up my bike and roared out of her quiet neighborhood without looking back.

CHAPTER SEVEN

Ranger

I was sitting on my favorite bar stool at the clubhouse watching the boys dart in and out of Phoenix's office while trying to decide if I wanted to see what had them running around or wait for them to come to me. After finishing my lunch, I decided to go see what in the hell was going on.

"Byte's trying to find the last location on his cell phone right now," Phoenix said into his phone.

"What's going on, Prez?" I asked and took a

seat without waiting for his invitation. He might be the President, but I was around when he was in diapers, so I commanded a level of respect the others didn't.

"We can't find Savior anywhere. Coal thought he might be sick because he hadn't come out of his room since the day before, but when he went in to check on him, he wasn't there. No one's seen or heard from him in almost twenty-four hours and his phone's turned off. Last time anyone saw him was when he left Precious Metals to give some girl a ride home."

"Shit," I cursed and pushed to my feet. "I know where he is."

"Where?" Phoenix barked.

I turned back to my Prez slowly and raised one eyebrow. "If you think about it for a minute, you'll know where he is, too. I'll go get him. You fuckers stay here. He don't need everybody seeing him like this."

"Fuck," Phoenix hissed. "Should I—?"

"No, don't do anything. I'll bring him back," I said and hoped like hell I could bring him back in more ways than one.

Twenty minutes later, I found him right where I thought he'd be—well, almost where I thought he'd be. Instead of sitting between his parents' graves, he was sitting beside the headstone of Officer Ian Parker, with an empty bottle of Jack beside him and a half-drunk one in his hand.

I watched him for a few minutes before I slowly made my way over to him. He finally noticed my presence and looked up at me with red-rimmed, bloodshot eyes. Making a grand gesture with his arm, he splashed liquor all over himself and the ground. "I killed him, and then I fucked his wife."

"Yeah, I figured it was something like that."

He shook his head. "No, no, no. See, I mean I fucked her. Like bent her over the couch, fucked her, and walked out while I was still putting my dick away. And then I did it again and again and again—"

He was going nowhere fast, so I cut him off. "Listen, I hate to say it, boy, but it probably would've been easier on you if you had been at fault. You'd be paying your penance with a prison sentence. But that's not what happened. And here you are, wallowing in your grief instead of living up to the name I gave you."

When he didn't respond, I continued, "You didn't earn the name Savior just for saving my grandbaby, though that was reason enough in my book. No, your Gramps told me all about what you've been doing for those kids and their momma. Working your ass off to give them every extra cent you had. And I knew the minute they left town because you changed. It's why I suggested that Phoenix send you to Devil Springs."

"What the fuck, Ranger?" he roared and got to his feet. "You should've fucking told me! You had no right to mess with my fucking life!"

"Be pissed. I did what I thought was right and I won't apologize for it. You wanna take a swing at me, boy? I'll let you have one, and then I'm going to put you on your ass right here in the cemetery."

CHAPTER EIGHT

Savior

I was so angry—at him, at myself, at the universe—that I didn't care about anything anymore. So, I took a swing at a man I loved and respected. And the motherfucker lied. He didn't let me have one. He dodged my punch and cold-cocked me with a left hook that I never saw coming.

When I came to, Ranger extended his hand to help me get to my feet. "I'll take you to your Gramps's place."

I let him help me up and rubbed the side of

my head once I was on my feet. "Thanks, man, but I can't go to Gramps's like this," I said and swayed on my feet.

Ranger studied me for a few long moments before he nodded. "Yeah, I suppose you're right about that, but you're coming with me anyway. You're in no shape to ride right now."

"Wasn't planning on riding anywhere. I was just fine where I was until you showed up," I mumbled.

"You weren't fucking fine, and you know it. Now, get in the damn truck and try not to puke."

I dropped into the seat and closed my eyes. As soon as he put the truck in gear to move, I felt like the world was spinning, and my stomach started to churn. I fought it for as long as I could, but it was futile. "Fuck, pull over."

Ranger pulled the truck over like his ass was on fire and barked, "Out!"

I pushed the door open and fell out onto my hands and knees where I proceeded to puke up a disturbing amount of alcohol with such force I almost choked.

My head shot up when I heard an unmistakable sound, "What the fuck are you doing?"

Ranger put his phone back into his pocket

and crossed his arms over his chest. "Taking a picture so you can see how pathetic you look when you're sober enough to process it."

"Fuck you! I didn't ask you to come get me!"

"No, you fucking didn't. Your brothers were coming. And don't you dare forget that I'm one of those brothers. This is what we do. Now get your ass up and get in the truck."

I couldn't get up. I didn't want to get up. Ever.

A meaty hand firmly gripped my bicep and pulled me to my feet. And I lost it. If Ranger hadn't been holding me, I would've dropped to the ground again as sobs wracked my body. Ranger held me against his chest like I was a child. He was a silent pillar of strength as every soul-crushing moment from the last few years came pouring out in torrents.

"About time you let some of that shit out. You've been dealt some shit cards in the last few years. Wasn't none of it your fault, but I know that doesn't make it any easier," he said.

I didn't respond. There was no need to because everything he said was absolutely correct, especially the part about it not being easier. Finally, he turned me by my shoulders and helped me into the truck.

I should've asked where we were going, but I assumed he was taking me to his place. I didn't even open my eyes when his truck came to a stop until I heard a small child shrieking, "Papa!"

After the piercing pain in my head lessened, I cracked one eye open and groaned, "Fuck."

"We weren't expecting you. Is everything okay?" Keegan asked her grandfather.

"Uh, Gabby, go on inside, and I'll be there in just a minute," Ranger said and placed the little girl on her feet.

"Shaky Jakey, Papa's here!" she squealed as she ran to the house.

"Everything's fine. Savior needs a little help, though. Will you send Shaker out here?"

"Of course. Is there anything else I can do?" she asked.

"He needs something to eat and will probably need a change of clothes."

"No problem. Let me get Jacob, and then I'll make him something to eat," Keegan said.

A few minutes later, I heard Shaker and Ranger talking quietly. Then, the passenger side door was yanked open. "Holy shit, I think I could get drunk just from the fumes coming off you," Shaker said and made a show of waving his hand in front of his face. "Can you walk?"

"Not sure," I grumbled. I managed to get to my feet and followed him to his garage.

"Welcome to my man cave. You can have a seat after you change clothes," he said with a laugh.

I looked down and noticed the splatters of vomit on my shirt and jeans. Without giving it much thought, I ripped my shirt over my head and dropped my jeans to the floor. "I'm not going to stay upright much longer," I confessed and dropped onto the sofa.

Keegan opened the door to the garage and gasped. "Why is he naked?"

"He's not naked. Did you need something?"

"Uh, Ranger said Kellan needed something to eat. I brought him a sandwich and some chips. Does he need some clothes, too?" she asked.

"He's right here. Clothes or a blanket would be great. It's freezing in here," I said and rubbed my arms.

Keegan returned a few minutes later with some drawstring pants and a T-shirt for me to wear. She'd also brought me a blanket. "Thank you," I said.

"Any time. I'll be inside if you need anything," she replied, though it was directed at her husband.

Shaker sat down in a recliner across from me and crossed his arms over his chest. "You want to tell me what in the hell is going on?"

I shook my head. "Want to? No. But I guess I have to."

"You don't have to tell me shit if you don't want to, but I'm guessing Ranger brought you here because he thought I could help."

I sighed and pinched the bridge of my nose. "You remember hearing about the cop that died when his patrol car was hit two years ago?"

"Yeah, if I remember correctly, they said the driver fell asleep."

"I was the driver," I said flatly.

Shaker sucked in a sharp breath. "Fuck, man. Why didn't you ever say anything?"

I snorted. "It's not something I enjoy talking about."

"Yeah, I get that. I've been through something similar," he said. "When I was deployed, my unit was assigned a certain area to patrol. We'd been there for over two weeks with little to no activity. Then, one night, this car came by and circled the area a few times. We reported it and received the order to take them out. Since I was a sniper, that job fell on me. I didn't hesitate to kill both men in the car." He paused and rubbed the back of his neck. "Hours later, when we searched the car, we found two eighteen-year-old boys with a trunkful of fruit. We never figured out what they were doing, but it looked like they were innocent. And they were dead because of me."

"I'm sorry that happened, man, but it's not the same. You didn't have a choice; you had to follow the command you were given."

He nodded. "Yeah, just like you don't have a choice when your body falls asleep."

I sat up and opened my mouth to argue, but he continued, "If sleeping was a voluntary action, the world wouldn't be full of people with insomnia. You can't tell me you've never tried to fall asleep and couldn't or tried to stay awake and couldn't."

Well, shit. I'd never thought about it like that, but it still didn't change anything.

"I fucked his wife," I blurted.

Shaker's eyes widened, and he made a faint choking noise. "You what?"

"I didn't know it was her. I only saw a few pictures of her right after the accident. She looks completely different now."

"You didn't recognize her name?"

I shook my head. "She said her name was Grace. The wife's name is Avery."

"How'd you figure it out?"

I sighed. "I fell asleep on her couch after I finished fucking her. Went to take a piss before I left and saw a picture of her kids hanging on the wall."

"Shit," he cursed. "You think she knew who you were?"

I shrugged. "I have no idea. If she did, I don't know what her game plan was. Doesn't matter anyway. I'm not going to see her again."

Shaker nodded. "That sounds like a good plan. But listen, man, you can't let this shit continue to eat you alive from the inside out. You've got to find a healthy way to deal with it."

"I'm not going to counseling," I stated. Gramps had already tried to get me to start therapy right after the wreck. I just couldn't do it. I couldn't bring myself to discuss my deepest and darkest of truths with a complete stranger—a stranger I was paying.

He pulled out his phone and quickly typed something before putting it away. "I just sent you Harper's contact info. She's a great therapist, and she's helped me deal with some of my own shit. Before you say no, think about it. No one has to know, and what could it hurt?"

I'd heard Harper was an excellent therapist,

but going to her with my own problems had never crossed my mind. If I was being honest with myself, I wasn't sure I wanted help.

"In the meantime, I think you need to find a way to channel your anger."

"I'm not angry."

"Yeah, you fucking are; you just do a damn good job of suppressing it. By the looks of it, I'd say you use alcohol as one way to hide your emotions."

"When did you become the all-knowing biker Yoda?" I snapped.

He laughed. "I'm not giving out all my secrets today."

The garage door opened and Keegan stuck her head in. "Sorry to interrupt, but, um, I need you to come inside. Right now," she said, and Shaker instantly got to his feet.

"What's wrong?" he asked as he followed her inside. Instinct kicked in, and I got up to see what was going on as well.

"Look, Jakey! Cheese and Whiskers had babies!" Gabriella squealed in excitement. "And they're pink!"

"Ranger!" Shaker bellowed.

Keegan started to laugh but slapped her hand over her mouth. "As soon as he saw them, he ran out of here like his pants were on fire."

"Yeah, I bet he did since he's the one who bought her two 'male' mice. I wonder if Copper and Bronze could feed them to Slither and Squeeze," Shaker mused.

Gabriella screamed in horror as tears ran down her face. "No! You big meanie!" Then, the spunky little girl junk punched Shaker with all of her might.

"Fuck," he groaned and hunched over while he cupped his balls.

"Tell him no, Sissy!" Gabriella wailed. "You won't kill my babies!"

Shaker's head shot up, and his eyes filled with pain. "I'm sorry, Gabby," he croaked. "It was a bad joke," he said and dropped down to his knees. "You can keep them all if that's what you want," he said and held his arms out to her.

Gabriella glared at Shaker for several moments before Keegan nudged her forward. "I'm sorry, sweetheart," Shaker said while he smoothed her hair and tried to comfort her.

"Hey, little slugger, where'd you learn to throw a punch like that?" I asked, hoping to distract her.

She pulled back and smiled proudly. "Papa taught me. He said if a man ever tried to make me do something I didn't want to, all I had to do was punch him in his zipper."

"Wifey, we're going to have to have a talk with your grandfather," Shaker grumbled.

Keegan was trying to hold in her amusement, but she cracked when I openly laughed. "I'll talk to her about it," Keegan promised. "Gabby, let's go find out what we need to do to take care of baby mice. Then, we need to go to the pet store and get another cage, because Cheese and Whiskers can't live in the same one anymore."

"But they're married, and they love each other. You can't make them get divorced," Gabriella said as they left the room.

Shaker chuckled and got back to his feet. "That kid can throw a punch."

"Looked like it."

"Speaking of throwing punches, you ever thought about getting into sparring or boxing at a gym? Hell, even just going to town on a punching bag is a great way to relieve some stress," he suggested.

I shrugged. "No, but I'd rather try that than talking to Harper."

CHAPTER NINE

Avery

Several weeks passed with no sign of Savior. We fell asleep on the sofa one night, and when I woke up, he was gone. I'd been back to the bar a few times hoping to run into him, but he was never there. I spent an embarrassing amount of time trying to figure out how to cross paths with him again before I realized I had something much bigger to focus on.

"Mommy!" my babies squealed as they came through the front door.

I knelt down and wrapped my arms around both of them. "Oh, I missed you so much! I'm so glad you're home. Did you have a good time?" I rambled through my tears.

They both started to chatter at the same time, rushing to tell me all about their summer vacation with Nana and Papa, who were grinning from ear to ear.

"You two go put your things in your room, and I'll get dinner started," I told them.

My mother followed me into the kitchen while my dad dropped onto the sofa and turned on the television. "How are you doing, honey?" she asked in a concerned tone.

"I'm okay," I answered quickly and started pulling things from the pantry.

"You don't look so good."

"Thanks, Mom," I replied sarcastically. Truthfully, I hadn't felt well in over a week, but not so much that I felt like I needed to go to the doctor. Since my husband died, I slept like shit, so I never truly felt great.

"I mean it, Avery. A mother knows when something is wrong with her child. What's going on?"

I shrugged. "You know I don't sleep so well anymore. It was a little worse with the kids gone."

"Honey, we could've come back early, or you could've joined us. I thought you wanted some time to yourself," she said.

"I did, Mom. I haven't felt great for the last day or two. I don't know; maybe I'm coming down with something."

"Well, go sit down. I'll take care of dinner," she insisted and shooed me away.

"Thanks, Mom. I'm going to go lay down until dinner's ready."

I felt like shit leaving my mother to cook dinner for my children when she'd been doing it all summer, but I was suddenly overcome with exhaustion.

The moment I crawled into bed, a wave of dizziness hit me and cold beads of sweat formed on my forehead. I closed my eyes and tried to remain as still as possible while taking slow, deep breaths. I had just gotten my nausea under control when my mother entered the room.

"Avery!" she gasped, and then I felt her cool hand on my forehead. "Frank! Bring me a glass of ice water and my purse!"

Mom's hands disappeared, and I heard the water running in the bathroom. Seconds later, she returned with a cool washcloth for my face.

"What's wrong, dear?" my dad asked.

"Avery's sick. Can you get the kids started on dinner?" she asked.

"Of course," my dad said and pressed a kiss to my forehead. "Let your mom take care of you, peanut."

"Here," my mother said and thrust something at my face. "You need to eat."

"I can't eat right now," I groaned and pushed her hand away.

"Honey, you need to try to eat something," she insisted.

"Mom, if I try to eat anything right now, it won't stay down for long. I'll try to eat something in a little bit. I just want to go to sleep."

"Okay, honey, but I'm going to stay right here with you. Your dad can handle the kids for the evening."

"Okay," I mumbled and drifted off to sleep.

I woke with the unmistakable feeling of impending vomit and bolted for the bathroom. I barely made it before what little was in my stomach came out followed by horrendous dry heaves. When it finally stopped, my mom helped me get cleaned up and back into bed.

For the next two days, all I did was sleep, wake up to puke, and go back to sleep. On the third day, I jumped out of bed and started for the toilet, but a wave of dizziness washed over me, and I hit the floor before I made it to the bathroom.

"Frank!" my mother screamed. I could hear the horror in her voice, but I couldn't make myself respond. Instead, I succumbed to the darkness.

Buzzing, beeping, and whispers woke me. Opening my eyes, I glanced around the brightly lit room in confusion. "Mom?" I croaked when my eyes landed on her.

"Avery!" she gasped. "You scared the shit out of me. How are you feeling, sweetie?"

"What's going on?" I asked.

My mother covered her mouth with one hand and shook her head while holding up one finger with the other. When she composed herself, she said, "You fainted and wouldn't wake up. You were so cold and still. I thought—" She shook her head again. "I thought we'd lost you."

"What? Where are the kids?" I asked and felt the panic rising. My babies would be terrified if they'd witnessed any of it.

"They're with your dad. They didn't see anything," she reassured me. "We told them I was taking you to the doctor."

Right on cue, a doctor entered my room. "Mrs.

Parker, I'm Dr. Alvarez. How are you feeling?"

"Like shit," I answered honestly.

She smiled kindly and nodded her head. "We'll see if we can do something about that. How long have you been sick?"

"Just a few days."

"I see," she said and directed her attention to Mom. "Ma'am, I need to do a quick physical. Would you mind stepping outside for just a moment?"

My mother whirled around and looked at the doctor as if she'd asked her to step outside naked. "Mom, it's fine. Go get some coffee or something," I suggested.

"Well, if you're sure, I could use a fresh cup of coffee."

As soon as my mother left the room, I asked, "What did you find? I'm only twenty-six. I'm too young for cancer. Wait, is it cancer? Am I dying?"

Dr. Alvarez shook her head. "No, we didn't find any cancer. And, technically, everyone is dying, but we didn't find anything to indicate death in your near future. I'm sorry if I scared you, but I've made it a policy to only deliver test results to the patient without an audience. With that said, you're severely dehydrated, you have a UTI that has spread to your kidneys, and you're pregnant."

If she'd told me aliens had landed and used magic to make pigs fly, I would've been less shocked. "That's not possible," I whispered.

She arched an eyebrow. "Do you have a uterus?"

"Yes, but—"

"Are you sexually active?"

"Fuck," I breathed.

"Yep, that's how it happens."

"I can't be pregnant," I cried. "I can't be."

She cleared her throat and lowered her voice. "Were you sexually assaulted?"

I gaped at her. "N-no, I wasn't. I'm just, I mean, this wasn't planned. Like at all." I cupped my hands over my face. "I don't know what to do," I whispered.

"You don't have to make any decisions at this time. Right now, we're going to treat your kidney infection and get you rehydrated. Your mother said you have two children; did you have severe morning sickness with either of those pregnancies?"

I shook my head, still reeling from the news. "Uh, no, not anything like this."

"Okay, well, we're going to keep you overnight to get some fluids and antibiotics in you. We'll also give you something for nausea. When you can keep food and oral antibiotics down, we'll let you go home," she explained.

"Thank you," I said. "Um, I would like to keep the news to myself for the time being."

"Absolutely. It's against the law for healthcare workers to discuss your medical information without your consent."

"Knock, knock. May I come in?" my mother called from the other side of the door.

"Yes, ma'am. We've just finished up. I'll go put some orders in for you. We'll also let you have some clear liquids and see how you do with those before letting you have anything heavier."

"Thank you, Dr. Alvarez."

"Well, what did she say?"

I sighed. "She said I have a UTI that has turned into a kidney infection and I'm severely dehydrated. They want to keep me in the hospital until they're sure I can keep the pills down," I explained.

"Oh, thank goodness it's something simple."

"Yeah," I said solemnly. It was anything but simple.

CHAPTER TEN

Savior

I tried to make sure I stayed busy because, whenever I wasn't, I found myself thinking about Avery Grace and her children. I would always look for ways to help the kids; it was just something I needed to do, but having any kind of relationship with her was out of the question—not that it was ever my intention in the first place.

I started hitting the gym hard. Coal began tagging along after the first week, and soon after, Grant joined us when he could. We hit the gym at least five days a week, and it was starting to show. The three of us were getting bigger, and my overall mood had noticeably improved.

I was just coming out of the locker room after my shower when a guy I didn't know stopped me. "You got a sec?" he asked.

"Nah, man. I gotta be somewhere in a few minutes."

"Wanted to know if you and your boys were interested in an opportunity to make some extra cash?" he asked, and I was instantly on alert.

"Appreciate the offer, but I'm good," I said and moved to step around him.

"Really? You don't want to know how you can make ten grand in less than an hour?"

"Nope. Cause chances are it's not legal, and that's not my thing," I said and continued on my way.

"What did he want?" Coal asked when I stepped outside the gym.

"Wanted to know if I was interested in making ten grand in less than an hour."

Coal snorted. "Shit. Are you serious?"

"Yeah, man. Told him thanks, but no thanks. Don't think he liked my answer, though."

"He's a recruiter," Grant said from the back seat.

"For what?"

"They have fights in the basement. He recruits new contenders," he explained.

"Underground fights?" I asked.

Grant nodded. "Yeah. They have one every other weekend, I think. I've never been to one, but I've heard they're brutal."

I glanced over at Coal before I focused on the road. "How long have they been doing this?"

Grant shrugged. "I don't know. The first time I heard about it was a few months ago."

After that, Coal changed the subject until we dropped Grant off at his place. He lived in the same complex as us, but his apartment was at the front of the complex while our building was near the back.

"You think we should tell Copper about the fights at the gym?"

"Yeah, I do. I doubt he knows about them, and I'm pretty sure he won't be happy knowing they're trying to recruit his members," I said. "But I think it can wait until the next time we're at the clubhouse."

"You think we should find another place to work out?"

I shook my head. "No. I like working out there, and I'm not going to let some slimy motherfucker keep me from doing what I like," I stated.

***

The following Friday, we were at the clubhouse for the monthly meeting with all the members. When Copper asked if there was anything that needed to be discussed, I stood from my seat and cleared my throat. "A guy from the gym where Coal and I work out tried to recruit us for the underground fights held there."

Copper's jaw tightened, and his hands clenched into fists. "And what did you say?"

I shrugged. "I told him thanks, but no thanks. He didn't seem happy with my answer."

"Is it that new place off Jefferson Street?" he asked. "I think it's called Pumpers."

I chuckled. "I didn't know it was new, but yeah, it's Pumpers off Jefferson."

"It's not exactly new. It wasn't turning a profit, so the previous owners shut it down. Somebody bought it and reopened it a few months ago," he explained.

"Yeah, Grant said he heard about the fights a few months ago."

"What else did he say?"

"He said they held them every other weekend,

and he'd heard they were brutal."

Copper nodded. "You boys find someplace else to work out for now. I'm going to go by there and have a chat with the new owner, but I don't want you getting wrapped up in whatever the hell is going on over there."

"Will do, Prez."

Copper continued to talk for another twenty minutes before dismissing us. I usually hung around the clubhouse after meetings to have a few drinks or shoot the shit, but I wasn't in the mood to be social.

"I'm gonna head out," I told Coal.

"Same here. That new routine we started this week has kicked my ass."

I laughed. "Yeah, man, I know what you mean. My arms were so sore yesterday I didn't think I was going to be able to wipe my own ass."

Coal threw his head back and laughed. "I wondered what the fuck was going on in there. Figured you ate something that fucked up your stomach."

I shook my head and laughed. "Let's go."

As soon as we pulled into the parking spaces in front of our apartment, it was obvious something was wrong. I pulled my gun from the waistband of my jeans and checked the chamber.

"Call Copper," I told him.

He already had the phone pressed to his ear. "Yeah, just pulled up to our apartment and the front door's been kicked in. Looks like the place has been trashed."

"Yeah, we're still outside. Yeah, got it. See you in a few," he said and disconnected the call. "Copper wants us to wait outside. He's on his way, and I'm sure he's not coming alone."

"I don't think anyone's in there," I said.

But as soon as the words left my mouth, a pained groan filled the air. "Help me. Fuck, please," a garbled voice said.

Ignoring my President's orders, I entered our apartment with my gun leading the way. I took two steps over the threshold and saw a bloodied and bruised Grant on the floor.

"Fuck! Coal, get in here, now!" I bellowed as I knelt down beside him. "Hey, man. It's gonna be okay."

"Shit," Coal cursed. "I'm calling an ambulance."

"Who did this?" I asked.

"Gym guys," he croaked before his eyes rolled back into his head.

"Grant!" I shouted. "Grant! Stay with me, man!"

A hand landed on my shoulder as someone else knelt on the other side of Grant. "He's all right. He's probably been fighting to stay conscious until someone got here," Judge said from behind me.

"Did he say who did it?" Copper asked.

"He said, 'Gym guys,' when I asked him."

"Motherfuckers are gonna pay for this," Copper grumbled.

"Splint's here," Batta called from the door.

Splint and his partner didn't waste any time. They had Grant loaded into the rig and were on the way to the hospital in less than three minutes.

"Judge, you and Batta go to the hospital. I'll meet you there after we finish up here."

"Got it, Prez. Officer Dunk and Officer Underwood just pulled up," Judge said.

"Thank fuck those two are working tonight," Copper said.

Officer Dunk entered the room and glanced around briefly before directing her attention to Copper. "We've got to stop meeting like this."

Copper shook hands with both officers. "Ain't that the truth. Not sure if you've met our newest members. This is Kellan Ward—we call him Savior—and this is my cousin Coal Martin-

Black."

"So, what happened tonight?" Officer Dunk asked.

After filling her in, we went through each room to see if anything was missing. Neither one of us had anything of real value in the apartment, but the television was busted and the living room furniture was ruined.

"Do you have any idea who could be responsible for this?" Officer Underwood asked.

"I asked them the same thing as soon as I got here," Copper said. "They haven't been in town long enough to piss anyone off."

"But the one who just went to the hospital is from Devil Springs, correct?" Officer Dunk asked.

"Yeah, he is," Copper said.

"Once we finish up here, we'll head over to the hospital to get his statement."

After another thirty minutes or so of answering questions, we were finally allowed to go check on our friend.

CHAPTER ELEVEN

Avery

"Avery Grace, I know there's something you're not telling me, and I want to know what it is right this instant," my mother demanded.

I knew I would eventually have to tell her, but I was putting it off until I absolutely had to.

I sighed. "Hi, Mom. Yes, I'm doing better today; thanks for asking."

"Don't try to distract me. I know you're doing better today because you're not the color of your grandmother's couch. Now, spill it. What in the hell is going on with you?"

I cupped my hands over my face and cried. My mom was by my side instantly, wrapping her arms around me. "Oh, baby, just tell me. Please. Is it cancer? We'll fight it. You're one of the strongest women I know. I'll be with you through it all."

I shook my head and cried harder. "It's not cancer," I managed to say through my sobs.

"Well, what else could it be that has you so upset?"

"I'm pregnant," I wailed.

"You're fucking what?" a male voice roared from behind my mother, startling both of us.

I gasped when my eyes landed on Savior. "What are you doing here?"

"Answer my question first," he fumed.

"Young man, I think you need to leave. Avery, do you want me to call security?"

"No, Mom, don't do that. Um, I need to talk to him, privately," I said with a grimace. I knew it would only take seconds for her to put the pieces together.

"Oh," she said. "I see. Well, yes, I'll just be in the visitor's area." She whirled around and pointed her finger at Savior. "But you keep your voice down and don't you dare upset her. She's been sick as hell, and this is the first day she's looked human in weeks."

Once she was gone, he stepped closer to the bed and crossed his arms over his chest while he glared at me. "You're pregnant?"

I cleared my throat and picked at the sheets on the bed. "That's what they tell me."

"Is it mine?"

I wanted to be offended by his question, but he had every right to ask it. We'd barely exchanged names before we fucked, and he had no way of knowing what kind of person I really was.

"It is."

"Were you going to tell me?" he snapped.

And that question did offend me. "Listen, I just found out a few weeks ago, and I've been in and out of the hospital ever since. I wasn't intentionally keeping it from you, but it's not like I had any way of contacting you."

"You could've gone to the bar."

"Did you hear me say I've been sick since I found out? This is the third time I've been admitted to the hospital."

His face softened just a touch. "Why have you been so sick?"

"They said I have hyperemesis gravidarum,

which basically means I have morning sickness on steroids. I can't keep anything down and end up with severe dehydration and a kidney infection," I explained.

"Is the baby okay?"

"Yeah, so far everything's fine."

"Did you get sick like this with your other kids?"

My entire body stiffened at his question. "How do you know about my kids?"

"You have pictures of them in your house," he replied quickly.

I did have pictures of my kids all over my house, but I didn't realize he'd taken notice. When he came over, it was for one reason, and he left as soon as we were finished.

After a few moments of awkward silence, he asked, "Are you going to keep it?"

"Yes," I snapped.

He held his hands up in a placating manner. "I wasn't suggesting anything. I mean, I want you to have the baby, and I want to be a part of his or her life."

"Oh, well, okay," I stammered. I wasn't expecting that from him.

"But, there's something you need to know," he said and pinched the bridge of his nose. "First,

I want you to know I had no idea, not until I saw the picture on the wall outside of your bathroom. And once I knew, I didn't come back."

An uneasy feeling settled in the pit of my stomach, and the nausea that had finally subsided started to return with a vengeance. "What is it?"

"You told me your name was Grace."

"It is. My name is Avery Grace."

He swallowed audibly and rubbed the back of his neck. "Yeah, I know that now. Um, my name is Kellan Ward."

Nothing could have prepared me to hear that name come out of his mouth.

Kellan Ward.

The man who killed my husband.

The man who took my children's father from them.

The man whose baby I was carrying.

No.

No.

No.

"Get out," I managed to say before vomit violently spewed from my mouth and nose. I coughed and sputtered as I blindly tried to grab for the emesis basin. It suddenly appeared in front of me as a large hand gently rubbed my back.

"I'm sorry, Avery. I'm so fucking sorry. I didn't know. I swear I didn't know."

"How could you not know?" I screamed between heaves.

"I only saw a few pictures of you, and you don't look the same," he explained.

It made sense; I'd never met him, and I hadn't seen any pictures of him, but I wasn't thinking logically. "Bullshit! Why are you doing this to me? What did I ever do to you?"

"I didn't know! You said your name was Grace!" he yelled back.

"My name is Grace!" I screamed.

"You didn't know who I was either!"

"I didn't kill your spouse and ruin your life!"

"The fuck is going on in here?" another male yelled as he entered my room.

"Security!" I heard my mother yell as she pushed her way into my room.

"Savior, outside, now. That's an order," the new man said.

Savior pinned me with eyes so full of pain and anguish. "This isn't over, Avery Grace," he vowed before he left the room.

"My apologies, ma'am. I'm not sure what's going on, but I'll make sure he stays out of your room if that's what you want."

"And you are?" my mother asked.

He cleared his throat and extended his hand to my mom. "I'm Copper Black, President of the Blackwings MC. Savior is a member of my club."

My mother shook his hand and said, "I think it's best if he refrains from visiting Avery for the time being."

"Understood," he said and reached into the pocket of his leather vest. "Here's my contact information. Please don't hesitate to call if you have any problems with him."

Mom plucked the card from his hand and briefly glanced at it. "Thank you, Mr. Black," she said. He nodded once before he turned on his heels and left the room.

"What in the hell is going on, Avery?"

"Mom," I gasped and choked on my own spit which started another round of vomiting.

She was right there by my side, just like she always was. She wiped my face and handed me some water to rinse my mouth. "Sweetheart, was that the father?"

I nodded and wiped the tears from my face. "The first one, not the second one," I clarified.

"Honey, you haven't done anything wrong. You're—"

"Yes, I have, Mom," I sobbed. "I've done the worst thing ever."

"Avery, don't be so dramatic."

"I'm not being dramatic. That man, the baby's father, is Kellan Ward," I cried.

My mother's mouth dropped open, and the color drained from her face as she gaped at me in horror. "I didn't know it was him. And he didn't know it was me. And now we're having a baby. What am I going to do?" I managed to say before I started gagging again.

Mom knew how to handle my frequent vomiting, so she sprang into action with the washcloth and water. "Oh, Avery, is this why you've been so sick?"

I shook my head. "No, I just found out who he was right before you started yelling for security."

"Well, clearly, stress makes it worse for you," she observed.

"I can't believe this happened. What am I going to tell people? I'll be the talk of the town."

"You're in a new town, and you don't have to tell anyone anything. It's no one's business but your own. Now, I've already discussed this with your father, and we were planning on renting a house nearby so we could help with the kids until you were better. We thought you had cancer. I'm so glad you don't, but you're still going to need help for a while." She pulled me against her chest and smoothed her hand over my hair. "We'll get through this, honey."

I wasn't sure I believed her, but I hoped she was right.

CHAPTER TWELVE

Savior

"What in the hell was going on in there?" Copper demanded.

"I, uh, fuck," I swore. "She's pregnant. It's mine, and I don't want to talk about it."

"You don't have to talk about it, but you do have to stay out of her room."

"Not a problem, Prez."

He arched an eyebrow and studied me. "You going to leave her high and dry?"

I shook my head. "I don't want to. But you

saw how she reacted. We, uh, we have a tangled past." I pinched the bridge of my nose. "Fuck, Prez, I don't know what I'm supposed to do. It's not like we planned this. I want to be involved and help her however I can; but I don't want to upset her any more than I already have," I confessed.

Copper's hand landed on my shoulder. "Maybe it's just her pregnancy hormones making things seem worse than they are."

"I wish it were that simple. Trust me, Prez, she has every right to be upset with me."

"You know, Phoenix never told me why he ordered your transfer. And really, it ain't my business if it doesn't affect the club directly. But, your brothers can't help you if they don't know what kind of help you need."

I sighed. He was right. I didn't want all the brothers to know about my past, but I was in over my head, and I needed some help. "Can we keep this between you and me for right now?"

"Of course."

"A little over two years ago, I was driving home from a long day at work. I even turned down an invitation to hang out with some friends that were in town because I was so exhausted. I was about halfway home when I fell asleep behind the wheel. My truck crashed into a police cruiser parked on the side of the highway and killed the officer inside. That officer was Ian Parker, Avery's husband," I said and gestured to her hospital room.

Copper sucked in a sharp breath and glanced at her closed door. "Shit, Savior."

"I didn't know it was her. I'd never seen her before. When I met her at Precious Metals, she said her name was Grace. I told her my name was Savior. Neither one of us knew who the other one was."

Copper rubbed his chin with his thumb and index finger. "I'm guessing you figured out who she was when you disappeared a few weeks ago and Ranger found you drunker than a skunk in the cemetery."

"Yeah," I rasped. "I saw a picture of her kids on the wall and figured it out. I, uh, I went to the cemetery to apologize to her husband."

"So, I don't get it. Why'd Phoenix send you up here?"

"It was actually Ranger's idea. He knew she moved to Devil Springs and thought it would be good for me to be here as well. After the accident, my lawyers told me not to contact the family in any way. But I had to at least do something for the kids. So, I found ways to make sure their school lunches were paid for, had things delivered to their house, prepaid for their meals at different restaurants around town, stuff like that."

"Fuck, Savior, if there's anything I can do for you, I will."

"Thanks, Prez. I appreciate it," I replied. It was a nice offer, but there wasn't anything anyone could do to help me.

"I'm going to go wait in the visitor's area. Will you let me know when there's an update on Grant?"

"Of course," he said and patted my shoulder.

I took a seat in the empty waiting room and slumped in my chair. How had my life become such a fucked-up mess? I couldn't blame Avery for not wanting to talk to me. I would hate me too if I were in her shoes. I hated myself as it was. Fuck! I wanted to hit something. Anything.

"Mind if I sit here?" a woman asked softly.

I looked up to see Avery's mother pointing to the seat beside me. For a brief moment, I was distracted by how much the two of them looked alike.

She didn't wait for me to answer before she dropped into the chair. "I'm Claire Cameron, Avery's mother. I'm not here to be hateful to you or to tell you to leave. I overheard you talking to your friend, and I understand what a tough position you're in. My Avery has always reacted defensively to hide her feelings. Once she's had time to process, she usually comes around."

"I don't think that's going to be the case this time."

"Well, if I know my girl, she'll come around and do the right thing. It might take her a little longer than usual, but she'll get there."

"We, um, we didn't exactly have a relationship, but I do want to be there for her and the baby. She can't do everything by herself and be as sick as she is."

"No, she can't. Her father and I are going to make arrangements to stay in town and help with the kids until she gets better, however long that may be. Your friend gave me his card, but let me get your phone number so we'll be able to get in touch with you."

I rattled off my cell phone number and looked at her curiously. "Why don't you hate me?"

She gave me a sad smile. "I think I did for a short period of time before we knew what happened, but it was an accident. And even as devastating as it was, it wasn't your fault. Avery knows that, too, but this sudden turn of events has thrown her for a loop. Well, I better get back to her room," she said.

"Can I get your number, too? Maybe I could text you and see how she's doing?" I asked.

"Of course. I'll send you a text from my phone."

"Thank you," I said. "I—"

She held her hand up to stop me. "You don't have to explain yourself. Not to me. And regardless of the other circumstances, I would never frown upon a man wanting to be involved in his child's life."

I sat there in stunned silence long after she returned to Avery's room. I couldn't believe how kind she was to me after my sheer existence ruined her daughter's life and the lives of her grandchildren. The more that I thought about it, I started to think it might be better if I wasn't involved in my child's life.

"Hey, brother. You okay?" Coal asked.

"Uh, yeah, I'm good. Any word on Grant?"

He nodded. "He's out of surgery and in recovery. He had some minor internal bleeding, but they were able to get it stopped. He's got a concussion, and his eye socket is fractured, but no other broken bones."

"Fuck, they really did a number on him."

"Yeah, they did. Copper is fucking pissed. He sent me to come get you. Said he had something he wanted to discuss before Grant gets back from recovery."

I got to my feet and followed Coal to what I assumed would be Grant's hospital room. Copper was standing front and center with his arms crossed over his chest. "I want a brother here with Grant around the clock. I don't think they'd be stupid enough to come to the hospital and try some shit, but I didn't think they'd be stupid enough to fuck with someone from my club. Coal, you're on duty tonight. Savior, you take tomorrow."

CHAPTER THIRTEEN

Copper

I was fucking pissed. How dare these motherfuckers come into my town and start fucking with my club? I didn't really give a shit about the illegal fights. I didn't even care that they'd asked a few of my members if they were interested. What pissed me right the hell off was them not taking "No" for an answer.

Once Grant was out of surgery, and we were sure he was stable, I sent everyone back to the clubhouse for Church, including Savior.

"We need to address the situation with the

gym. I know how I'd like to go about it, but I'm open to suggestions."

"Why don't you tell us how you'd like to go about it first?" my pain in the ass little brother asked.

"I thought Judge and I would stop by and have a chat with the owner. Tonight. Let him know where he went wrong and see how he wants to go about unfucking his fuck-up."

"All in favor?" Bronze asked.

Unanimous "ayes" sounded around the table.

"All right. Judge, let's roll. The rest of you stay here in case things don't go according to plan."

Bronze laughed. "You mean in case we have to bail you two out of jail."

"Suck it, bitch."

Twenty minutes later, Judge and I pulled into the parking lot of the gym. Spazz did some digging and found out the owner's name but not much else which seemed shady as shit.

We walked through the front doors and went straight to the first employee we found. "Need to speak with the owner," I rumbled.

"I'm sorry, you'll have to make an appointment for that," the twerp squeaked.

I slammed my fist onto the counter. "This is me making an appointment. Where's his office?"

He pointed a shaky finger to a hallway along the far wall of the building. "Thanks," I said and wasted no time heading in that direction. I laughed to myself when his makeshift security guard stepped out into the hallway blocking our path.

"Can I help you?"

"Are you Todd Russo?"

He shook his head. "No, I'm his security."

"Then step aside. I have a meeting with your boss."

He arched an eyebrow. "And you are?"

"Copper Black."

"Uh-huh. And him?"

"He's my security. Let's go. I ain't got all day," I said impatiently. His amateur intimidation tactics were doing nothing but pissing me off even more.

He stuck his head inside the office and mumbled something before straightening and opening the door for us to enter.

Todd Russo was everything I expected him to be—a slender man with slicked-back hair in a cheap suit. He stood from behind his desk and extended his hand. "Good evening.

I'm Todd Russo. What brings you into my fine establishment this evening?"

I glanced at his hand in disgust. "You know damn well why I'm here."

He feigned surprise. "I'm afraid I don't."

"Three of my boys have been working out here. When they declined your invitation to fight for you, you put one of them in the hospital and trashed the apartment of the other two. Now, I wouldn't have given a shit what you've got going on here as long as it didn't affect me and mine, but it has, and now I'm pissed."

"Again, I'm afraid you have me at a disadvantage. Your boys?" he asked.

I grinned. "Oh, you really don't know who I am. Allow me to introduce myself. Copper Black, President of the Blackwings MC. Your cronies fucked with two of my patched members and a prospect."

He tried to hide his reaction, but I saw his body slightly stiffen at the mention of the club. We were well-known in the area and you'd have to be new in town or completely clueless to not know who we were.

"I can assure you none of my employees or associates were responsible for the unfortunate situation your friends found themselves in."

"Cut the shit, Todd," I snapped. "We both know that's bullshit. When's your next fight?"

His eyes widened in surprise, but he answered quickly. "Tomorrow night."

"Good. We'll see you then," I said and turned to leave.

"Excuse me?"

"You wanted a fight, and you're going to get one."

"You can't just—"

"Yeah, I fucking can. We'll be here tomorrow night."

He grinned. "All right, but if my guy wins, your boys will fight for me."

I returned his grin and extended my hand. "And if my guy wins, I get your gym and you find a new town to play in." When he didn't immediately shake on it, I added, "What? You don't have faith in your fighter?"

He smirked. "Of course, I have faith in my fighters, Mr. Black. I'm just not sure you understand what you're agreeing to."

I snorted, "I know exactly what I'm agreeing to."

He stuck his sweaty hand in mine and limply shook it like the pussy he was. "Well then, we'll see you tomorrow night."

Judge managed to keep a straight face until we made it back to our bikes. "This is going to be fun," he laughed.

I smiled. "Yeah, it fucking is."

CHAPTER FOURTEEN

Savior

I spent the entire day at the hospital with Grant. He was doing much better than the day before, but he slept most of the time I was there because of the pain medication they were giving him.

It killed me to have to sit in his room knowing Avery was down the hall and I couldn't visit her. Part of me wondered if Copper had intentionally assigned me to stay with Grant to test my willingness to follow his orders; but, the more I thought about it, the more I didn't think that was the case.

"Hey, man," Splint said quietly as he entered the room. "Your shift is over."

"I was expecting Coal," I blurted.

"Yeah, well, I can't be involved in the activities this evening, so I volunteered for guard duty."

"What activities?" I asked.

"You'll have to ask Prez about that. He wants you to head to the clubhouse as soon as you leave here," he said.

"Will do."

With that, I left Grant's room and forced myself to walk past Avery's door without looking inside. I knew she was still in the hospital because I'd seen her mother walk down the hallway a few times, but I never called any attention to myself. I knew she needed some time, and I did, too. I'd give it a few days and then check in with her mother if I hadn't heard anything from her.

When I arrived at the clubhouse, the whole crew was already on their bikes in the forecourt ready to roll. Copper waved his hand, and I fell into formation as we rolled through the gate. Once we hit the main street in downtown Devil Springs, I knew exactly where we were going.

I pulled into a parking space and glanced around, only then noticing that Bronze, Batta, and Coal were pulling up in a cage. "What's going on?" I asked Judge.

Judge smirked. "Prez agreed to a fight."

"He what?"

"Relax. He knows what he's doing," he said.

I wasn't so sure about that, but I kept my opinion to myself and followed the rest of the club into the gym.

"You know what's going on?" I asked Coal.

He shrugged. "Just that Copper agreed to a fight between a club member and one of the gym's fighters."

"Why would he do that?" I wondered out loud.

"Guess we'll find out in a few minutes."

We were escorted to the basement and led to a dingy locker room. "We'll come get you five minutes before the fight starts. Stay in here until then," some guy said before he disappeared.

Copper turned to me and Coal. "You two go with Tiny and scope out the setup. Text Spazz if you see anything we need to know about. I have no doubt they'll try to pull some bullshit, and I want to be ready for it."

"Prez, if this is because they tried to get me to fight, I can't let you do whatever you're about to do," I blurted.

Copper turned to me with an unreadable expression on his face. "You don't let me do anything. But, I understand where you're coming from, and it's not on you. Now, go with Tiny and Coal."

"Yes, Prez."

I didn't agree with him; it was on me. If I'd had my shit together, I wouldn't have needed to find a gym to deal with my fucked-up life, and none of us would be in the mess we were in. I shook my head and tried to focus on the task at hand.

The setup was exactly what you'd expect for a place that held illegal fights—dark, musty, and overran with cheap everything. Even the ring looked like it would fall apart with one good kick. I continued to scan the area when something caught my eye.

"Tiny, two o'clock," I mumbled low enough for only him to hear.

Tiny brought his hand up to his face and mumbled something before he started coughing. He finally stopped and cleared his throat. "Thanks, man."

I furrowed my brows in confusion and started to ask what in the hell was wrong with him when I caught the ever so subtle shake of his head.

And then I noticed the watch he was wearing, and everything started to make more sense. I guess Copper did know what he was doing after all.

The lights flashed on and off, and the announcer instructed the crowd to find their seats. We claimed the first two rows directly behind what we assumed was our corner.

"Ladies and Gentlemen, tonight we have a treat in store for you. Our reigning champion, Dez De Santis, will be defending his title against newcomer, Bronze Black."

I don't know what I was expecting, but it sure as shit wasn't for the crowd to laugh.

"Give it up for Dez 'The Destroyer' De Santis!" the announcer shouted and the crowd went wild.

"And now, Bronze Black." Once again, the crowd laughed, but it didn't seem to faze Bronze in the slightest. Bronze kept his head down as he walked to the ring, surrounded by Copper, Judge, and Batta.

He climbed into the ring and started preparing for his fight. Just before the announcer called them to the center, Bronze glanced over his shoulder at us and winked. "Holy shit, does he—?"

"Yes, the fucker's always doing stupid shit

like that. He knows it's not a good idea to wear contacts during a fight, but he says it's part of his strategy or some shit," Tiny explained.

I couldn't help but laugh. Bronze was wearing red contacts that made him look like he was possessed by a demon.

After stating the rules, which were minimal at best, the bell rang and the fight began. When Bronze blinked up at his opponent, Dez paused for just a second, but it was enough for Bronze to get three solid hits in—two to the head and one to the body.

Bronze worked him over and ran him all over the ring. I'd never seen anyone fight as well as he did. He was quick and moved strategically. He didn't waste energy on throwing punches he couldn't land. Instead, he kept his opponent moving to wear them down and struck when an opportunity presented itself.

"Does he have professional training?" I asked Tiny.

"Not like you're thinking. He was on the Marine Corps Boxing Team. That's a whole different kind of training."

I continued to watch in awe as Bronze wiped the floor with Dez round after round. It was during the fifth round when things went to shit.

I guess Todd Russo realized his guy wasn't going to win, and according to Tiny, that meant he would lose his gym to the Blackwings.

Suddenly, another fighter was entering the ring with Bronze and Dez.

"Fuck," Tiny swore and got to his feet. "Keep an eye on Russo." I was going to do one better than keeping an eye on him.

With everyone focused on the ring, I was able to go around the back side and come up behind Russo without anyone noticing. I pulled the blade from the horizontal sheath at my back and brought it up to his neck.

"Breathe wrong, motherfucker, and you're dead," I growled.

I glanced at the ring just in time to see Batta swing his bat at the unwelcomed contender's leg resulting in a crack that echoed above the roar of the crowd.

I pressed the blade harder against Russo's neck and wiggled it just enough for him to feel the sting of his skin being broken. "Keep that hand where I can see it, or I'll pin it to your chest with my other knife."

He held his shaky hands out in front of him where I could clearly see them. More sounds of flesh hitting flesh and wood breaking bone sounded from the ring.

The announcer had long since fled the ring, but the crowd eagerly watched the chaos unfolding before them. Bronze was still fighting Dez like there weren't four other people in the ring with him. Batta was beating the fuck out of another fighter with his bat, and Tiny had some other guy in a chokehold. But Copper, Judge, and Coal had disappeared.

Moments later, Bronze threw one hell of a punch and Dez hit the floor. Apparently, that was the signal for the crowd to disperse. People immediately began making their way to the stairs and, within a few minutes, the basement was cleared out.

Judge appeared with Todd's bodyguard in tow, and right behind them, Coal was frog-marching another man to the ring. We heard the distinct sound of a heavy door being closed and locked before Copper came down the stairs.

He clapped his hands together and grinned, "Well, looks like I just got myself a gym. Thanks, Todd. This was fun."

"Fuck you," Todd spat. "I'm not signing over my gym to you."

Copper rubbed his chin and nodded. "Yeah, I thought that might be the case." He paused before adding, "Good work, Savior. You can let him go."

I released Todd and took a step back, but kept my knife in my hand in case things went south again.

Copper hooked his thumbs in his belt loops and rocked back on his heels. "Had my tech guy do a little digging into your records," he said casually. "Want to take a guess at what he found?"

I watched Todd's entire body stiffen. "Y-you didn't find shit," he stammered.

Copper grinned wickedly and held up his cell phone. "Wanna see if the Feds find shit? Got a buddy in the Bureau on speed dial."

"Fuck," Todd cursed and actually stomped his foot.

"Sign over the deed and get the fuck out," Copper demanded. "Leave a forwarding address, and we'll send your shit to you. And let me make one thing perfectly clear; you fuck with me and my club again, I'll let my boys have some fun with you before we feed you to the wild pigs."

We escorted Todd upstairs to his office, and he told us where we could find the deed. As soon as he signed it over, Batta and Judge escorted him out and locked the doors. "Judge, you and

Tiny get started on the security install. Savior and Coal can help. I'm going to go check on Bronze and Batta," Copper said.

I snorted and pointed behind him. "We're just fine, oh fearless leader," Bronze said jovially.

Copper pulled his younger brother in for a half-hug and slapped him on the back. "I can see that. Fuck, man, you stink," he said as he moved to do the same with Batta.

"That's the smell of victory, Prez," Batta chuckled and rubbed his sweaty armpits all over Copper's shirt.

"You motherfucker," Copper growled and shoved Batta away.

"Nice fight, man. Never seen anyone as good as you are in person," I told Bronze.

"Thanks, brother. I'm a little rusty, but I'd love to start some light training again."

"If you're ever looking for someone to spar with, let me know," I offered. "You'll probably whoop my ass, but I'd love to learn some of what you know."

Bronze smiled. "I'd be happy to teach you some of my secret moves."

"Will you take those fucking contacts out already? You're creeping me out," Tiny said.

Bronze laughed. "Yeah, that was the point."

"Quit fucking around and start helping us get this place secured. I want to get home to my woman," Copper ordered.

Judge snorted. "She's over at my mom's house, Prez. She didn't tell you?"

"No, she fucking didn't. Doesn't surprise me since I wouldn't tell her where I was going tonight. That woman," he said and grinned.

CHAPTER FIFTEEN

Avery

After a week in the hospital, I was finally allowed to go home. I still felt awful and threw up several times a day, but the medicine the doctor prescribed had helped make it bearable. She also assured me that even though I was surviving on Coke and Cheez-Its, my baby was okay.

I still hadn't fully come to terms with the fact that I was even having a baby, much less who the child's father was. My main focus every day was to throw up as little as possible so that

I could take care of my children. The first few days were rough, but by the end of the week, I had developed somewhat of a routine.

I was sitting at the kitchen table staring at a bowl of grits trying to decide if I really wanted to test fate when my mother dropped into the chair beside me. "Sweetheart, remember what the doctor said. Don't force yourself to eat if you don't think you can keep it down."

I sighed and sat back in my chair. "Mom," I whined. "I'm the only pregnant person in the world who can't gain weight. Look at me," I said and waved my hand up and down my body. "I look like the pregnant chick in that vampire movie."

Mom scoffed. "You most certainly do not. She was much farther along in her pregnancy than you are when she looked so sickly."

I rolled my eyes. "Thanks, Mom."

"Any time, dear," she said and patted my hand.

"Mommy! Mommy!" my daughter squealed as she came running into the kitchen.

"Good morning, Riles! Did you have a good sleep?" I asked.

"I did! I dreamed I was a fairy princess and lived in a big castle by the sea. Nana was my fairy grandmother, and you were the fairy queen. We had big, fluffy dresses, and we got to eat ice cream whenever we wanted. Even for breakfast!"

"Sorry, little princess, but you're not having ice cream for breakfast," I laughed.

"That's okay. I love Nana's breakfasts," she said excitedly.

Riley was a morning person, just like her father. My son, however, was just like his mother and took a little longer to be pleasant in the morning.

Right on cue, he stumbled into the kitchen and fell into the chair. Then, he proceeded to lay his head on his folded arms. "Morning, Mommy," he grumbled.

"Good morning, Brax. Did you have a good sleep?"

"Yes," he sighed.

"Sit up, honey. Here's your breakfast," my mom said and placed a bowl of cereal in front of him.

The kids wolfed down their food while I continued to look at mine like it might contain poison. "After you put your dishes in the sink, go upstairs and get dressed. Wash your faces and brush your teeth, too. We have a few errands to run today," Mom said to the kids.

"Where do you have to go?" I asked.

"They both have doctor's appointments today for their yearly checkup. Then, I'm taking them shopping for back-to-school clothes. We'll be out most of the day."

"Mom," I said. "You don't have to do that. I can take them once I get better."

Mom shook her head. "Honey, school starts next week. And besides, I don't mind helping. I just wish your father was in town so I didn't have to leave you here all alone."

"I'll be fine," I assured her. My dad was going back and forth between Croftridge and Devil Springs. Most of the time, he could work remotely, but occasionally he needed to be on-site in Croftridge for a few days.

An hour later, I was resting on the couch while Mom was herding the children out the front door. "We'll be back later this afternoon. You call if you need anything."

"I will," I promised.

I picked up my e-reader to continue reading the debut novel by Teigh Byrd when the front door opened. "Sorry, honey, it's just me. Uh, I forgot to tell you that a visitor would be stopping by. Well, gotta go," she said and disappeared right before Savior stepped into the room.

"You've got to be kidding me," I mumbled to myself.

"If you want me to leave, just tell me. I don't want to upset you, but your mom said you would be at home alone today and thought it would be a good time for us to talk," he said.

I closed my eyes and exhaled slowly. "Fine. Come in and have a seat." I didn't want to talk to him, but I knew I would have to eventually.

"How are you feeling?" he asked.

I shrugged. "I've only puked once today."

"You're still sick?"

I snorted. "Yeah, and apparently I'm going to be sick for a while, possibly through the entire pregnancy."

"I'm sorry," he said sincerely.

"It's not your fault. It's just something that happens sometimes."

"I mean about everything. I—"

I cut him off. "We're not talking about that today. One thing that was blatantly clear when I was in the hospital is that stress makes things worse for me."

"Okay," he agreed quickly. "Um, is there anything I can do to help?"

"Thanks, but I'm good right now."

"I didn't mean just right now. I meant any

time. I get that we don't really know each other, and we have a complicated history, but I want to be involved. I want to go to appointments, or at least know about them, and I want to be there when the baby's born."

I closed my eyes and leaned my head back, taking a moment to process his words. I knew, deep down, that regardless of our past, I couldn't and wouldn't keep him from his child. I also knew, deep down, that the accident wasn't his fault. But none of that made the situation any easier. "Maybe we should start by getting to know each other," I suggested.

He nodded. "What do you want to know?"

"Why did you move to Devil Springs?" I asked.

He grimaced and rubbed the back of his neck. "I'm a member of the Blackwings MC. I joined the Croftridge Chapter but was transferred to the Devil Springs Chapter at the beginning of the summer. It wasn't my choice to move here."

"Did you know I was here?"

"No, I didn't. I knew you weren't in Croftridge anymore, but I didn't know where you went, and I didn't try to find you."

"How did you know I left Croftridge?"

He sighed heavily. "Because I was doing

things for your kids. I wasn't trying to make up for what happened, but I was trying to help out where I could."

I gasped and slapped my hand over my mouth. "That was you?"

"The school lunches, the Christmas fund, the random packages on your porch, the complimentary meals at restaurants. Yeah, those were all from me," he confessed.

My eyes filled with tears as my heart ached in my chest. "Disney World?" I whispered.

He nodded once. "Yeah, that was me, too."

I couldn't contain my emotions any longer. The tears spilled down my cheeks, and I curled in on myself while I desperately tried to choke back the sobs. I didn't know where the gifts came from, but I never suspected they were from him. In my mind, he was a faceless man driving a truck, not a real person who struggled just as much as I did with the aftermath of the wreck.

Savior's strong arms surrounded me and pulled me against his firm chest. "I'm sorry. I didn't mean to make you cry," he said softly while he gently rubbed my back.

"Why did you do all that?" I mumbled against his shirt.

"Because I lost my parents when I was

younger. I was lucky enough to have a grandfather who was able to raise me and provide for me. I just wanted to help them have the same thing."

His reply had more tears leaking from my eyes and soaking his shirt. And then it happened. I choked on some rogue snot and threw up all over him. I quickly turned and grabbed the small trash can that traveled from room to room with me, but it wasn't necessary. Everything in my stomach was all over the man on my couch.

My cheeks flamed with mortification. "I'm so sorry. Oh, kill me now."

He pulled his shirt away from his body and said, "It wouldn't be so bad if it wasn't warm."

"Stop talking," I ordered and covered my mouth with my hand. Gross.

"Sorry," he laughed.

"Let me get you a towel or something."

"No. I'll get it. Are your towels in the bathroom?" he asked and pointed down the hall.

I cocked my head to the side and slowly nodded. "Yeah, it's the second door on the left."

"I know. I've used it before," he said and disappeared down the hall.

I managed to make it to my own bathroom to brush my teeth and wash my face. Miraculously, I didn't have any vomit on my clothes but decided to change into something fresh anyway.

When he returned to the living room, I was on my knees scrubbing the few smalls spots on the couch. "I could've done that," he said from above me.

I turned to look at him, and my mouth dropped open. He was standing beside me in nothing but a pair of boxer briefs, and I was eye-level with the goods. "Oh, I, um, you, it's, yeah," I stammered and turned back to the task at hand.

He chuckled. "I tossed my clothes in the washing machine. It's not like you haven't seen it all before."

Yes, I had seen it all before; well, most of it. But, I was pregnant, and although I was sick, my sex drive wasn't. I blinked up at him and couldn't hide the want I was feeling.

"Fuck," he cursed. "Don't look at me like that."

"Like what?" I asked, even though I knew exactly what he meant.

"Like you want me to fuck you."

I bit my lower lip and contemplated what to say next. Did I want him to fuck me? My vagina certainly did. Was it a good idea? Again, my vagina was all for it, but my brain had a different opinion.

"Sorry. Pregnancy hormones," I said with a shrug.

"Pregnancy hormones?" he asked, sounding confused.

"Well, this is slightly awkward," I laughed. "Um, pregnancy hormones sometimes send a woman's sex drive into overdrive."

He sucked in a sharp breath. When I glanced up at him, he was staring at me with an almost feral look in his eyes. And his hard cock was making my mouth water.

"Avery, I don't think this is a good idea." He took a step back, and when the backs of his legs hit the sofa, I rose to my feet and planted my hands on his chest. With one firm shove, he went down, and I climbed on top of him.

"I do," I said before I covered his mouth with mine.

His hands came up and threaded through my hair while I devoured his mouth. His fingers tightened, and he gently pulled my head back, breaking the kiss.

"Not like this," he breathed. Before I could argue, he stood with me in his arms and started for the stairs. "Where's your bedroom?"

"The door at the end of the hall," I mumbled against his neck. I couldn't get enough of him.

He smelled divine and tasted even better.

He kicked the door closed and carefully placed me on the bed before he climbed over me. "You're so fucking beautiful," he said softly.

I looked away from him and shook my head. "I'm—"

He stopped my words by capturing my lips in a soft kiss that quickly intensified. He carefully pulled my top over my head and tossed it to the floor. I was a little uncomfortable because we'd only had sex in the dark and he could see all of me with the light streaming in from my bedroom window.

My insecurities vanished when his hands cupped my breasts and he rubbed his thumbs over my extremely sensitive nipples. I moaned loudly, causing him to grin. He lowered his head and flicked one with his tongue while he continued to pass his thumb over the other. My nipples had always been sensitive, but they were a hair-trigger when I was pregnant.

"Please don't stop," I begged.

I felt him smile against my skin before he moved to the other side. I was writhing beneath him and shamelessly grinding myself on his thigh.

All too soon, he released my nipple. I wanted

to cry out in frustration, but he didn't give me a chance. He quickly removed my shorts and panties, and then he was on his stomach between my legs. With his hands holding my thighs wide open, he slowly licked the length of my center. Over and over again, until I was ready to explode.

"Please, please, please," I chanted.

He rose to his knees and shoved his boxer briefs down his legs. He came down on top of me and froze. "Fuck," he whispered.

"What?" I gasped somewhat frantically.

"My wallet's downstairs."

"So?"

"Condom," he said simply.

"I'm already pregnant," I stated.

"I'm clean."

"Me, too."

"You sure?" he asked.

"Yes! Please, just—" My words morphed into a sigh of contentment when he slid his length into me. "Yes," I breathed when he started to move.

His movements were slow and controlled, almost restrained. "You won't hurt me or the baby," I said softly.

"I know," he said and kissed me as he continued his gentle pace.

He broke the kiss and pressed his forehead to mine. With his intense gray eyes locked on mine, we reached our climaxes together. And I knew, once again, everything had changed.

CHAPTER SIXTEEN

Savior

A few days later, Coal and I were in Copper's office, at his request, when he delivered news neither of us was expecting. "I'm putting you two in charge of running the gym. I've had our lawyer look over the paperwork and everything's in order. You start tomorrow."

I gaped at him. "I don't know anything about running a business, Prez."

"I'll handle the business side of things. All you two need to do is work out a schedule so that at least one of you is there to open and the other is there to close. Once Grant is back on his feet, he can help cover the hours in between. Oh, and two of the staff members contacted me about continuing their employment. After Spazz ran background checks on them and I personally interviewed them, I agreed to let them continue working at the gym, but you're probably going to need to hire a few more people," he said.

"Okay. Wow. Um, thanks, Prez. What time do we need to be there tomorrow morning?" I asked.

"It previously opened at five and closed at eight. Let's keep the same hours for a week or two and see how it goes. If you're not doing a lot of business during the early hours or the later ones, we can readjust the opening and closing time."

"Got it. Thanks again, Prez," I said.

"Thanks, Copper," Coal added.

"You're welcome. Coal, you're good to go. Savior, I need a minute before you leave."

Coal nodded and left the office. As soon as the door closed, Copper leaned back in his chair and folded his arms over his chest. "What's going on with your girl?"

"She's not my girl, Prez," I corrected.

"She's carrying your baby."

"Yeah, she is," I agreed. "She's home from the hospital. She still gets sick several times a day, but the medicine they gave her seems to be helping."

"And how are things between you and her?" he asked.

"Less fucked up than they were."

"Well, I suppose any improvement is better than none. Is she going to let you be a part of the baby's life?"

"She says she is."

He nodded. "Good. You let me know if that changes and we'll get Tina to handle the custody agreement."

"Thanks, Prez."

***

Beep.

Beep.

Beep.

I groaned when my alarm clock went off at four o'clock in the morning. I wasn't one to sleep extremely late, but I wasn't one to rise before the sun was up either. I stumbled into the kitchen and managed to get a pot of coffee going before I made my way back to the shower.

When I returned to the kitchen, Coal was standing at the counter with two mugs in front of him. Without a single word, he shoved one in my direction. Yeah, it was going to be a long day for both of us. After our meeting with Copper, we'd agreed to work open to close for the first few days to see how things went.

"I don't know about you, but my ass is going to be taking a nap in one of the offices sometime today."

He laughed. "Yeah, same here. This ass crack of dawn shit is going to suck."

"Maybe the place won't be busy and we won't have to do this much longer," I mused.

Coal and I arrived at the gym fifteen minutes before it was supposed to open. I was a little on edge when we first got there, but everything was fine. We disarmed the alarm, turned on all the lights, and sat there for almost two hours before anyone showed up.

For the next two days, no one showed up before seven o'clock, but people were rushing to get out the door at eight o'clock when we closed. Coal and I discussed it with Copper and we decided to move the gym's opening and closing time two hours forward.

Coal and I were still opening and closing the

gym together, but we each took extended breaks during the day. For mine, I usually went back to our apartment for a nap, but it had been over a week since I'd seen Avery, so I texted her and asked if I could stop by for a visit. She replied instantly saying I could, and fifteen minutes later I was knocking on her front door.

When she opened the front door, I knew she wasn't feeling well. "Are you okay?" I asked.

She nodded. "Yeah. I had a rough night last night, and this morning wasn't much better."

"Is there anything I can do?"

She flopped onto the couch in her living room and covered her face with her hands. "I don't think there's anything anyone can do," she said and sniffed.

I gathered her in my arms and smoothed my hand over her very tangled hair. "There's got to be something I can do. Whatever it is, just name it."

She pressed her face against my shirt and hiccupped. "There is one thing, but I hate to ask."

"What is it?"

"Will you help me wash my hair?" she asked and started to cry again. "The hot water from the shower makes me sick, and I can't tolerate a cold shower. Leaning over the tub makes me sick. Everything makes me sick. I'm sorry. I'm just so miserable right now."

"Where's your shampoo and conditioner?"

"Upstairs in my bathroom."

I ran upstairs and grabbed the bottles from her shower as well as a towel. After putting them by the kitchen sink, I scooped her from the couch and placed her on the kitchen counter.

"What are you doing?" she asked.

"Washing your hair. Turn around and I'll help you lean back."

Once she was situated, I used the sink sprayer to wet her hair with cool water and proceeded to wash and condition her hair while she groaned in pleasure. I willed my cock to behave, but he'd heard those noises come from her mouth in very different circumstances and he was ready to recreate those memories.

After rinsing her hair, I squeezed the water from it and carefully wrapped a towel around her head before I helped her sit up. "Thank you," she said softly.

"I'm not finished yet. Come on," I replied and lifted her from the counter. I carried her back to the living room and sat on the couch with her in my lap. Then, I picked up the comb on the coffee table and started combing the tangles from her long, auburn hair.

The whole time, she watched my every move but never said a word. When I was finished, I put the comb down and pulled her against me so her head was resting right under my chin. "Better?" I asked.

"Much," she sighed followed by a yawn.

"Sleep, baby. I've got you."

***

Muffled laughter followed by the sound of a door opening woke me. It only took me a few seconds to get my bearings and remember where I was, but it was too late to react. Avery's front door swung open and her mother stepped inside followed by her children.

"Nana, who's that?" Riley asked.

Claire didn't miss a beat. "That's the Sandman, sweetie. He's helping your mommy sleep. You and Braxton run upstairs and be quiet until she wakes up." Riley glanced at me, as did her brother, before they both quietly went upstairs.

I started to move, but Claire held her hands up to stop me. "Don't get up on my account. She needs to sleep. I'll just be in the kitchen starting dinner."

I probably should have objected and moved Avery to the couch so I could leave, but I was damn comfortable where I was. And she was right; Avery did need the rest. And apparently so did I, because I closed my eyes and went right back to sleep.

My phone buzzing in my pocket woke me, as well as Avery. She shot up with a look of panic on her face. Then, she was up and running for the bathroom. I pulled my phone out and cursed when I saw the time. "Sorry, man, I'll be there in fifteen minutes," I said by way of greeting.

"Just checking in. You don't usually stay gone this long," Coal replied.

"I forgot to set the alarm on my phone."

"It's all good, man. Listen, why don't you take the rest of the day off. I don't mind closing tonight. We were planning on starting the new schedule tomorrow anyway," he offered.

"You sure? Because I'm not going to say no."

He laughed. "I'm sure. I'll catch ya later."

I got to my feet to go check on Avery when her little girl appeared in front of me. "Hello, mister," she said cheerfully. "Thank you for helping Mommy sleep."

"Oh, um," I stammered, unsure of what to say.

"What's your name?" she asked.

"I go by Savior."

She scrunched her nose. "That's a funny name."

I laughed. "Well, it's more of a nickname."

"Oh, how'd you get it?"

"I helped save someone, and her grandfather started calling me Savior. Pretty soon, everyone else did, too," I explained.

"See, Braxton. I told you he wasn't really the sandman," she yelled with her hands on her hips. I turned to see her little brother quietly sitting at the top of the stairs watching us.

"Hi," I said and gave him a little wave.

"Hi," he said and waved his hand excitedly. He jumped to his feet and hurried down the stairs, but his little feet wouldn't move as fast as his body was trying to go. I saw it before it even started to happen—his torso went forward while his feet were still planted on the stair behind him.

"Shit!" I yelled and dove for the boy, knocking over a lamp in the process. By sheer luck, I caught him and cradled him against my chest while I landed on my side with a loud thud.

As soon as we hit the ground, he began to scream and cry. "Hey, little man, you're okay. I know that was scary, but I got you."

"What in the world is going on in here?" Claire called out as she came running into the room with Avery right behind her.

"Savior saved Brax! Can he stay for dinner?" Riley squealed.

"What?" Avery gasped and took her crying son from my arms.

"He tripped coming down the stairs. Sorry about your lamp, but I didn't think I was going to be able to catch him," I told her.

"I don't care about the lamp," she said and hugged her son while she swayed from side to side. "Are you hurt?"

"He's fine. He never touched the ground."

"I meant you."

"Oh," I said and waved my hand dismissively. "I'm fine. I'm just glad he's okay."

"Braxton, what did Mommy tell you about running down the stairs?" Avery asked her son.

"That I'm not supposed to do it," he said quietly.

"That's right. Now do you understand why Mommy tells you not to run down the stairs?"

He nodded his head and sniffled. "Yes,

Mommy."

Riley grabbed my hand and started pulling. "Come on, Savie; you can sit beside me." I glanced at Avery for help, but she completely ignored me. "Nana! Savie's having dinner with us," Riley yelled.

"Well, I guess it's a good thing I made some extra, isn't it?" Claire said with a smile.

The backdoor opened and an older gentleman stepped inside. "Papa!" Riley squealed and barreled toward the man.

"Hey, peanut! How was school today?" he asked as he picked her up and swung her around.

"Frank, put her down. You'll upset her stomach before dinner," Claire scolded.

"Yes, love," he said and placed Riley on her feet. "And how was your day, dear? How's our girl?" he asked and pecked his wife on the cheek.

"She had a rough night and morning, but her afternoon has been much better."

"Great! Was it something specific? Because if it was, we need to keep doing it."

"It was Savie, Papa. He put Mommy to sleep," Riley informed him.

"Who?" he asked as his eyes landed on me for the first time.

I cleared my throat and extended my hand. "That'd be me, sir. Savior."

"Your name's Savior?" he asked with a raised brow.

"Nickname," I clarified.

He took my hand and shook it. "Frank Cameron."

"Nice to meet you, sir."

"So, you put my girl to sleep?"

I laughed nervously. "I came by to check on her after work and helped her wash her hair. She fell asleep as soon as we were finished."

"Is that right?"

"It is, Papa. She was asleep right on top of him when we got home from school. She was drooling on him, too, like Brax does to his pillow."

"Riley Grace Parker," Avery called, but in a teasing tone. "It's not polite to tell people your mother drools in her sleep. Even if it might be true."

Riley crossed her arms over her chest and stuck her bottom lip out. Braxton had stopped crying but was still in Avery's arms. "Honey, let me take him. You don't need to be putting any extra strain on your body," her father said.

Braxton lifted his head and pointed to me. "Savie." He extended his arms toward me with his little hands opening and closing.

"No, baby, we're getting ready to eat dinner."

"I can take him," I said and reached for the little boy.

Avery made a plate of food for her children and then she made one for me, too. Once everyone was seated, I noticed she didn't have anything in front of her. "You're not going to eat?"

She grimaced. "Over the last few weeks, I've learned it's better if I wait until everyone else is finished before I try to eat anything."

"So, Savior, what kind of work do you do?" Frank asked.

"I manage a gym that just opened up last week," I said as I took a bite of my food with Braxton perched on my lap.

"I thought Avery said you worked security at the bar."

"I did. I'm a member of the Blackwings MC. I do whatever job I'm assigned."

"You get steady work?"

"Yes, sir."

Seemingly satisfied with my answer, Frank focused on his meal and the conversation turned toward the children. Once they were finished, Claire scooted them out of the room and Frank followed her, leaving Avery and I alone in the kitchen. Without a word, I got up and made her a small plate of food.

"I don't know if I can eat that," she confessed.

"Will you try? You've got to get some nutrition in you."

"I know. But the doctor said it was okay right now. That it was more important for me to stay hydrated than to worry about my food intake."

"What about some protein shakes? Do you think you could drink one of those?"

Her forehead wrinkled while she thought it over. "I don't know. Maybe."

"Stay right here. I'll be back in just a few minutes," I said and darted out the back door.

I hauled ass to the gym and ran inside to grab a few different flavors of the premade shakes we had in stock. I waved to the guy at the desk—Adam, I think—and ran back out to my bike.

When I walked back into Avery's house, she was sitting exactly where I left her. "Here you go. Which one would you like to try?"

"Where did you get these?" she asked.

"I work at a gym. We have tons of these in stock."

"Can I try the vanilla one?"

"You can try them all. Whichever ones you can keep down, I'll bring a case over for you," I offered.

"Cross your fingers," she said and brought the bottle to her lips. She took her time, taking small sips, but she managed to drink the entire bottle.

"I don't want to jinx it, so I'm not going to ask."

She laughed lightly. "That's probably a good idea."

"Well," I said and clapped my hands together. "I should probably get going."

"Thank you."

"You can call me, you know? If you need anything," I trailed off. "Or if you just want to."

She nodded. "Okay."

"Okay," I said and kissed the top of her head before I left.

CHAPTER SEVENTEEN

Avery

I wiped my mouth and flushed the toilet before I carefully stood up. I'd been getting dizzy when I changed positions too quickly and was making an effort to take things slower. Surprisingly, I had gotten used to the nausea to some extent, but I felt awful all the time. It was all I could do to get my kids ready for school in the morning. Thank goodness my mom was able to take them to school for me because there was no way I could have driven them.

"Honey," my mom said and cupped my

cheeks. "I think you need to call the doctor. You can't keep going on like this. There has to be something they can do for you."

I sighed. "Yeah, you're probably right. I'll give them a call this morning."

"Good. Let me know if they want to see you. I have a few appointments this morning, but your dad can take you," she said and turned to the stairs. "Grandbabies! If we leave now, we can stop for donuts on the way to school!"

"But don't run down the stairs!" I shouted; at least, I tried to.

"Go sit down, sweetie. I'll bring you a protein shake and a Coke before we leave."

I collapsed onto the couch and pulled the blanket over me. "Bye, Mommy," Riley said quietly. "I hope you feel better soon. You've been sick for a long time."

I pulled her in for a hug. "I feel better already, baby girl. I'll be fine. You have a good day at school, okay?"

"Okay. I love you."

"I love you, too," I said and kissed her cheek.

"Bye, Mommy. Love you," Brax mumbled.

"Love you, too. Have a good day," I said while I hugged and kissed my little man.

Mom placed my drinks on the end table

beside me, as well as my cell phone. "Call the doctor as soon as they open and let me know what they say."

"Will do," I promised and fell asleep right after they left.

When I woke, I was covered in sweat and vomit was already on its way up and out. I leaned forward and barely managed to get my hands on the little trash can my children affectionately named Hurley.

Something was different. I usually threw up once and that was it. But this time, I kept heaving and heaving and couldn't seem to stop. And there was a new pain in my stomach that felt like someone was squeezing something inside of me. I screamed in frustration before I started to cry.

Grabbing my cell phone from the end table, I called Savior. Just as he answered, another round of heaving hit me hard.

"Avery! Answer me!" he yelled into the phone.

"Sick," was all I managed to say while dry-heaving and gasping for breath. There was a strange pressure on my chest that made it hard for me to catch my breath.

"I'm on my way. Stay on the phone with me," he said.

"Yeah," I choked out and pressed my hand over the place where it hurt.

When the pain finally eased off, I collapsed into a heap on the floor, clinging to Hurley and crying hysterically.

The front door crashed open and Savior stepped into my living room with a look of sheer panic on his face. "Oh, Avery. Fuck! What happened, baby?"

"Sick," I cried. "I'm so sick."

He scooped me and my disgusting trash can off the floor and started walking. "Where are your keys?" he asked.

I pointed to the hook by the front door where I always hung my keys. He grabbed them and closed the door behind us. "I'll have one of the guys come by and fix the door."

I honestly didn't care at that point. I just wanted to feel better. He maneuvered the seat belt around me and Hurley and got into the driver's seat. Before I could ask where he was taking me, he was on his phone. "Hey, man, did River work last night?" There was a pause, and then, "Will you call her and see if she'll wait for me? I'm on my way there now with Avery. Thanks, brother."

"Who's River?"

"My brother's girl. She's an ER nurse, and I trust her," he said.

She was waiting by the door when Savior carried me inside. "What's going on, Savior?"

"She won't stop throwing up and it's getting worse."

"Follow me and we'll get you checked in. How long has this been going on?" she asked.

"For about six weeks," I said.

"What?"

"I'm pregnant and have HG. But this is different."

"When did the different stuff start?"

"I'm not sure. Maybe a few days ago."

"All right. I'm going to get an IV started and get some fluids going. Then, one of the doctors will be in to see you."

"Knock, knock," a woman called from the door. "Hi, I'm Dr. Daniels. Why are we seeing you today?"

I started gagging again before I could explain. Savior placed Hurley in my hands and answered the doctor for me.

"Have you had any other symptoms?"

I nodded and held up one finger. As soon as I could speak, I said, "I have this dull ache in my chest. I didn't really notice it until I was trying to catch my breath, but I think it's been there for a few days. I woke up covered in sweat last night and this morning, and the nausea and vomiting has been significantly worse over the past few days."

She nodded and walked to the sink to wash her hands. "I'm just going to check a few things," she said and proceeded to feel all around my neck and shoulders. Then, she brought out that damned light and shined it in every orifice above my belly button.

"I know this probably won't be pleasant for you, but I need to feel your abdomen. I'll try not to press hard," she said, not waiting for me to agree. She was true to her word and was finished quickly.

"Okay, we're going to give you some fluids. I'm going to order some lab work, and we'll get you something for nausea. Is there anything else you need?"

"I would do just about anything for a toothbrush."

"I think we can arrange that. But, I don't want you to eat or drink anything for right now."
"No argument here," I promised.

"Do you want me to call your mom?" Savior asked.

"Yes, but tell her not to come up here just yet," I said.

I closed my eyes and tried to breathe through the nausea. I knew there was nothing in my stomach and I dreaded dry-heaving.

"Yes, ma'am. I'll call as soon as we know something, and I won't leave her side," Savior said.

"You don't have to stay with me. You probably need to get back to work."

"I'm not leaving you here. Bronze and Batta were already there working out, so they're going to cover for me."

"Thank them for me."

"I will," he said and paused. "I've been meaning to ask you…are you okay financially? Because I can help out if you're not."

"Thank you, but I've got everything under control," I replied and didn't offer any other explanation. I didn't want to think about the fact that I was fine because of my husband's life insurance, and I'm sure he didn't want to think about that either.

"Do you have a job?"

I snorted and shook my head. "I've really kept you at a distance," I mumbled to myself. "I'm a graphic designer. I create book covers, logos, and promotional graphics for authors."

"So, you work from home?"

I nodded. "For the most part, but I can work from anywhere if I have my laptop," I explained.

"Can you show me some of your designs?" he asked.

"Sure. Let me see your phone."

I internally smiled when he handed it over without an ounce of hesitation. I pulled up my website and clicked on my premade covers section before handing it back to him. "These are some that I currently have for sale."

He spent a good ten minutes scrolling through my designs, zooming in and out on several. "These are really good. Did you say you do logos, too?"

"Yeah. Scroll back up to the top and click on the logos tab."

After scrolling through that section, he looked up with a smile. "Will you design a new logo for the gym?"

"If you're serious, yes. But, if you're just asking because you feel some sort of obligation to me, then the answer is no."

"Avery, I do have an obligation to you, or at least to our child, but that's not why I asked. The gym needs rebranding, and I like your work," he said sincerely. "Actually, the bar and the property management businesses probably need logos, too. I think Judge already has one, but he might be interested in upgrading."

"What do you think my man already has?" River asked as she entered the room with what I hoped was a syringe full of anti-nausea medication in her hand.

"A logo for Jackson Security."

She laughed. "No, he has 'Jackson' in all capital letters on top of 'Security' with only the first letter capitalized, all in white. Why do you ask?"

"Avery is a graphic designer and she just showed me some of her work. I'm going to hire her to design something for the gym."

River nodded and reached for my arm. "This is Zofran. It's for nausea," she said before she gave me the medicine.

"Oh, thank you, thank you, thank you," I chanted.

"That bad, huh?"

"It's been absolutely awful. I'm having my tubes tied after this one," I vowed.

"It'll take about fifteen minutes for the Zofran to kick in and start working," she explained. "Now, about this logo. I want to see what you showed Savior."

I pointed to him. "It's on his phone."

Savior handed over his phone and she scrolled through my site, oohing and aahing every now and again. She tapped the screen a few times and then another phone dinged before she handed it back to Savior. "I sent the link to myself so I can show Jonah when I get home. He'll definitely be interested."

"Savior said you worked last night. You must be exhausted. Please don't hang around on my account," I told her.

She waved me off. "There have been plenty of times I didn't leave here until three hours after my shift ended, and that was not by choice. This, I don't mind whatsoever. Plus, he's like family, so that makes you and your little bean family, too."

"Well, thank you. I appreciate you staying and getting us back here so quickly. I'm starting to feel a little better."

"Good. I'll hang around for a little bit longer before I head home."

"Didn't the doctor say she was going to order some lab work?" I asked.

"She did. You have nice, juicy veins, so I pulled some blood when I started your IV to save you a stick."

"Thank you," I said again.

She hung around for another thirty minutes or so before she left. She also made sure to introduce us to the nurse that would be taking over for her.

Savior sat quietly in the chair in the corner of the room while I stared at the ceiling. When I couldn't take it any longer, I said, "We have got to talk or something or else I'm going to go crazy just sitting here."

He stood and came to sit on the edge of the bed by my feet. "What would you like to talk about?"

"I don't care. Anything."

"Why'd you decide to move to Devil Springs?" he asked. "I mean, why did you choose Devil Springs?"

"I wanted to live somewhere close enough to easily visit with my parents, yet far enough away that I wouldn't know anybody in town. Devil Springs was the only place like that with good schools and low crime rates," I said honestly.

"Why did you want to live in a town where you didn't know anyone?"

I gave him a pointed look. "You know why."

"Oh. The pity looks," he said knowingly.

"You seem to know something about—"

A knock on the door interrupted me. "Hi, Mrs. Parker, I'm Dr. Cadet-Destil. I have some test results to go over with you. Sir, would you mind stepping outside for just a moment?"

"It's okay. He can stay."

"Okay, then. Well, we ran a few tests and you are dehydrated. Your white blood cell count is also elevated as well as other labs that we commonly see with gallbladder problems. Since you're pregnant, I'm going to start with an abdominal ultrasound before ordering something more invasive."

"And if it is my gallbladder?" I asked.

"Depending on what the ultrasound shows, I'll refer you to GI or a general surgeon. It's not uncommon for gallbladders to go bad during or right after pregnancy. So, I'll get this ordered and we'll go from there."

"You have got to be kidding me," I groaned and flopped back into the bed. My gallbladder? Really? Being pregnant with hyperemesis wasn't enough?

"How will this affect the baby?" Savior asked.

"We won't know for sure until we've clearly diagnosed the issue but, in general, gallbladder surgery during pregnancy is fairly common.

Sometimes you can wait until after delivery to have the surgery, but each case is different. I can assure you, we will make sure you are aware of all the risks and benefits before we decide on a treatment plan," she explained.

"Great. This is just fucking great," I grumbled.

"We're going to give you another bag of fluids. After the ultrasound, we'll see about letting you have some clear liquids."

"Thank you," I said even though I didn't mean it. I knew it wasn't her fault, and she was trying to help me. But, damn it, I was sick of being sick.

Once she was gone, I turned my head into the pillow and cried. "Hey, it's not that bad," Savior soothed as he wrapped his arms around me.

"I can't do anything," I sobbed. "I can't take care of my kids. I can barely take care of myself."

"You were doing much better until this happened. It's just a little setback. You'll be back on your feet in no time," he said softly and gently rocked me from side to side.

"I feel so useless," I confessed.

"You're not useless. You're raising a family and growing a baby. You accomplish more than most people every single day by merely existing."

I looked up and saw the sincerity in his eyes. He really believed what he said. Before I realized what I was doing, I leaned forward and gently pressed my lips to his, even as the tears still ran down my face.

"It's going to be okay," he whispered against my lips.

"Thank you," I whispered back.

"For what?"

"For being here. And for being you."

CHAPTER EIGHTEEN

Savior

Several hours later, Avery was discharged from the hospital with a handful of new prescriptions and an appointment for the following day with a general surgeon to discuss having her gallbladder removed. I dropped her prescriptions off on the way back to her place and told her I would pick them up when they were ready.

When I pulled into her driveway, she was sound asleep. I quietly got out of the car and unlocked the repaired front door before I went back to carry her inside. "What are you doing?" she asked through a yawn.

"Taking you inside. Do you want to go to the couch or your bed?"

"Bed, please," she said and snuggled against my chest.

After I placed her on her bed and pulled the covers over her, I kissed her forehead and turned to go back downstairs, but she grabbed my wrist. "Stay with me."

The pleading tone of her voice had me agreeing instantly. "Okay, I'll stay."

She smiled with her eyes closed and scooted over, patting the bed beside her. I shrugged, kicked my shoes off, and climbed in the bed beside her. She wiggled closer and fit her body right next to mine with her head resting on my chest.

"I love the way you smell," she said dreamily causing me to laugh.

"Go to sleep, baby."

I was in the middle of a hot as hell dream featuring Avery when something woke me. I cracked my eyes open to find her staring at me with a mischievous grin on her face. And the next second, I realized why.

I reached down and grabbed her hand that

was rubbing my dick. "Avery, what are you doing?"

"If you have to ask, I'm clearly not doing it right."

I moved her hand up and down my hard length. "Oh, you were doing it right. But we're not doing this. Not while you're sick."

She dropped her head and mumbled something against my chest. "What was that?"

"My vagina isn't sick," she said more clearly.

I threw my head back and laughed until I felt her body start to tremble. "Fuck," I cursed and rolled to my side so I could see her face. "It's not that I don't want to, but I'd feel like a complete asshole."

"I don't care. I'll just lay here. Please don't make me beg."

"Come here," I said and slid my hand around to the back of her neck to gently pull her to me. I cupped her cheek with my other hand and kissed her softly. I had no intention of doing anything other than kissing her, but things became heated rather quickly, as they tended to do between the two of us.

Before my rational mind could stop me, we were both naked and she was guiding me into her. She groaned loudly. "Oh, Savior, you feel so fucking good."

I paused and said something I'd wanted to say to her since I found out she was pregnant. "I want you to call me Kellan."

She locked eyes with me and nodded. "I want to call you Kellan."

"Okay," I said with a smile and started to move. It was probably the strangest sexual experience of my life. On one hand, I was terrified of causing her some kind of harm; but, on the other hand, I was enjoying every second of having her body wrapped around mine.

"Kellan," she gasped. "More. I need more."

"Not giving you more, baby," I said and dropped my mouth to her breasts to lavish her sensitive nipples.

She wiggled and writhed beneath me, and then she was coming with my name on her lips. With a contented sigh, she gripped my hair and tugged my mouth to hers, kissing me through my own release.

"You okay?" I asked while I smoothed the hair from her face.

"Much better," she smiled.

"Good. Let me get cleaned up and I'll help you wash your hair before I go pick up your medicine," I said.

She tightened her arms around my shoulder. "You really are a good man."

I dropped my head and swallowed past the emotion trying to clog my throat. "I try to be." My parents and my grandfather had raised me to be a good man and I tried to live up to their expectations every day of my life.

With that, I went to the bathroom and returned with a washcloth for her. Once we were both dressed, we went downstairs and I helped her onto the kitchen counter.

"Where'd you learn how to do this?" she asked.

"I remember seeing my dad do it for my mom when she was sick. She said no matter how bad she felt, having her hair washed always made her feel better."

"Was she sick often?"

I shook my head. "No, she wasn't. But somehow, she ended up getting the flu every year."

"Can I ask what happened to your parents?" she asked carefully.

I nodded and focused on rinsing the shampoo from her hair. I didn't like talking about it, but I'd gotten to the point where I could say what happened to them and be okay. "They died in a boating accident."

"Oh, Kellan, I'm so sorry. Were you with them?"

I squeezed the conditioner in my hand and smoothed it over her hair. "No, I was spending the night at my grandfather's. I usually did go with them, but fishing season had just started and it was still too cold for me to be out there that early in the morning. They were heading back to the dock when a guy on a jet ski cut in front of them. His buddy did the same thing to another boat beside my parents. Both boats swerved to miss the jet skis and hit each other. My parents were in a fishing boat which was much smaller than the boat that hit them. I don't know all the details, but Gramps said they were killed instantly and the people in the other boat were seriously injured."

"What happened to the people on the jet skis?"

I cleared my throat and focused on rinsing her hair. "My parents, Blake and Sienna Ward, were well known in the boating and fishing community of Croftridge. Some boaters stopped to help, while several other boaters chased down the jet skis and corralled them until the authorities got there. They were both drunk and ended up going to prison."

Avery reached up and placed her hand on my cheek. "I'm so sorry, Kellan. Thank you for sharing that with me."

I couldn't find the words to respond, so I leaned down and placed a kiss on her forehead before I went back to rinsing her hair.

The sound of a camera had me turning around and reaching for my knife before I realized Avery's mother was standing behind us. "Isn't this just the sweetest thing? I'll even forgive you for not calling me back with an update."

"Oh, shit. Sorry, Claire. We fell asleep as soon as we got back to the house."

"It's okay. I figured no news was good news, but thought I'd swing by and check on things before I went to pick up the kids. So, what did the doctor say?"

I finished rinsing Avery's hair while she filled her mother in on what the doctor said.

"Your gallbladder? No one in our family has gallbladder problems," she stated. "Are they sure?"

"I don't think it's necessarily a genetic thing, but yes, they're sure," Avery explained. "I have an appointment with a surgeon tomorrow to discuss when to have it removed, but based on what Dr. Cadet-Destil said, it needs to come out sooner rather than later."

"Well, hopefully, you'll start feeling better after it's out," she said cheerfully. "I'm going to go pick up your prescriptions before I get the kids. Do you need me to get anything else while I'm out?"

"No, thanks, Mom."

Claire turned her attention to me. "You know, you could make a killing if you were willing to do that shirtless," she said and held her hands up. "I'm just saying."

"Mom!" Avery scolded, but then burst into laughter while pointing at my shirt. "She's not wrong." I glanced down to see that I had unknowingly soaked the front of my white T-shirt while I was washing her hair.

I reached behind me and yanked my shirt over my head by the collar. "Woo! Nana's gotta go!" Claire said and headed for the door.

"Sorry about her."

I shrugged. "Doesn't bother me. I'm going to toss this in your dryer."

"Do you end up washing and drying your clothes at other people's houses or is it just mine?"

I couldn't help but laugh. "Oh, it happens

way more than it should, but the women of the club are always good about helping a brother out."

Avery stiffened and turned her anger-filled eyes to me. "I didn't need to know all that."

It took me a minute to realize what she meant. "Oh, I meant the Old Ladies, not the club whores."

"You're not helping."

I stepped between her legs and circled my arms around her waist. "You're the only woman I've laid a hand on since I moved to Devil Springs." From the moment my eyes landed on her when she was staring into her drink at Precious Metals, the thought of another woman hadn't so much as crossed my mind.

"Oh," she said and averted her eyes. "Well, it's not like I have any right to say anything about what you do or don't do. I'm sorry."

"Yes, you do."

When she brought her eyes back to mine, they were filled with a mix of hope and fear. "What?"

"You want to do this now?"

"I'm not sure I know what you're referring to," she hedged. She knew exactly what I meant.

"Do you want to have this conversation now?

Because of our past, I haven't brought it up. I didn't want to push you, but it seems like you're ready to be pushed a little."

"What do you mean?" she asked and wrinkled her forehead.

"I'm not just here because of the baby," I said softly and ran my hand up her arm until I reached her jaw. "I'm here for you, too. But you need to let me know if you're not ready for that."

She nodded and a tear slipped down her cheek. Taking in a shaky breath, she said, "I honestly don't know if I'm ready. And I'm scared."

I smoothed my thumb along her cheek and swiped away the few tears that had spilled over. "I hope you know that I would never ask you to forget him. I know I wouldn't be standing here with you right now if he was still here."

She started shaking her head rapidly and cupped her hand over her mouth. She jumped off the counter and ran for the bathroom. "Fuck!" I yelled and ran after her.

I expected to find her bent over the toilet, but she was sitting in the floor hugging her knees and breathing heavily. "We were separated. No one other than my parents knew about it," she confessed. "So, there's a very real chance that you would be standing where you are right now," she said between breaths.

"Are you okay?" I asked.

She visibly swallowed and nodded. "I'll be okay. Just a little panic attack," she said dismissively and wiped the faint sheen of sweat from her face. "I'm sorry. I've held that in for so long. I did love him, and it hurt like hell when he died, but we didn't have the picture-perfect life everyone made it out to be—at least not at the end. In the weeks before he left, he was rarely home because he picked up extra shifts, and when he was home, he barely spoke to me."

I had no idea what to say. Her confession didn't change anything for me. I was still responsible for the death of an innocent man. I was still responsible for her children growing up without their father. And I was still responsible for making her a widow.

"I was really angry after he died. For a lot of different reasons, but one of them was because I knew our issues would never be resolved. He, um, he left me, and he never gave me a reason. And for a little while after his death, I completely blocked out the part where he'd left and convinced myself that we did have a picture-perfect life. But, my mother and my therapist put a stop to that as soon as they realized what was going on. So, once I figured out that I was grieving for something that wasn't real, I had to start over and grieve for what I'd actually lost."

She slowly got to her feet and nervously smoothed her hands over her hair. "You must think I'm crazy."

I shook my head and opened my arms for her. She didn't hesitate to come to me. "I don't think you're crazy. I think you've had a lot to deal with over the last few years."

"You can say that again."

"Let me ask you something. Earlier you said you were scared. Is it because you're not sure if you're ready or is it because you don't know why he left?"

"Because I don't know why he left," she confessed.

"Thought so. Listen to what I'm about to say and hear it. I will not do that to you. I will tell you why I'm doing something before I do it. Communication is everything in a relationship."

"Okay."

"Okay, what?" I asked and had to force myself to breathe.

"Okay, we can do this you and me thing."

"Hell, yes, we can," I said and kissed the shit out of her.

When our lips parted, she placed her hand on my chest. "There's just one thing. Um, I don't want the kids to know we're anything more than friends right now. Are you okay with that?"

I covered her hand with mine and nodded. "Yes, I'll go along with whatever you think is best, but what are you going to tell them about the baby?"

She grimaced. "I haven't figured that out yet. I've been putting it off, but I don't have much longer before I start showing."

My hand dropped to her stomach and I smiled. She was already showing, but I wasn't about to point it out. "I can't believe my baby's in there," I whispered in awe.

She laughed, "A part of me can't either. Even before everything happened, I didn't think I'd have any more kids."

I was silent for a few long moments, trying to formulate my words. Finally, I asked, "How do you feel about having another one?"

She didn't hesitate to answer. "I'm not going to lie; at first, I wasn't thrilled about it. But, I've always believed things happen for a reason, even the things that are hard to accept. I've had some time to come to terms with it, and I'm happy about it." She laughed lightly. "I'll be much happier once I start feeling better."

I leaned in and kissed her forehead. "Speaking of, you need to rest," I said and lifted her into my arms.

"What are you doing?"

"Taking you to the couch. Or, would you rather me take you to your room?"

"The couch is fine," she said.

CHAPTER NINETEEN

Avery

Kellan carried me to the couch and helped me get settled. "I'm going to head out before your Mom gets back with the kids. Do you need anything else before I go?"

"Would you grab my laptop for me? I need to get some work done while I can." Between being in the hospital and being sick at home, I'd fallen behind on my work. Thankfully, most of my clients had been with me for a while and were very understanding.

Kellan returned with my laptop and charger

and kissed the top of my head. "I'll call and check on you later, but you call me if you need anything. I don't care what it is or what time it is."

"Thank you, Kellan. I really appreciate everything you're doing for me."

He gently brushed his fingers against my cheek. "I care about you. I'd do anything for you," he said and softly kissed my lips.

I spent the next hour working on finalizing two book cover designs and answering multiple queries from my social media pages. When my children came through the front door, I was ready for a break.

"Mommy!" Riley yelled. "Jenna lives on our street! Can I go over to her house and play? Pleeeease!"

"Hold on just a minute. Who is Jenna?"

My sassy little girl huffed and planted a hand on her hip. "My best friend," she said as if she'd already told me this new bit of information.

"Well, I'm happy you have a best friend that lives so close, but I will need to meet Jenna's parents before you can go over to her house."

Riley stuck out her bottom lip and stomped her foot. "I'll never get to play with her. You're too sick to do anything!"

She started to run to her room, but stopped when I yelled, "Freeze!" I took a deep breath and lowered my voice. "Riley, you do not talk to me like that. Go sit down for five minutes and then we'll talk about this."

With a scrunched face, she crossed her arms over her chest and stuck out her bottom lip, but she managed to quietly walk to the love seat and sit. I turned my attention to my son. "And how was your day, Braxton?"

My little man smiled broadly. "It was great, Mommy. I kissed Lucy on the lips and now we're getting married."

"You did what?"

"I kissed Lucy. We're gonna get married and have a baby. Like you and Savie!"

I gasped in horror and slapped my hand over my face. "I'm not...we're not..."

My mother reached out to take Braxton's backpack from his shoulders. "You can tell Mommy the rest of your story in a little while. Go put on some play clothes and come to the kitchen for a snack."

She jerked her head in Riley's direction and gave me a pointed look. "Riley, go change into some play clothes, too. We'll talk after you've had your snack," I said.

Once both kids were upstairs, my mom said, "He doesn't know anything. He's just verbalizing his assumptions about you and Savior."

"He asked me today when I was going to tell the kids about the baby."

She sat down beside me and clasped her hands in her lap. "And what did you say?"

"I said I didn't know yet. Mom, I have no idea how to tell them I'm pregnant," I confessed.

Mom nodded knowingly. "Listen, Avery, you're approaching it like they're going to have adult reactions. They're not going to automatically know you were diddling the hot guy and got knocked up."

I groaned. "Mom! Please don't say it like that."

She laughed. "Excuse me. Would you have rather I said 'fucking the hot guy'?"

"Anyway," I said and rolled my eyes. "You're right; I was anticipating adult reactions from them. And, judging by Riley's outburst just now, I think she needs an explanation as to why I've been so sick."

"I agree. Do you want me to stick around while you tell them or would you rather it just be the three of you?"

I thought about it for a moment before

answering. "Thanks for offering, but I think it would be better if it was just me and the kids. That way, they can talk to you about it if they need to without feeling like you are on my side."

"I am on your side, sweetie."

"I know, Mom. And I'm so grateful for everything you've done to help me over the last few years. I wouldn't have gotten through this without you."

"Yes, you would have. You're a strong woman, but I'm glad I was able to make a bad situation a little more bearable for you."

I cleared my throat and shifted uncomfortably. "I, um, I told Kellan about Ian today." When her forehead wrinkled, I added, "About us being separated."

"What made you decide to do that?"

"We were talking and he said something like, 'I know I wouldn't be standing here with you if he was still here.' So, I told him there was a very good chance he would be because things weren't what they seemed."

Mom nodded. "Are you glad you told him?"

"Yes, I am, surprisingly. Of all people, I think he deserved to know. He's still carrying around a lot of guilt about the accident, and I felt like it was wrong to allow him to continue believing a misconception. He's been so careful of my feelings, about everything, and I just wanted him to know the truth. It doesn't change anything, but I don't know, maybe that knowledge will help him, at least where I'm concerned."

Mom exhaled slowly. "Avery Grace, I love you, honey, but I don't know how in the hell you get yourself into situations like this."

I shook my head. "I don't know either. It's definitely not something I did on purpose."

"Well, I'll go make the kids a snack and get them started on their homework before I start cooking dinner. Do you need anything right now?"

I shook my head. "No, I'm fine right now. I'm going to try to finish a few things for work."

I didn't get any more work completed. Within minutes after my mother went into the kitchen, I was fast asleep on the couch.

"Avery. Wake up, dear."

I reluctantly opened my eyes and blinked up at my mother hovering over me. "Sorry," I croaked. "I guess I fell asleep. Is it time for dinner?"

She smoothed her hand over my hair and shook her head. "No, honey. I've already fed the kids and gave Braxton a bath. They're upstairs playing before bed. Do you want me to stay tonight?"

"No," I said and put my laptop on the coffee table. "I can get them in the bed."

"Are you sure? I really don't mind staying," she said worriedly.

"I'm sure. I promise I'll call if it's too much."

"Okay," she sighed. "I'll see you in the morning."

After she left, I took a few minutes to find the courage to go upstairs and face my children. Once I found it, I got to my feet and slowly climbed the stairs. By the time I reached the top, I was ready to fall to the floor, but I forced myself to make it down the hall to my room.

"Riley! Braxton! Y'all come in here for a minute," I called down the hall.

I had just flopped down in the middle of the bed when they came running in excitedly. Both bounded onto the bed and dropped down with a bounce.

"What do you want, Mommy?" Riley asked with wide eyes full of excitement.

"I want to talk to you both about why I've been sick," I said slowly and cleared my throat. "As it turns out, there are two things that are making me sick right now. One is my gallbladder that I have to have a doctor work on—"

"What's the other thing?" Riley interrupted.

"Well, when the doctor was looking for what was making me sick, they found out that I'm going to have a baby," I said carefully and braced for their reactions.

Riley squealed excitedly. "Oooh, I'm going to be a big sister again!"

Braxton was less enthusiastic. "Will I have to share my toys with it?"

I laughed and ruffled his hair. "Only if you want to. And it's a baby, not an 'it'."

"You just called it an 'it'," Braxton pointed out.

I sighed in exasperation. "You're right, son. I did."

"Are we getting a little brother or a little sister?" Riley asked.

"I don't know yet."

"When will you know?"

"Probably in a few weeks."

"Can I go play now?" Braxton asked. He didn't seem to care one way or another about having another sibling as long as he didn't have to share his beloved toys.

"Not yet, son. We need to talk about something else. It is not okay to kiss little girls.

You can be friends with them, and you can even call one your girlfriend; but, you're only allowed to hug her if you ask her and she says it's okay. Do you understand?"

"Yes, Mommy. But she asked me to kiss her," he said.

"Did she now?" He nodded his head several times. The little hussy. "Well, if she asks you to do that again, you politely tell her no."

"Okay. Can I go play now?"

I sighed. "Yes, son. Go play."

He scampered off to his room and I turned my attention to my daughter. She was a clever child and already knew what I was going to say. "I'm sorry for being sassy. I just wanted to play with Jenna. I didn't know a baby was why you can't do anything with us anymore."

I pulled her in for a hug so she wouldn't see the tears welling up in my eyes. "I'm sorry, honey." I sniffled and took a few slow, deep breaths to get my emotions under control. "I know it's a school night, but how about you and Braxton go pick out a movie and we'll have a slumber party in here tonight?"

"Can I pick the movie?"

"Yes, but you can't pick something you know your brother won't like. So, no Barbie movies," I told her. We had plenty of other movies that they both enjoyed. Personally, I was hoping she'd pick one of the ones I enjoyed, too.

"Braxton!" she yelled as she ran down the hall. "We're having a movie night in Mommy's room!"

Ten minutes later, we were all settled in my bed watching Ice Age. Even though I cherished the time spent with my kids, I couldn't help but wish Kellan was there with us, too.

CHAPTER TWENTY

Savior

After leaving Avery, I went straight to the clubhouse to talk to Copper. When I arrived, the clubhouse was surprisingly quiet. Layla and Leigh were in the common room hunched over a laptop but no one else was in sight.

"Is Copper in his office?" I asked causing both of them to startle.

"Shit, Savior," Layla gasped. "You scared me."

"I'm sorry, Layla. I didn't mean to," I

apologized and held my hands up.

"It's fine," she said. "He should be in his office."

I knocked on the door and waited for the okay to enter. "Savior, what are you doing here?"

"I wanted to talk to you about something if you have a few minutes."

"Have a seat," he said and gestured to one of the chairs. "What's going on?" he asked and leaned back in his chair to study me.

"I spent the morning at the hospital with Avery. She's been pretty sick during the majority of the pregnancy and now they're saying she needs to have her gallbladder removed," I explained.

"Shit, man. Is the baby okay?"

"The doctor says the baby's fine. But I'm worried about her. When she called me this morning, it took me ten minutes to get to her. I wanted to know if I could work at the bar or something so I can be closer to her while she's recovering from the surgery."

Copper nodded and rubbed his chin. "When is her surgery?"

"She'll find out tomorrow, but it will probably be some time this week."

"Let me know when it is. You can take a week

off to be with her and don't worry about working. Bronze can help out at the gym."

"Thanks, Prez, but I don't know if she wants me there the whole time."

Copper smirked. "Don't give her a choice."

I laughed. "Got it."

With that, I left the clubhouse and headed to the gym. I felt like shit for dumping all of my new responsibilities on Coal, and I wanted to make sure he knew that.

When I arrived, I expected to find him in the office, but it was empty. After searching the entire place, I found Steve at the front desk. "Is Coal here?"

"Yeah, he's downstairs with Bronze and Batta."

My eyes widened in surprise, but I kept my thoughts to myself. What in the hell were they doing downstairs? Two minutes later, I had my answer.

"Keep your fucking hands up, Coal!" Batta yelled as Bronze's fist connected with the side of Coal's head. "So that right there doesn't fucking happen! You can't block him if your hands aren't up!"

"What're y'all doing down here?" I asked and leaned on the ropes beside Batta.

He snorted. "Giving Coal some sparring lessons without a damn audience. Did you see those bitches upstairs? Even I felt violated by the eye-fucking that was going on."

I laughed. "I'm sure you did. How long you been down here?"

Batta shrugged. "Twenty minutes or so. Why?"

I grinned. "Because I want a turn."

Batta threw his head back and laughed. "Go grab some gear. And for fuck's sake, make sure you have a good mouthguard. I'll do a lot of shit, but I am never searching for part of a tongue again."

I held my hands up. "I don't want to know."

When I returned with my gear, Coal was climbing out of the ring. "Fuck me. That's him going easy?"

Bronze laughed. "Yeah, and I'm out of practice." He turned to me. "Come on, boy. Come get you some."

"That sounds like a line from a bad porno," I said as I vaulted myself over the ropes into the ring.

Bronze threw his hands in the air. "Damn it, Savior. You ruined my next line."

"Which was?"

He grinned. "I'm about to pound that ass."

"Just stop," I chuckled.

"Yeah, yeah. All right, let's see what you got."

We moved around the ring while sizing each other up. I'd paid attention when Bronze was fighting Dez. He was methodical and selective with the punches he threw. Funnily enough, so was I.

"Will one of you nut up and throw a damn punch? This is the most boring match I've ever seen!" Batta shouted.

I kept my eyes on Bronze and grinned around my mouth piece. He rolled his eyes giving me the perfect opportunity to strike. I landed a solid right hook to the side of his helmet. Initially, I was proud of myself but quickly realized my mistake when a pissed off Bronze came at me full force. I barely got any hits in because it was all I could do to deflect him.

A bell sounded and Batta shouted, "Time!"

I stepped back and fell against the ropes as I removed my helmet and gloves. Coal was suddenly in front of me squirting water into my mouth and over my head.

"Holy shit, Savior, where'd you learn to fight like that?" Batta asked.

"Like what?" I panted. "He was whooping my

ass."

"No, I wasn't," Bronze said, sounding far less winded than I was. "You weren't landing any hits, but neither was I. You're one hell of a defensive fighter. We just need to strengthen your offensive skills." He chuckled and added, "And work on building up your stamina."

I couldn't help but laugh, too. "My stamina's fine when I'm not up against a fucking freight train."

"Let's go again. I'll ease up on you."

Once I had my gear back in place, Batta rang the bell to start round two. We went a total of four rounds before we called it quits.

"We need to make this a regular thing. You've got some serious potential," Bronze said as we walked to the downstairs locker room.

"I don't know about all that, but it's a great workout, so count me in."

After I showered, I realized that my change of clothes was upstairs in the office. Shrugging, I quickly ran a towel over my hair and wrapped it around my waist. The door leading to the basement was just down the hall from the office, so I could get to it without running into anyone, or so I thought.

When I emerged from the stairs and turned

to the office, my eyes landed on the one woman I never wanted to see again. The corners of her lips curved up into a sly smile when her eyes landed on my bare torso. "Kellan," she purred and swung her hips out while she sashayed toward me.

"Stop right there, Kelly," I barked. "What the fuck are you doing here?"

She froze and her mouth dropped open. Dramatically bringing a hand up to the cold heart residing behind her fake tits, she did a piss poor job of pretending to be surprised by my reaction. "Are you upset with me about something?"

I half-laughed/half-scoffed. "Are you serious right now?" When her only response was to blink her clumpy, black eyelashes at me, I threw my head back and laughed for about five seconds before I schooled my expression and glared at her. "Yes, cunt, I'm serious. I'm only going to tell you one time. Get. The. Fuck. Out. Of. Here!"

She took a step back. "You're scaring me."

"The devil himself couldn't scare you, bitch. Now, go!"

Bronze appeared in the hallway behind the she-bitch. "What's going on?" He came to a stop between us and gave Kelly a once over. "Why are you yelling at this pretty little thing?"

Kelly beamed proudly while I scowled. "Because she's been told many times before that I have no desire to breathe the same air as her soul-sucking ass. And yet, here she is again. I don't know how you found out where I was—and I honestly don't give a shit—but you will leave, and you will not come back. Are we clear?"

She arched an eyebrow while one side of her mouth tipped up in a devious grin. "Okay, Kellan, have it your way."

Bronze's posture changed at her words. "Who is she, brother?"

I sighed and pinched the bridge of my nose. "She's the cunt that keeps on cunting."

"Gonna need a little more than that, man."

"She's my ex-wife."

CHAPTER TWENTY-ONE

Savior

I pushed through the office door and grabbed my clean clothes from my duffle bag in the corner. I knew Bronze followed me, but I didn't give the first fuck if he saw my bare ass.

"She's your what?"

"You heard me. She's my ex-wife."

"How do you have an ex-wife? I thought you and Coal were the same age."

I laughed. "My baby face fools everyone. I'm twenty-six."

"Shit, you don't look it. So, how long were

you married?" he asked while making himself comfortable in the office chair.

Before I could answer him, the door flew open and Coal stuck his head inside. "Need some help up front!"

"Fucking hell," I grumbled to myself. I just knew whatever was going on involved Kelly.

"Here," Bronze said and shoved something into my hands. "You don't say a word and make sure you record everything that happens."

When we arrived at the front desk, Kelly was on the floor with her hands wrapped around her ankle and great, big crocodile tears streaming from her eyes. "I think it's broken!" she wailed.

"What happened?" Bronze asked Adam.

Steve walked up with an ice pack and a bottle of water. "Here you go, ma'am."

I watched as Kelly tossed the ice pack aside before she opened the bottle of water and poured it onto the floor. Then, she pulled her phone from her purse and started taking pictures. "I'm going to sue you!"

Batta rounded the corner and took in the scene. Bronze knelt down beside Kelly and said loud enough for all to hear, "Ma'am, if you'll kindly turn your head and look right over there." She followed the finger pointing to me. "Now, smile for the camera before you get your lying, scamming ass off the floor and walk the fuck out of here. Unless you'd prefer I call the cops and we make this no trespass order official."

She slapped her hands against the floor and pushed to her feet. "I just wanted to talk to you!"

"And he clearly doesn't want to talk to you. Batta?"

Batta chuckled and stepped forward. "You gonna go on your own or am I taking you?"

"You will not touch me!" she screeched.

Batta inhaled deeply causing his chest to puff out. Then, he bent forward and roared, "GOOOOOOO!"

Kelly snatched her shoes from the floor and bolted out the front door while the rest of us erupted into fits of laughter. "Holy shit, Batta! You sounded like a damn lion."

"You fucking looked like one, too!" Bronze added.

Batta held his hands up in the air. "And I didn't fucking touch her!"

Steve finished wiping the water off the floor and picked up the ice pack. "Sorry, sir. When she asked for ice and water, I had no idea she was going to do that."

"It's all good. We were already aware of her

crazy bitch status. Speaking of, if she shows up here again, call the police and have whichever one of us is here come out to deal with her," Bronze told Adam and Steve.

"Who was she, anyway?" Coal asked.

"Let's talk about it in the office," Bronze suggested.

Once we were in the office with the door closed, I leaned against the far wall and faced the others. "Kelly is my ex-wife. We were only married for two years before we filed for a divorce. And as you can see, she takes great pleasure in making other people miserable."

"You were married?" Coal and Batta asked at the same time.

"Yes. For two years. To the bitch you just met. Before you ask, I'm twenty-six," I snapped.

"Do you have any idea what she wanted?" Coal asked.

I snorted derisively. "You mean other than fucking with me just because she can? No, I don't have a clue what she could want."

Bronze got to his feet. "Well, I guess we'll have to wait and see if she comes back." He laughed, "But I think Batta might have scared her off for good. Did you see that bitch's face?"

"Send me that video. I want to see how I

looked," Batta said excitedly.

Bronze pulled his phone from his pocket and dropped back down into the chair. He wiggled the mouse and made a few clicks. "Let's watch it on a bigger screen."

We watched it at least four times. "Oh, fuck, man. It gets better each time," Bronze laughed. "I can't wait to show this to Copper."

"Thanks, brothers," I said seriously.

"Any time, man. She's not the first crazy bitch we've dealt with and I'm sure she won't be the last," Batta said and clapped me on the shoulder.

CHAPTER TWENTY-TWO

Savior

It was still dark outside when I arrived at Avery's house. Instead of knocking on the front door, I sent her a text message to let her know I was outside. Not even thirty seconds later, Claire opened the front door.

"Good morning, Kellan," she said quietly. "Avery's still getting ready. Would you like some coffee?"

"Yes, please," I said almost desperately.

She laughed. "Come on in the kitchen. She should be ready in just a few minutes."

She brought two cups of coffee over to the kitchen table. "Listen, Kellan, I'm going to tell you something about my Avery," she said and lowered her voice. "She's a strong woman, and most of the time, that's a good thing, but it's not such a good thing today. She's scared and she's got it hidden so well you'd think she was getting ready to go to the grocery store, not headed to the hospital to have surgery. Please try to reassure her, even if you don't think she needs it."

I reached over and clasped her hand. "I can do that."

"Thank you. I hate that I can't be there when they take her back," she confessed.

"Would you rather I take the kids to school and you go with her to the hospital?" I offered.

"Yes, that's exactly what I'd rather do, but Avery prefers the plan we have now. I'll be there as soon as I drop the kids off."

Avery walked into the kitchen with a smile on her face. "Good morning. Are we ready to go?"

"I'm ready when you are," I said and glanced at Claire.

"See," she mouthed.

I nodded and took my mug to the sink. Avery hugged and kissed her mother before turning to me. "Ready," she said with a wide smile.

"After you," I said and gestured for her to lead the way.

I opened the passenger door for her and helped her up into my truck before going around to the driver's side. Reaching over, I pulled her into my arms. "Cut the shit, Avery. No one is as happy as you are to be having surgery. It's okay to be nervous. Quite frankly, it's not okay to not be nervous."

She inhaled deeply and fisted my shirt. "I'm scared," she admitted. "I've never had surgery before, and if something happens to me, my babies will be all alone," she confessed.

"They won't be all alone. They'll have your parents, and you know I'll always watch over them, but that's not going to be an issue because you're going to be okay."

"What if something happens to the baby?"

"The doctor assured us the baby would be just fine. Actually, I believe they said there was more risk to the baby if you didn't have the surgery," I reminded her and kissed the top of her head. "You ready to go?"

"No, I wasn't earlier, and I'm definitely not now," she said.

"Well, I hate to break it to you, but if we don't leave now, we're going to be late."

"Fine," she huffed. "Let's get this over with."

When Claire arrived at the hospital, Avery was out of surgery and being moved to recovery. "You just missed the doctor. He said the surgery went according to plan and Avery and the baby are doing fine."

"Oh, thank goodness. Did they say when we can see her?"

"He said someone would come out and get us once they have her situated in recovery."

Thirty minutes later, a nurse took us back to the recovery area. Avery was propped up with her eyes half-open and a pink cup on its way to falling out of her hand. "Let me help you with that, sweetness," I said and reached for the cup.

"Hey, my sexy, badass biker man," she slurred.

"Oh, I see they've given you the good stuff."

"No siree. Only you give me the good stuff. You fu—"

"Your mother is here," I interrupted.

"Well, she knows we've fucked seeing as how your kid is in me," she blurted.

Claire slapped her hand over her mouth to try and stifle her laughter while I looked away completely mortified. "Avery, can we not talk about that in front of your mother, and, you know, the hospital staff?"

"I'm sure they know how babies are made, Kellan. And, look at you. They know your sexy ass can give it good." Then, to my absolute horror, in the loudest stage whisper ever, she asked, "Can I tell them you've got a big dick, too?"

"Avery!" I snapped. "Stop talking."

At that point, Claire was laughing hysterically. "Damn it. I should have been recording this."

"Mom," Avery started in her loud whisper voice. "Kellan's—"

"Kellan's going to spank your ass if you don't shut your mouth," Claire giggled.

"Oh, I love it when he does that."

"Fucking hell," I grumbled.

"I love a lot of things about him," Avery said dreamily and my head shot up. "He's a good man. He's a fucking good man and a good fucking man," she said and started giggling again.

"How are we doing over here?" one of the nurses asked.

"Chatty Cathy here seems to be doing great," I answered.

The nurse laughed. "You must be sharing some good stuff."

"Please don't encourage her," I pleaded.

"Trust me, we've heard it all before," she said

and turned to Avery. "Are you ready to go home?"

"Hell, yes. Have you seen what I get to go home with?" she asked and pointed to me. "He washes my hair for me when I'm sick."

The nurse turned to me and smiled. "Aw, that's so sweet."

"Hey, don't you be getting any ideas, nursey, nurse, nurse. He's taken."

"Oh, honey, you don't have a thing to worry about. I prefer the ladies," she said.

"Really? How does that work exactly? I mean, I think I would miss the dick, you know?"

"Avery Grace!" Claire scolded. "Eat your ice chips and shut your mouth."

"What?" Avery asked innocently. "I was just having a little girl talk."

"You were prying into the private life of the nurse taking care of you. That does not constitute as girl talk. Now, be quiet so we can get out of here before they put in for a psych consult."

The nurse couldn't stop laughing, even while she went over Avery's discharge papers. "Oh, you guys have been so much fun. Avery, you behave yourself on the way home."

"Where's the fun in that?" Avery retorted.

Blessedly, Avery fell asleep as soon as I pulled out onto the road.

CHAPTER TWENTY-THREE

Avery

The first two days after my surgery were a bit of a blur, but by the fourth day, I was feeling much better. I was even able to help Mom get the kids ready for school, which hadn't happened since the school year started.

Once they were out the door, I made my way back upstairs to take a shower and get dressed for the day. It was the first time I'd felt human in weeks and I planned to cherish every second of it. With my hair dried and flat-ironed and a touch of makeup on my face, I went downstairs geared up for a productive day.

I opened up my laptop and started working on the logo design for Jackson Security. I was almost finished with it when Kellan knocked on the front door. He'd been coming by to check on me at least twice a day since the surgery and he usually stayed for a few hours each time.

I walked to the door with an extra pep in my step and pulled the door open with a wide smile on my face. "Good morning," I said before realizing the person on my porch wasn't Kellan. "Can I help you?"

The beautiful woman smiled, but it didn't reach her eyes. "Yes, actually, you can. I would find it extremely helpful if you would stop fucking my husband."

I gaped at her for several moments before my brain processed what she'd said. "Excuse me?"

"Are you deaf or stupid?" she spat.

"You need to leave," I said and started to close the door.

"No, you need to keep your dirty snatch away from my husband. Kellan is and always will be mine!"

Complete and utter devastation ripped through me like a hot knife. I clutched my stomach and took a stumbling step back. Kellan was married? I was the other woman? The other woman carrying his baby?

My hand automatically dropped lower to protectively cradle my unborn child. Her eyes followed the movement and she added, "You can get rid of that thing, too. I won't have it looming over us for the rest of our lives."

"Kelly!" Kellan roared. "What in the absolute fuck are you doing here?"

"Introducing myself to your whore," she sneered.

Kellan said something I couldn't hear into his phone before shoving it into his pocket. He came to a stop between his wife and me. "I don't know what you're trying to do here, but it won't work."

"Judging by the look on her face, I'd say it already has."

"You both need to leave," I said and was proud of how strong I sounded despite how weak I felt.

Kellan whirled around and took a good look at me. "I promise it's not what you think. Give me two minutes and I'll prove it to you," he said softly.

She laughed cruelly. "Are you still showing those fake divorce papers to your little playthings?"

A quick chirp and a flash of blue lights

caught my attention. I looked past Kellan and his wife to see two police officers exiting their vehicle and approaching us.

"Savior, what's going on?"

"This is my ex-wife, who is not welcome here and refuses to leave. She pulled the same shit at my place of employment a few days ago," Kellan said.

"Is this your home?" the officer asked.

"It's mine," I chimed in.

"And you are?"

"Avery Parker," I said at the same time Kellan said, "My woman."

Kelly's eyes widened and filled with a menacing glee when she heard my name. "Oh, Kellan, this is rich. You're having a baby with the good officer's wife?"

"Ms. Parker, have you asked this woman to leave your property?"

"Yes, I have," I said.

The officer nodded and turned to Kelly. "I need to see some identification."

"For what?" she snapped.

"I was trying to be nice," the officer grumbled.

The other officer approached Kelly from behind. "Place your hands behind your back."

The next few minutes played out as one would

expect. Kelly screamed, yelled, and ultimately resisted arrest, which led to her being taken to the ground and handcuffed before being shoved into the back of the police cruiser.

"I'm assuming you want to file some trespass notices, possibly a restraining order?" the officer asked.

Kellan nodded. "Yes, I do. She's been a nuisance since we divorced, but I will not tolerate her showing up here and harassing Avery."

"No problem. We'll get her down to the station and then I'll swing back by with the paperwork. We'll also arrange to have her car towed," the officer said.

"Thank you," Kellan said.

The two officers got back into their car and drove away with Kelly in the back seat, clearly screaming at the top of her lungs.

"Come on, sweetness; let's go inside," Kellan said and started to usher me back into my living room.

"Are you married?" I asked shakily.

"No, Avery. Not anymore. I was married to her for about two years before we divorced."

"She said you have fake divorce papers," I pointed out. I hated that her words had so easily created a river of doubt between us.

He shook his head. "I can show you how to pull them up from the county's judicial records online if you want to see them for yourself."

"I do. I'm sorry, but I just—"

"Don't apologize. If I had a problem with you wanting to see them, I wouldn't have offered to show you."

"Why did you get divorced after only two years of marriage?" I asked.

He sighed and sat down on the sofa. "She was my high school girlfriend. And believe it or not, she used to be different. She wasn't the greedy, gold-digging evil bitch that she is now. I'm not sure when she changed, but I didn't notice it until it was too late. Or, hell, maybe she was always that way and hid it very well. Anyway, I got off work early one day and came home to surprise her, but the surprise was on me because I found her fucking a neighbor from down the street in our bed. As soon as I saw them, things clicked into place and I knew right away it wasn't the first time she'd cheated. After that, I filed for divorce. She fought it every step of the way, and it took me almost two years to get rid of her."

"I'm sorry that happened to you," I said.

He gave me a small smile. "Thank you. I was

pretty devastated by it at first, but it didn't take me long to realize I was in love with the idea of her, not her."

"So, she's done stuff like this before?" I asked.

He nodded. "She has. When I filed for divorce, I moved in with my grandfather because she refused to leave the house and I couldn't stand to be around her. She started showing up at his place at all hours of the night. When we put a stop to that, she started calling. She showed up at my job, the grocery store, restaurants. It was exhausting. I picked up an extra part-time job so I could get out of my grandfather's place and spare him from her bullshit."

"She hasn't left you alone since your divorce?" I asked in surprise.

"She disappeared for a few years and I thought that was the end of it until she showed up at the gym yesterday."

"Why do you think that is?"

"Well, she drug our divorce out for two years. We had a decent house and two cars, but no kids. She was just trying to get every cent she could from me. But after the accident, my grandfather pointed out that she could be held liable in a civil suit since we were still married. She agreed to the terms and signed the divorce papers within a week. I'd heard she found herself a sugar daddy, so I'm guessing her relationship with him has ended and she's looking to replace him."

"Please don't take this the wrong way, but you don't strike me as the sugar daddy type," I said honestly.

He laughed. "I'm not," he said and then a look of realization washed over his face. "Fuck. I know why she's back. She's after my money."

"What money?" I asked and slapped my hand over my mouth. "I'm sorry. It's none of my business."

"It's fine. When my parents died, their life insurance money went into a trust for me. I started receiving monthly payments when I turned eighteen and would get a lump sum every five years on my birthday once I reached twenty-one," he explained.

"Does she really think you'll go back to her when you're having a child with someone else?" I asked, partially in disbelief and partially because I needed the reassurance.

He moved closer and pulled me against his chest. "Yes, she thinks that highly of herself, but, sweetness, there's no way in hell I'd ever go back to her."

CHAPTER TWENTY-FOUR

Savior

Avery's surgery did wonders for her. She went from being sick multiple times a day and feeling miserable in general to being the stereotypical glowing pregnant woman. Since she was better, I wanted to introduce her to my brothers and their women. Layla, River, and Leigh had been hounding me about bringing her to the clubhouse.

Coal and I were still alternating morning and evening shifts at the gym, so I usually stopped by Avery's house to spend some time with her before I went in for an evening shift. She always answered the door happy to see me, except for one particular day.

"Hey," she said with a huff and immediately turned to stomp back to the kitchen.

"Something wrong?" I asked and followed her after closing the door.

"Yes! Look what these idiots have done!" she fumed and waved something in front of my face.

I took it from her and glanced over it, but I had no idea what I was looking at nor what was wrong with it. "I'm going to be honest, babe, I have no idea what the problem is with whatever this little paper thing is."

"It's a bookmark that I designed for one of my clients. And that is one of the most well-known models in the indie romance community. He has been on ninety-something book covers. And they cut off his nipple! They maimed a legend! Now, she has five hundred bookmarks with a uni-nip!"

"It's like a reverse nip slip," I chuckled.

"It's not funny!"

"It so fucking is!" I laughed so hard I bent forward and held my stomach. "Oh, shit, sweetness, this is classic."

"Stop laughing," she giggled. "Her book is coming out soon and she has an event this weekend. She can't give these out."

"Sure she can. Make it a thing like they do with those stuffed animals that have errors on the tags. Do you have the rare bookmark with a one-nippled version of Romancelandia's hottest cover model?"

Her mouth dropped open and she held one hand up. "Hold on; how in the hell do you know about Romancelandia?"

"Fuck," I breathed. "Uh, that term came up when I was looking at some of your designs online."

"So, you were cyberstalking me. Should I be worried?" she joked.

"I was not. I was showing Judge and Copper your work, and I couldn't remember the name of your website. So I searched your name, and that's where I saw that term," I explained.

"Mmhmm, I'm not sure I believe that story."

"You can ask Judge and Copper this weekend."

She cocked her head to the side. "This weekend?"

"Yes. Three brothers are getting married the weekend after next and they're having a huge combined bachelor/bachelorette party this Saturday. It's an all-day thing starting with a family barbeque. Then, they're going to have a big slumber party set up in one of the rooms for all the kids so the adults can have their fun once the kids have gone to sleep. I want you, Riley, and Braxton to come with me."

"There will be other kids there?" she asked.

"There will be a lot of kids there. Several of the brothers from the Croftridge Chapter have children. Actually, I think Keegan's little sister is around the same age as Riley. They'll probably be the oldest kids there."

"And this is a safe environment for kids?" she asked carefully.

"I wouldn't have asked if it wasn't. I know motorcycle clubs get a bad reputation, but just because some are bad, it doesn't mean all are bad," I explained.

Her cheeks flushed and she looked away from me. "I'm sorry; you're absolutely right. I've only had a few interactions with the members of your club and they've been nothing but nice to me."

"That's part of why I want you to come spend some time at the club and get to know everyone. They're not just my friends; they're my family," I explained.

"Okay," she agreed. "Do I need to bring

anything?"

"Just whatever you and the kids will need to spend the night. Oh, and bathing suits. I heard Layla talking about renting one of those inflatable water parks for the kids to play on."

"Oh, the kids will love that," she said excitedly.

And they did. A few days later when we went to the clubhouse for the party, the kids had a great time playing on the inflatables. Layla had arranged to have a large inflatable waterslide as well as an inflatable water park/obstacle course. I don't think we would've gotten them to go inside if Leigh hadn't thought to set up an ice cream sundae bar.

"Are you sure you don't need some help getting them to bed?" Avery asked Leigh.

"Oh no, as soon as the sugar rush wears off, they'll all crash from how hard they played today. I've been doing this for years and I've never had one last more than twenty minutes into the movie," Leigh said proudly. "But I'll be sure to come get you if there's a problem."

Just as Leigh disappeared into the clubhouse, Batta shouted, "Let's get this party started!" I turned to see him at the top of the waterslide. He jumped in the air, landed on his stomach, and went head first down the slide.

"Oh, shit!" I said and pressed my fist to my mouth. Batta's big body shot down the slide like a rocket, hit the landing pool, and went straight over the inflatable barrier. He slid across the wet grass and came to a stop twenty feet away.

He groaned and rolled to his back. "Fuck! Can somebody see if they can find my nipple? I think I lost it at the halfway mark."

Avery slapped her hand over her mouth trying to hide her amusement. But I couldn't let the opportunity pass. "Batta, you ever thought about being on a book cover? I hear there's a new one-nipple trend."

Batta sat up with a confused look on his face. "How much have you had to drink, brother?"

Avery lost it. She started laughing and then suddenly slapped my arm and took off for the clubhouse. "You're going to make me peeeeee!"

"You're in big trouble now," Annabelle laughed. "You never make a pregnant woman laugh that hard."

I pointed at Batta like a petulant child. "He did it!"

Batta threw his hands in the air as he walked toward us. "All I did was ask where my nipple was. I'm too scared to look. Is it still there? Fuck it, I'll have it tattooed back on if I lost it."

"Yes, it's still there you big fucking baby," Bronze said and proceeded to give Batta one hell of a titty twister.

"Owww!" Batta yelled and grabbed Bronze. "Ooooey! I got your barbell. Whatcha gonna do now, fuckhead?"

"Knock it off before one of you gets hurt," Copper ordered. "Besides, I think the ladies have some party games they want to play."

"Listen up!" Layla shouted. "No bachelor/bachelorette party is complete without a few games. And since this is a combined party for three couples, we worked really hard on putting together some new games to play. For the first one, we want to see just how tough our big, scary bikers are. So, I need five of you boys to volunteer."

When no one moved or uttered a word, Layla sighed. "Bronze, Judge, Carbon, Duke, and Shaker, get your asses over here."

"What about me?" Batta asked.

Layla arched an eyebrow. "Have you and your nipple recovered enough to play?"

"You're lucky I like you," Batta joked as he grabbed a chair and made his way over to Layla. He placed it beside the other guys and dropped into it while crossing his arms over his chest. "I'm playing, too."

"Suit yourself," Layla teased.

River stepped forward with a bowl in her hands. "Each one of you will reach into the bowl and pull out one piece of paper. You can look at it, but don't tell us what it is until we ask."

"Okay, starting with Batta, each one of you tell us what your paper says," River instructed.

"Forehead and cheeks," Batta said.

"Armpits," Bronze shared.

"Legs," Judge called.

They continued with Duke having chest, Carbon's was stomach, and Shaker had arms.

"Keegan, Reese, Harper, and Annabelle, we need your assistance."

"What are they doing?" Avery asked.

"I have no idea, but I can't wait to find out."

A few minutes later, the girls returned to their seats after smearing something black onto the body part assigned to each man.

Layla cleared her throat and struggled to stop giggling long enough to explain the game. "We have smeared the guys with a blackhead removing face mask. It's supposed to do wonders for your skin, if you can stand to peel it off. Since I know none of you will be able to peel it off without crying out in pain, the winner will be whoever can go the longest without making a sound. Are you ready?"

"Fuck, yes!" Batta roared.

"Go!" Layla shouted.

"Ahhh! Motherfucking son of a cocksucking bitch!" Batta blurted. "Oh, fuck! Do over! Do over!"

"Sorry, Batta, you're out!" Layla laughed.

"Need help, Bronze?" River teased.

He frantically shook his head and waved her away with his hands. He was visibly struggling to pull that from his armpits without making a sound.

"Fuck this shit," Duke announced. "I give up."

Judge was doing well until River grabbed what he had pulled up and yanked. "Fuuuuccck!" he bellowed.

A high-pitched, ear-piercing shriek filled the air and we all looked to see Bronze hopping in a circle on one foot. "Put it back! I want my skin and hair back, right now!"

Keegan had snuck up behind Shaker during the commotion. She ripped the mask from his arm causing him to shout out in pain.

Carbon stood proudly and flashed us all a

wicked smile before he silently ripped the mask from his chest and tossed it aside. "Looks like I win, motherfuckers!"

I was laughing so hard I had tears running down my face. Avery was cradling her stomach and desperately trying to catch her breath. Bronze came over and sat down beside her. "What about one bald pit? Is there a trend for that?"

CHAPTER TWENTY-FIVE

Avery

I had so much fun at the combined bachelor/bachelorette party for Kellan's friends that I didn't want the night to end. We talked and laughed until the wee hours of the morning.

To my surprise, the party continued the next day. As soon as the kids were up, they were outside playing on the inflatables. "When do you have to return those things?" I asked Layla while we were eating breakfast.

She shrugged. "Any time in the next day or two. Copper is friends with the guy who owns the rental company. He let us have those for free and told us to call when we wanted to have them picked up."

"Do you have his contact info? I know both of my kids will be asking to have something like that for their next birthday party."

"I don't have it handy, but I'll ask Copper to give it to Savior for you."

"Thank you."

River came barreling into the room with a frantic look on her face. When her eyes landed on me, she made a beeline for the table. "There you are! I was afraid you'd already left."

I immediately went into mommy mode. "Why? Did something happen to Riley or Braxton?"

"Oh no, nothing like that," she said quickly. "I wanted to ask you if Riley and Braxton could be in the wedding. Riley would be a flower girl with Gabby, and Braxton would be a ring bearer with James."

"Um, it's fine with me, but they've never done anything like this before, so I can't guarantee their behavior."

River laughed. "Oh, don't worry about that. This is a biker wedding; we don't expect anyone to behave."

"Okay, then, but I did warn you and I have

witnesses."

"Leave me out of this," Layla joked.

"Just let me know when and where they need to be."

"Let me get your phone number and I'll text you all the details. I know it's super short notice, but could you meet me tomorrow afternoon for a dress and tuxedo fitting for the kids?"

"Sure. Any time after they get out of school will be fine."

She blew out a slow breath and leaned back in her chair. "Thank you so much. We did a trial run this morning, and Gabby couldn't pull the wagon with little Raven in it by herself. Then, James would only walk down the aisle if someone was holding his hand. I had a moment of panic."

"Do you want them to come inside and do a practice run with you?" I asked. I loved my children, but they could be just as stubborn as any other kid from time to time.

"We're actually practicing outside. They've been looking over like they were interested, but I wanted to run my idea by you before I asked if they wanted to join us."

I pushed to my feet and picked up my plate. "Let me drop this in the kitchen and we'll go see if my monsters will cooperate."

"I got it, sweetness," Kellan said and took the plate from my hand. "Grab a bottle of water and sit in the shade. It's already hot as hell."

"Bossy," I teased.

"Concerned," he said and rubbed my stomach. "I'll be out there in a few minutes."

To my surprise, my children were thrilled to be included in the wedding. They both listened attentively and carefully followed the instructions they were given. James was thrilled to walk down the aisle with a friend and Riley and Gabby could easily pull the wagon down the aisle together.

***

I was a bit nervous about the wedding. The wedding ceremony was going to be at Judge's mother's house with the reception to follow at the clubhouse. Since my children were part of the wedding party, we needed to arrive early. Kellan offered to come with us, but I told him there was no sense in him getting there early just to make me feel better. However, I was suddenly overcome with nerves when I pulled into Leigh's driveway.

Fortunately, I didn't have much time to worry

about being nervous because Riley jumped out of the car as soon as I turned the engine off. "I want out, too!" Braxton shouted.

"Riley! Get your little butt back here right this instant," I scolded and went around to help Braxton out of his booster seat.

"But I have to put on my princess dress and get beautiful for the wedding," she whined.

"And we have plenty of time for that, but you know better than to jump out of a car and run off."

"I'm sorry, Mommy, but I'm so excited," she squealed.

By that point, she'd attracted the attention of others. "Do you need help with anything?" Leigh called from the front porch.

"No, I think we're good," I said and closed the car door. "But thank you for offering."

"You're welcome. It's a madhouse in there, so enter at your own risk."

"I can't even imagine. If there's anything I can do to help, please don't hesitate to ask," I offered.

She showed us to the room where we would be getting ready. Keegan, Ember, Layla, and Annabelle were already inside as were several children in various stages of dress. "Good luck,"

Leigh said before she disappeared down the hall.

"I am so sorry," Layla said with her eyes fixed on me.

"What? Why?"

"Because you can't have any wine, and you're going to need it."

"That bad, huh?"

"Ignore her. She doesn't have any kids yet," Annabelle laughed.

"Shut it, sister dearest," Layla joked.

After two meltdowns, snacks for everyone with teeth, and bottles for those without, it was time for the pre-ceremony pictures. Thankfully, the kids were excited about the ceremony and were full of smiles for the photographer.

"You look gorgeous," Kellan said from behind as he slid an arm around my waist and pressed a kiss to my cheek.

"Thank you," I replied and turned to face him. "Look at you," I breathed and felt my body start to react. He was dressed in a pair of black slacks with a button-down shirt that appeared to be the same color as his beautiful gray eyes. "You look delicious," I said and ran my hand over his firm chest.

His hand came up and circled my wrist to yank me closer. "Don't, sweetness."

I couldn't help myself. He looked so damn good and I was ready to go like the horny, pregnant hussy I was. I licked my lips and stepped closer to press my breasts against him. "Don't what?" I breathed.

"Coal, can you watch the kids while I show Avery where the bathroom is?" Kellan asked.

Coal smirked but nodded. "Sure, brother."

"Thanks," Kellan clipped and pulled me down the hall to the bathroom. Once inside he pulled me close and put my hand on his cock. "Feel what you did. Now, bend over so I can fix it."

I groaned as I turned around and placed my hands on the counter. Kellan shoved my dress up over my hips and palmed my cheek giving it a squeeze. "This is going to be quick, sweetness."

"Please," I begged.

A shiver of anticipation ran down my spine when I heard his zipper. He pulled my panties to the side and plunged inside. With a firm grip on my hips, he thrust forward while pulling me back.

When a low moan escaped from me, he brought one hand up and covered my mouth. "Shhh, baby, unless you want everyone to know what we're doing."

Something about the thought of others knowing Kellan and I were having a quickie in the bathroom was extremely exciting for me. "You like that?" he rasped near my ear. "You want them to know you can't wait to have my cock?"

"Kellan," I mumbled against his hand.

"Too bad, sweetness, no one hears the sounds you make when you come but me. Now, give it to me," he demanded, and I did. I bit down on my cheek to keep the whole house from hearing my moans of pleasure.

Kellan groaned quietly and stilled when he found his own release moments later. When he stepped back, he pulled my panties back into place and smoothed his hand over my center. "Fucking love that you'll be full of me during the wedding ceremony."

I gasped at his dirty words, "Kellan!"

"Don't act like you don't like it; I know you do," he whispered and nipped my earlobe. "We need to get back or they really will know what we were up to."

***

I was slightly uncomfortable leaving the kids

with the wedding party, but the women promised to watch after them and Kellan assured me they were in good hands. We sat near the front so I could have the kids come sit with us if they started misbehaving.

I anxiously watched as the procession began. The entire time I was silently chanting "Please do it right." Suddenly, the music cut off followed by the low rumble of pipes. Then, there was a collective gasp from the crowd that quickly turned into chuckles as Bad to the Bone began to play.

I looked down the aisle to see Braxton riding a battery-operated motorcycle toward the altar with James in a sidecar. Right behind them, Riley and Gabby were also riding battery-operated motorcycles with little Raven in a sidecar attached to Riley's motorcycle.

When they reached the front, Braxton parked the motorcycle and helped James out. Ember went to get Raven while Riley climbed off her bike and got on the back of Gabby's. They circled back around and came down the aisle again, this time with Riley tossing out flower petals.

"Where did they get those?" I asked and looked over to see Kellan recording the whole thing with his cell phone.

"I don't know, but since Bronze and Batta aren't anywhere in sight, I'm guess they had something to do with it."

When Gabby parked the tiny motorcycle off to the side, she and Riley climbed off and walked hand-in-hand to stand with the bridesmaids.

Right on cue, the infamous song began to play and the audience stood. Ranger appeared with Reese on his arm. "Are they related?" I whispered.

"No. Reese's father was a member of the Devil Springs Chapter before he died years ago. Ranger is the last living original member and was good friends with Tank. Since her brother is also getting married today, Ranger proudly stepped in to fill those shoes."

Next, Phoenix appeared with Harper on his arm. "Before you ask," Kellan whispered, "Harper's father is also deceased. She doesn't trust easily, but she's always trusted Phoenix, so she asked him to walk her in place of Duke."

It amazed me how they acted as a family even though they weren't all blood related. I'd never witnessed anything close to the love and loyalty they shared.

I was pulled from my thoughts when River

came down the aisle on her brother's arm. River's genuine happiness radiated from her as she walked toward the man she loved.

I wasn't sure what to expect from a biker wedding featuring three separate couples, but surprisingly, it was very much like a traditional wedding and each couple had their own moment to shine.

After the ceremony, they had a huge reception at the Devil Springs clubhouse. Once again, my family and I were welcomed with open arms. Everyone treated us like we were and always had been a member of their family.

CHAPTER TWENTY-SIX

Savior

After the wedding, life settled down into more of a stable routine for a few weeks. Coal and I finally moved into the rental house. Since it was a three-bedroom, we asked Grant if he wanted to move in with us, but he opted to keep his apartment. As soon as he recovered from his injuries, he was back at the gym working out with us like nothing ever happened. Since he spent so much time there, Copper had us hire him to help run the gym.

When I wasn't at work or at the clubhouse,

I spent most of my time at Avery's house. Our relationship was slowly growing stronger. I went to doctor's appointments with her. Riley and Braxton started calling me Kellan. We took the kids trick-or-treating together. I even ate Thanksgiving dinner with her and her family. For the first time in a long time, I was happy, and I think she was, too.

As I was walking back to the office to take my lunch break, my phone buzzed in my pocket. I smiled when I saw Avery's name on the screen.

"Hey, lil' mama."

"Kellan," she sniffed. "I'm at the hospital with my mom. Is there any way you can pick up Riley and Braxton from school and bring them here?"

"Yeah, I can get them, but what's going on with your mom?" I asked and grabbed my keys to head to the hospital.

"Someone ran over her," she cried.

"What?"

"That's what they told me. They said she was walking to her car in the grocery store parking lot and someone ran over her," she hiccupped. "I don't know anything yet. They won't let me go back to see her."

"Sit down and take some deep breaths. I'm on my way. Have you called your dad?"

"I haven't, but someone from the hospital did. He's the one who told them to call me. He's on his way from Croftridge now."

"Good. I'll be there in ten minutes," I said and disconnected the call.

I didn't bother to slow my pace as I passed the front desk. "Gotta go. Family emergency."

When I arrived at the hospital, I found Avery sitting in a chair in the corner of the waiting room looking scared to death. She threw herself into my arms the moment she saw me coming toward her. "Oh, Kellan, they won't tell me anything," she sobbed.

"They probably don't know anything yet, sweetness," I soothed.

"Why can't I see her?"

"Because they're working on her. Let me see if I can get ahold of River." I didn't want to wake her in case she worked the night before, so I sent her a text message and asked her to call me if she was awake. Thankfully, my phone rang seconds later.

"Hey, Savior. Is everything okay?"

"Not really. Avery's mother was hit by a car earlier today and is in the ER. They won't let Avery go back to see her and she's kind of freaking out. I didn't know if there was something you could tell her that might help."

"Sure, let me talk to her."

"Here, baby," I said and handed her the phone. "It's River."

She reluctantly took the phone from me and spoke to River for several minutes. "What did she say?" I asked when she handed my phone back.

"She said this is considered a crush injury, and it's actually a good thing they aren't letting me go back because it means they're still working on her and getting her stabilized. She did say it could be anywhere from thirty minutes to a few hours before they let anyone see her."

"I'm sorry, sweetness," I said and wrapped my arm around her shoulders.

We sat quietly waiting for any news about her mother. Finally, a nurse came out and told Avery she could come back and wait with Claire until they took her to surgery. "You go on back. I'm going to go swap my bike for my truck and go pick up Riley and Braxton," I said and dropped a kiss on her forehead.

"Thank you. I called the school before you got here and let them know you would be picking them up. Cars will already be lined up when you get there. Just get in one of the lines and have your driver's license handy to show whichever teacher is working the car line," she said quickly. "Oh, you need to get the booster seat from my car," she added and handed me her car keys.

"I got this. You go be with your mom," I said and gently nudged her toward the waiting nurse.

Avery wasn't kidding about the car line. Cars were lined up at least five hundred feet down the street even though I was twenty minutes early. I put the truck in park and pulled out my phone to let Coal and Copper know what was going on while I waited.

Finally, the doors opened and children poured from the school. Moving at a snail's pace, I gradually rolled closer to the front of the school. As expected, a woman with a clipboard walked up to my window and asked who I was picking up.

"Riley and Braxton Parker. Avery said she called the office to let them know," I said as I handed her my driver's license.

She took it and wrote something on her clipboard. "She did," she said and handed my license back. "Once the children are in your vehicle, please wait until the teacher signals you to move forward. Then, you will pull forward and merge into one line with the other cars."

When I reached the front of the line, a teacher

opened the back door and helped Riley, then Braxton into the back seat of my truck. "Kellan!" Riley squealed. "You surprised us!"

I smiled at her enthusiasm. "I sure did. Sit down and get buckled so we can get moving," I said and glanced over my shoulder to see Braxton watching me carefully. "Hey, Brax."

"Where's Mommy?" he asked. The kid didn't miss a thing.

"She's with Nana. We're going to see them right now. Is everyone buckled in?"

"I am!" Riley yelled. "And so is Braxton!"

With that, I pulled out onto the road and pointed my truck in the direction of the hospital. "Did either one of you learn anything fun today?"

"I did!" Riley said excitedly and raised her hand in the air. "We learned that a starfish's mouth is on the bottom. Isn't that gross?"

"Why is that gross?"

"Because mermaids put them on their boobies!" she said in horror.

I couldn't hold in my laughter. "What are they teaching you at that school?"

"They teach us all kinds of—"

Riley's words morphed into an ear-piercing scream as the world around us flipped on its axis and then everything faded to black.

CHAPTER TWENTY-SEVEN

Savior

I could hear screaming, or maybe it was crying. Possibly both. "Kellan!! Help me! Kellan!!"

Who was screaming? "I'm stuck! My arm hurts!"

Was that Riley? My eyes flew open at the same time I yelled, "Riley?"

"Kellan! Get me out!!" she cried.

I tried to turn to so I could see what was wrong with her, but I couldn't move. I tried to turn the other way and quickly realized something was very wrong when I looked out the truck window.

"What the hell?" I said to myself. The entire view was off, almost like the world was turned on its side. I suddenly realized the pressure on my chest was from the seat belt holding me in place as gravity tried to pull me forward. Fuck, the truck was somehow on its nose.

"Hey! Can anybody hear me?" a man yelled and an overwhelming sense of unwelcomed déjà vu washed over me.

"Yes! I can hear you," I yelled back.

"Try not to move! We've got help on the way!"

"I've got young kids in here!" I said and realized I hadn't heard a sound from Braxton. I forced myself to turn so I could see him. His little body was being held in place by the seat belt, but I couldn't see his face. "Braxton! You okay, little man?"

Nothing.

"Riley, is Braxton okay?"

"I don't know!" she cried. "Braxie-boo, please wake up."

Fuck.

Fuck.

Fuck.

I felt around for my phone and wanted to cheer when I found it in my pocket. I managed to get it out and called Copper.

"Copper Black," he answered.

"Need help, Prez. Had a wreck. Trapped in the truck with Avery's kids."

"Be right there," he clipped and I heard him yell for Spazz before the call ended.

"Good," I thought. I knew Spazz would be able to ping my location on the way.

"Riley, sweetheart, are you hurt?" I asked and prayed she didn't have any injuries.

"My arm hurts and I'm scared," she cried.

"I know, princess. Try not to move, okay? Help is on the way; we just have to be patient and wait for them to get here," I said and hoped like hell I wasn't lying to her.

I turned my body as far as I could and tried to reach Braxton but only the tips of my fingers grazed his shirt. "Braxton!" I bellowed. "Wake up! Please, wake up," I begged.

Nothing.

Not a fucking peep. I couldn't even tell if he was breathing.

And that's when I broke. I screamed in anger and frustration. "Why?" I bellowed. "Why is this happening again?"

I slammed my head back against the headrest as the tears ran down my face. "Why?" I cried. "I cannot go through this again." And then, tiny little fingers sifted through my hair.

"I love you, Kellan."

Fuck me. I cried even harder. "I love you, too, baby girl. I love your mother and I love Braxton, too."

The truck shifted and metal groaned causing Riley to shriek. "What was that?"

"Savior!"

I breathed a sigh of relief when I heard Copper's voice. "Thank fuck, Prez."

"Are you all secured?"

"We're still strapped in by the seat belts," I answered.

"Good. Don't move. We're using a winch to stabilize the truck. Then, we'll get you out. Is anyone seriously injured that you know of?"

"You need to get Braxton out first," was all I said. I didn't want to upset Riley any more than she already was, but he needed to know things were not okay inside the truck.

"Understood. How's Riley?"

"My arm hurts really bad and I can't move, Mr. President."

"We're going to fix that for you in just a few minutes, sweetheart. How's Kellan doing?" he asked.

"He's hurt. He was crying and his hair is all

sticky and red," she said.

I reached up and felt all around my head. When I brought my hand back in front of my face, sure enough, it was covered in blood.

"Riley, I need you to do me a big favor right now. I want you to squeeze your eyes closed as tight as you can and hold your breath. There's going to be a loud noise and then you can open your eyes and stop holding your breath. Are you ready?"

"Yes, sir," she said.

"Okay, sweetie. Close your eyes and hold your breath, now," Copper said. There was a brief pause and then the sound of glass shattering filled the truck. "Okay, baby girl, it's all done," he said and sounded much closer than before.

"I'm going to get Braxton out, and then we'll get you out, okay?"

"Okay," she said shakily and I could tell she was crying again.

"Riley, did you know that Copper and Bronze have pet snakes that live at the clubhouse? Their names are Slither and Squeeze and they've had them since they were kids. Would you like to go see them sometime?" I asked, hoping to distract her while they pulled her brother from the truck.

"No! I don't like snakes!"

The truck moved and there was a loud scraping sound followed by a curse from Copper. "His name is Braxton Parker and he's four years old. He's been unconscious since the collision. His mother is already at the hospital," Copper relayed.

"Thank fuck," I whispered. If he was relaying Braxton's details, then that meant he was alive.

"All right, princess, let's get you out of here," Copper said. "I need you to put your hands on Kellan's seat and be very still. I'm going to cut your seat belt and you might move forward, but I'm going to catch you."

"I can't move my arm," she cried. "It's stuck."

"Shit," Copper grumbled. "It's okay, honey. It's just going to take us a few more minutes to come in a different way, okay?"

"Wait!" I called out. "Pass me that knife so I can cut myself out."

"Savior, just give us—"

"No! We need to get her out of here!" I screamed. I was trying not to panic, but I needed both kids out of the truck before anything else happened to them.

"Okay, brother. Reach back and get the handle."

I took the knife from him and sliced through

my seat belt. I was able to raise the steering wheel, but I couldn't move my seat at all. It took some maneuvering, but I was able to slide over to the passenger seat and turn myself around.

"Riley," I breathed when my eyes landed on her. She seemed to be okay, except for her arm. "I'm going to get you out."

"Please don't hurt my arm."

I grimaced. "I'm going to try my hardest not to." I didn't want to hurt her, but if I had to in order to get her out, I would.

Carefully climbing over the center console into the back seat, I wrapped one arm around her waist and held her steady while I sliced through her restraints. She screamed when her torso fell forward.

Looking over her shoulder, I could clearly see what the problem was. "Fuck, Copper. Her arm is pinned between the seat and the door."

"One second," he said and disappeared. Moments later he stuck his head through the back window. "Hold her steady," he said firmly and held up a crow bar.

I tried to brace for what I knew was coming. Copper forcefully pried the door away from the frame, allowing Riley's arm to slip free, which also allowed blood flow to return to the area with a vengeance. Her screams of pain broke my heart. "I'm so sorry, baby girl. I'm so fucking sorry."

Reluctantly, I carefully passed her through the broken glass into Copper's waiting arms. "Riley Parker. Six years old. She's been conscious the entire time. Left ulna and radius are clearly broken. She's a princess, so handle her with care," he said.

"Kellan!" she screamed. "I want my Kellan! No! I'm not leaving him!"

"I need you to go with the fireman so I can get Kellan out. Okay?"

"Right now?" she asked.

"Right now," Copper promised.

"Okay," she sobbed.

Copper came back to the window and stuck his hand through. "Can I pull you out?"

"I'm not sure," I said honestly. "I'm not sure what's hurt."

He nodded knowingly. "Adrenaline. Let's not waste it."

I reached out and firmly clasped his hand and used my other one to push myself up and out while he pulled.

"Fuck!!" I bellowed as pain ripped through my body, but Copper didn't relent.

"Almost there," he said. "I need a basket!" he yelled. "I'll strap you in and they can pull you up."

"Pull me up?" I asked.

"Your truck is hanging off the Lakeview Road bridge by the rear axle," Copper said. "Come on; let's get you ready to go up."

I was all for letting them pull me up until I heard Riley crying for me. "I got it, Prez," I said and used every bit of strength I had left to push myself the rest of the way through the window. I braced my feet on the window frame and my hands on the truck bed as I stood.

"Forget the basket!" Copper shouted. "He's out and we're coming up!"

Something wasn't right. My vision was darkening at the edges and I was extremely light headed. The last thing I saw was Copper's eyes filling with horror as I tipped sideways and fell from the bed of the truck.

CHAPTER TWENTY-EIGHT

Copper

"No! Fuck, no!" I bellowed as my brother's eyes rolled to the back of his head and he plummeted to the water below.

I didn't even think about it. I unclipped the line from my harness and jumped out of the truck bed to follow him down. My jump was intentional and controlled; I was going to be perfectly fine. Savior was going to be hurt worse than he already was.

It felt like it took forever to hit the water and

the entire way down all I could hear were the terrified screams coming from a little girl who had no business watching what was happening.

As soon as I plunged into the cold water, I kicked and swam as fast as I could to the surface. "Where is he?" I bellowed.

No one answered me.

"Where the fuck is he?" I yelled even louder.

Still nothing.

I frantically turned in the water, scanning the surface for any sign of him.

"Kellan!" I called. "Kellan!" No, this couldn't be happening. Not on my watch. I inhaled deeply and dove under the water to search. When I came up to take another breath, I noticed Bronze, Judge, and Coal had joined me in the water.

"I can't fucking find him!"

We all turned to the sound of a splash. Before Batta's head had fully surfaced, he was yelling, "I got him! I fucking got him!"

The five of us held a still and silent Savior on top of the water and quickly swam him to the shore where the first responders were waiting to take him. Splint immediately started CPR as they ran with the stretcher to the waiting helicopter. I didn't have a clue when the fuck that arrived.

I didn't waste any time pulling myself out of

the water and running for my bike. "Sir, I need to make sure you're okay before I can let you leave."

"The only person who won't be okay will be you if you try to stop me," I growled and roared away from the scene. A quick glance in the mirror confirmed my brothers were right behind me, as I knew they would be. And I knew they'd be praying for Savior, Riley, and Braxton, just like I was.

We pulled into the parking lot and stormed into the waiting room as a unit. "We're Kellan Ward's family," I told the receptionist. "He was just brought in via helicopter."

She clicked around on her computer and nodded. "Yes, sir. Have a seat and the doctor will update you when they can," she said and turned back to her computer.

"I'm not finished. Riley and Braxton Parker were also brought in. If their mother isn't here yet, I'm going back there," I stated.

"Only family—"

I held my hand up to stop her. "Save it. I'm their uncle. Where are they?"

"Just a moment, sir," she said and picked up the phone beside her.

"Family of Riley and Braxton Parker,"

someone called from behind me.

"Right here," I said and stepped forward with Bronze by my side.

"Follow me, sirs."

"Has someone gotten in touch with their mother?" I asked. I knew Avery was in the hospital with her own mother.

"I don't believe so, sir."

"What? Avery is here in the hospital with her mother. Can you find out where Claire Cameron is?"

"Of course. I'll check in just a moment." She stopped in front of a room with an open door and gestured inside. "This is Riley's room. Braxton is in the one beside her."

"I'll go to Braxton," Bronze said and clapped me on the shoulder as he passed.

"Little Princess!" I said and tried to sound cheerful.

"Mr. President!" she cried. "I want Mommy and my Kellan!"

"I know, sweetheart. The nice nurse is going to find your mommy right now," I assured her and gave the nurse a pointed look.

"Where's my Kellan?"

"He's here, but the doctors are giving him a checkup right now, so it'll be a little while before you can see him. But, I'm going to hang out with you until then if that's okay."

"Please don't leave me," she cried and reached for me with her uninjured arm.

"I won't leave you. I promise," I said and scooped her into my lap.

"You're all wet," she said.

I hadn't even realized it until she pointed it out. "Sorry, Riley," I said and placed her back on the bed. "Let me see if I can get someone to bring me something dry to wear."

I picked up the phone in Riley's room and called my woman. I don't know how she knew, but Layla was already on her way to the hospital with Leigh, and they were bringing dry clothes for all of us.

Not even two minutes later, I knew Avery had arrived in the ER. I heard the scream of pain that erupted from her outside of Braxton's room. "My baby!" she sobbed.

"Mommy!" Riley screamed. "Mommy! Mommy!"

I turned to look out into the hall and froze as I watched the scene in front of me play out in slow motion. I quickly blocked Riley's view as Avery bent forward and clutched her stomach. Then, her knees buckled and she dropped to the floor. Two nurses were there instantly helping her to her feet. And that's when everyone except Avery saw the blood trickling down her legs and onto the floor.

"Ma'am, how far along are you?"

"I'm thirty weeks. It's false labor. I just wasn't expecting it," she said.

"Let's get you to a room and see what's going on."

"No! I need to make sure my kids are okay. My son and daughter were just brought in," Avery insisted.

"Avery," I called out. "I'm with Riley, and Bronze is with Braxton. We won't leave them."

"Kellan?" she asked and her fear was evident.

"We don't know anything yet. But I'll make sure someone updates you as soon as we know something," I promised.

She grimaced and clutched her stomach. "Shit," she cursed.

"Ma'am, we really need to get you upstairs. I think you might be in labor," the nurse said carefully.

"This is my third child. I know what labor feels like," she grunted.

"Call labor and delivery. Let them know we're coming up with a woman in premature labor and visible bleeding."

Avery gasped at the nurse's words before she turned back and met my eyes. "Please take care of my kids."

"I will. I'll bring them to you as soon as they're released," I promised.

"Thank you," she said and reluctantly sat in the wheelchair waiting to take her away.

"Is Mommy having her baby?" Riley asked quietly.

"I'm not sure, sweetie. But the nurses upstairs will take good care of her and we'll go see her as soon as they make sure you're okay."

River and Kennedy came running through the doors and I'd never been so happy to see another female who wasn't my woman. "Copper, what do you need us to do?"

"Can you find out what's going on with Braxton Parker and Savior?"

"Of course," she said and disappeared into the fray.

To my surprise, Kennedy was the one who came back with an update. "Braxton has a concussion and is going to be admitted to the hospital for overnight observation. He's awake and talking," she said and shook her head. "Well, he's talking to everyone except Bronze."

"What about Kellan?"

She cleared her throat. "River's in there helping them prep him for surgery," she said and looked down at her feet.

"Kennedy?"

She shook her head. "He's in bad shape," she whispered.

"How bad?"

"Bad enough that they're considering waiting for his grandfather to get here because they don't think he'll make it through surgery," she whispered.

"No!" I bellowed and got in her face. "You go back in there and tell him he has to make it. His baby is being born right now. He has a little girl and little boy sitting here in this hospital crying for him. Go tell him that. Right now!"

With tears in her eyes, she nodded and went back to the room. Kellan flatlined thirty seconds later.

CHAPTER TWENTY-NINE

SAVIOR

"Avery's having the baby," someone said in the distance. "Riley and Braxton are asking for you."

"Good. They were all okay," I thought and felt my body relax.

CHAPTER THIRTY

Avery

I cradled my stomach as they wheeled me up to the labor and delivery unit. The pain was getting worse and I could feel blood pooling underneath me. I was losing everything. My children, my love, my unborn child.

"Ms. Parker," someone called. "Can you hear me? Ms. Parker!"

"Get her to the OR, stat. We've got to get this baby out before we lose them both. Does she have family here or on the way?"

"They're in the ER with injuries from an

MVA."

"Ms. Parker, if you can hear me, we're giving you anesthesia to put you to sleep while we deliver your baby."

I may or may not have nodded before I faded away.

CHAPTER THIRTY-ONE

Ranger

When Phoenix called, he told me the last thing I ever expected to hear. Savior had been in a car accident and they didn't think he'd survive.

"Can you pick up his grandfather and bring him to the clubhouse? Shaker will be waiting in the bird to take you both to Devil Springs."

"Yeah, Prez," I rasped. "We'll be there soon."

I didn't want to be the one to tell Mack about Kellan, but I also didn't want anyone else to tell him either. Kellan was the only thing that helped him get through the loss of his daughter and son-in-law. He wouldn't survive losing Kellan, too.

I knocked on his front door twice before I pushed it open and announced my presence. "Mack! It's just me."

"Ranger! I wasn't expecting you," he said cheerfully, but the smile dropped off his face when he saw the look on mine.

"No," he said and took a stumbling step backward.

"He's hurt, but he's alive. I need you to come with me. One of the brothers is going to fly us to Devil Springs."

"No," he said and shook his head.

"Yes! We don't have time for this. Let's fucking go!" I roared and that seemed to snap him out of it.

He grabbed his keys and his shoes and bolted for his truck.

"I'll drive," I told him and ran to the driver's side.

We hopped in and I peeled out of his place leaving a cloud of dust behind us.

"What happened?" Mack asked.

"I honestly don't know. Phoenix called and said he had a wreck. Then he told me to get you to the clubhouse. We'll find out more when we get there."

"I can't…"

"I know, Mack. I know. Let's not go there yet, okay?"

He nodded and we rode the rest of the way in silence. I didn't stop in the forecourt when we arrived. Instead, I drove the truck straight to the field where Shaker kept his helicopter.

Phoenix ushered us to the door and climbed in behind us. The moment we were strapped in, Shaker was lifting us off the ground. I reached forward and patted my grandbaby on her shoulder before I put my headset on. I should've known she'd be with Shaker. She and Kellan had become good friends when he was her assigned bodyguard.

"Do you know anything?" Mack asked.

Phoenix shook his head. "Not much. Layla called and told me he'd been in a bad accident, but she didn't know any details. I haven't been able to get any of the Devil Springs members to answer the phone, and the hospital won't tell me shit. What I do know is from the little bit on the news station's social media page."

Phoenix grimaced and braced his hands on his knees. "Kellan picked up Avery's kids from school. On the way home, they were hit by another vehicle. The truck rolled and went up over the guardrail, but the rear axle got caught and kept them from going all the way over. He got the kids out, but he fell when he climbed out."

"How far? Where?" Mack blurted.

"They were on a bridge that runs over a small lake. He fell about forty or fifty feet into the water. He wasn't in the water long..." Phoenix said and trailed off at the end.

"But what?" Mack asked.

"Someone commented and said he wasn't breathing when they pulled him out, but I don't know that to be true. I'm sorry, Mack. I should've kept that part to myself."

"I'd rather know how bad it is up front, to be honest," Mack said.

"He'll be okay," Keegan said confidently.

"I hope you're right, sweetheart," I said and something occurred to me. "Where's Gabby?"

"We were over at Reese's house when Shaker called. Reese offered to watch her for us."

We fell silent when Shaker started communicating in his fancy pilot codes with someone over the air waves. "Yes, Mr. Marks, we'll kiss your ass and let you land your helicopter anywhere you want because you donate large sums of money to us," Keegan mocked.

Shaker snorted. "Caught that, did ya?"

"How could I not?" she retorted.

"Hell, I'll kiss his ass for getting us to the hospital so fast," I said. "But just this one time."

We fell silent until we landed on top of the hospital fifteen minutes later. Someone was waiting at the door to the stairwell to let us in and tell us where to go. Mack and I didn't wait for the others. As soon as the bird was on the ground, we were on the move.

The stairwell opened into the ER waiting room where we found Judge, Batta, Coal, Tiny, Spazz, and Leigh. "Give us an update," I barked.

"We haven't heard anything," Coal said.

"Where's Copper and Bronze?"

"They're back there with the kids."

"Why the fuck aren't any of y'all answering your phones?" I demanded.

"Because we all jumped into the lake after him," Coal shared. "Everyone's phone is either lost or fried."

Mack walked up to the receptionist. "My grandson, Kellan Ward, was in a car accident. I'm his next of kin and was told I needed to get here quickly. Can someone take me to him?"

"One moment, sir," she said and picked up the phone beside her.

A door opened and River appeared. "You must be Kellan's grandfather. Follow me," she said and held the door open for him.

"I'm his other grandfather," I said and followed Mack like I had every right to do so.

I was bracing myself for the worst when we arrived in a patient room with Copper, Layla, and a young girl who appeared to be sleeping. River closed the door and said, "They've already taken Kellan to surgery. His injuries were too extensive to wait. I don't know all of his injuries, but I can tell you his heart has stopped twice—once when he was in the water, and once right before they took him to the OR. They believe he has a liver laceration which is bleeding into his abdominal cavity. I'm sorry, that's all I know right now."

"Was he awake when you saw him?" Mack asked.

"No, sir," River said and looked down at her feet. "I'm sorry I don't have better news to give you."

"Thank you, dear. Any news is better than not knowing," Mack said softly. "How are the children?"

"Riley has a broken arm and is sleeping

off the sedative they gave her before setting it. Braxton has a concussion and has been moved to the pediatric floor for overnight observation."

Someone knocked on the door before immediately pushing it open. Another nurse rushed inside, heaving in breaths like she'd just finished running a marathon. "They just delivered Savior's baby. A little girl. She's going to the NICU, but she's doing okay for how early she is."

"And Avery?" Copper asked.

"Um, Avery had some complications that I can't discuss, but she's going to be okay, too."

"Thank you, Kennedy," Copper said and stood to shake her hand.

"Can I see my great-granddaughter?" Mack asked.

Kennedy shook her head, but River stepped forward and took his hand. "I think I can sneak you in for a quick peek."

"Take a picture!" Layla shouted after them.

As soon as they were gone, I focused on Copper. "Tell me what happened."

"I'll be happy to as soon as Phoenix gets here. I don't want to tell it again," he said and I could tell whatever happened was weighing heavily on him.

When Phoenix was brought back to the little girl's room, Copper told us every excruciating detail of the accident and the subsequent rescue.

"So, what happened to the person that hit them?" I asked.

Copper shook his head. "Don't know. The cops were talking to witnesses and trying to see if anyone had a dash cam that caught the wreck, but it appears to be a hit-and-run."

"Well," I scoffed, "they can run, but they can't hide."

CHAPTER THIRTY-TWO

Avery

Pain.

I was in a lot of pain. And I felt like I was going to be sick. I tried to move, but that made the pain worse. I placed my hand over my stomach, where it hurt the worst, and gasped at what I felt, or didn't feel.

"My baby," I rasped.

"Ms. Parker, you're just waking up from surgery. You're in the hospital."

Right. I was in the hospital because my gallbladder crapped out on me. "Mom? Kellan?"

A warm and familiar hand gripped mine. "Hey, peanut," my dad said.

"Daddy? Where's Mom?"

"She's upstairs in her room."

I managed to crack an eye open and looked at my father. "What are you talking about?"

"Your mom had surgery today. You don't remember?"

"Why would mom have surgery on the day I scheduled my surgery?"

"Is this normal?" my dad asked someone across the room.

"Yes, sir, it's very normal for a patient to be confused when they wake up, especially in emergent situations like hers."

"What emergent situation?" I asked, starting to get alarmed.

"Ms. Parker, you had a placental abruption. We had to do an emergency c-section to deliver your baby."

My hands returned to my empty abdomen. "My baby! What did I have?"

"A beautiful little girl," my dad said proudly.

"Where is my daughter?" I screamed.

"She's in the NICU, but she's doing better than expected."

"What in the actual fuck is that supposed to

mean?" I snapped.

"Avery Grace," my dad chastised. "She meant your little girl came into this world earlier than expected in the middle of a stressful situation and she could be doing far worse than she is."

His words triggered my memory and everything came rushing back. "My babies! Where are my babies? Are they okay?" I started pulling at the covers and trying to get out of bed so I could go find my children.

"Avery, stop! You can't get up right now. They're okay. Riley's arm is broken and Braxton has a concussion, but they're okay," my dad said vehemently.

"What about Kellan?"

Dad grimaced and shook his head. "The last I heard, they were taking him to surgery."

"And Mom?"

"Your mom's going to be okay. She's got a few broken bones and some bumps and bruises, but nothing she can't handle," he assured.

"You need to go back and stay with her. She doesn't need to be alone."

"You know good and well your mother would whoop my ass if I left you alone. But before you start, she's not alone. One of Kellan's friends is staying with her and I have strict instructions to call them as soon as they move you to your room."

I nodded as my lower lip started to tremble. "This can't be happening," I whispered.

My father squeezed my hand. "You've got a waiting room full of people who love you and are ready to help in any way they can. You will get through this."

I closed my eyes and relaxed into the pillow until they moved me to my room. To my surprise, Copper, Layla, and Riley were waiting inside when they wheeled me in.

"Riley," Copper rumbled. "Your Mommy's here."

"She's still sleepy from the medicine they gave her before they set her arm," Layla explained.

My eyes landed on the bright pink cast on her left arm. "Is it bad?"

"Both bones in her forearm are broken, but she didn't need surgery," Copper shared.

"Riley," I called. "Wake up, baby."

"Mommy," she said through a yawn.

"Hey, sweet girl. You okay?"

She nodded and immediately started to cry. "Can I put her on the bed without hurting you?" Copper asked.

"Yes," I said and patted the bed beside me.

"Riley, your Mommy just had surgery on her tummy, so you have to be gentle," Copper instructed.

"Okay," she said and carefully scooted up beside me. I breathed a small sigh of relief when I had her in my arms. "Did you have the baby?" she asked.

I swallowed past the emotion clogging my throat. "Yes, I did. You have a little sister."

Riley sat up and looked around the room. "Where is she?"

"Well, she's in the special nursery for babies who come early," I explained.

"Can we go see her?"

"Yes, we can, but not right now."

"Can we name her Elsa?" she asked excitedly.

I smiled but shook my head. "No, sweetie, her name is Sienna Blake Ward," I said.

"I wanted to name her after my favorite princess," she pouted.

I kissed the top of her head and looked up as Copper handed me his cell phone. "Mommy!" Braxton shouted from the screen.

"Hey, little man!" I said and struggled to fight back my tears. "I'm so happy to see you. Are you okay?"

"Yes! Bronze is my new best friend," he said

proudly. "He gets me ice cream and tells me funny stories. And he has a pet snake he said I could play with."

"Knock, knock," I heard from the phone. "Did someone order an X-box?"

"Bye, Mommy!"

"I want to play with the X-box," Riley whined.

"If it's okay with your mom, I'll take you to Braxton's room," Layla offered.

"Yes, thank you," I said sincerely.

As soon as they were out of the room, I asked, "Tell me about Kellan."

"He's still in surgery," Copper said.

"Tell me about the accident. What happened?"

"They were hit on Lakeview Road. The truck rolled and started to go over the guardrail, but the rear axle got caught on part of the rail and stopped them."

"They were hanging over the bridge?" I gasped.

Copper nodded solemnly. "I pulled Braxton out, but Riley's arm was pinned between the seat and the door. Savior cut himself out of his seat belt so he could free her and hand her out to me."

"Then what?"

"Fuck, Avery. I'm so fucking sorry," he said

and shook his head. "I thought he was okay. I pulled him through the back window and he stood on his own two feet. We were about to climb up and he— Fuck! I couldn't catch him!"

I held my hands up and frantically waved them. "No more. I don't want to know anymore."

"If there's anything I can do, anything you need, you got it."

"Thank you," I said. "I'm going to need help with the kids for the next few days."

"Not a problem. Riley can spend the night with me and Layla tonight if that's okay with you. And we can keep Braxton when he's discharged from the hospital. Or we can stay with them at your house. Whatever you want."

I nodded and closed my eyes. "Thank you."

"Rest, Avery. I'll wake you as soon as we know something."

CHAPTER THIRTY-THREE

Savior

My eyes fluttered open and I immediately closed them to block out the piercing bright light. When I tried to raise my hand to use it as a shield, I discovered I couldn't move either one of them. I opened my mouth to speak, but nothing came out.

"Mr. Ward," someone said. "You're in the hospital. You were in a car accident. We have your hands tied down so you can't pull the breathing tube out."

A soon as I heard the words "breathing

tube," I became hyperaware of its presence and I immediately began coughing. All I could focus on was the tube in my throat and I wanted it out.

"Settled down, boy," Gramps said and I instantly obeyed his command.

"Mr. Ward," another voice said. "I'm going to remove the breathing tube now. When I tell you to, cough." I did as he said and coughed while he pulled the tube and what felt like the majority of my insides out of my mouth causing me to groan in pain.

"You're okay, Kellan," Gramps said.

It was only then I realized I'd never opened my eyes again. Slowly cracking one open at a time, my eyes landed on Gramps.

"You look like shit," I blurted.

"So do you, you little shithead."

"What happened?" I rasped and tried to clear my throat.

"Mr. Ward, I'm Dr. Abernathy. Do you know where you are?" he asked and shined a bright light in my face.

"In the hospital."

"What year is it?"

I looked over at Gramps. "Is he fucking serious?"

Gramps chuckled and nodded. "Yes, now,

answer the question."

He asked me several other questions before giving me a quick exam and mumbling something about writing some new orders. When he was gone, I turned my attention back to Gramps. "So, what happened?"

"You were in a bad car accident two days ago," he said cautiously.

"Was anyone hurt?" I asked as my stomach started to churn.

"Yes, but they're going to be okay and this was one hundred percent not your fault."

I frowned. I didn't remember anything about being in a car accident. "Who was hurt?"

Ten minutes later, I knew every horrible detail about the wreck, but I could tell there was something he wasn't telling me. "And what else?" I asked.

Gramps shook his head. "Relax, Kellan. It's not exactly bad news, but it's not my story to share. You'll know soon enough."

I wasn't happy about it, but I trusted Gramps implicitly, so I kept my mouth shut and closed my eyes.

I woke to the sound of muffled voices and sniffles. When I opened my eyes, I saw Gramps first. Then, my eyes landed on Avery sitting in a wheelchair crying. "Avery? What's wrong, baby?" I asked and reached for her.

"Kellan," she cried and gripped my hand firmly. She tipped her head back and whispered, "Thank you."

"Why are you in a wheelchair? Wait, are you wearing a hospital gown?" I asked and tried to sit up.

"No!" Gramps barked. "You can't get up. I was going to step out to give you two some privacy, but you have to stay put."

"Understood," I said with a nod.

When Gramps stepped outside, I met my woman's tear-filled eyes and spewed question after question. "What's going on? How are Riley and Braxton? Are they really okay? Gramps said they were, but I know he's not telling me something. And what's wrong with you? I know you weren't with us, and I—"

"Kellan," Avery interrupted and wiped a few tears from beneath her eyes. "You have a daughter."

It felt like my heart stopped for a few moments upon hearing her words. A daughter. A little girl. I was overwhelmed with feelings of love, happiness, and pride, but also fear, as the purpose of my entire being shifted to a new focus—family.

"When did you find out?" I asked. "I thought you wanted it to be a surprise."

More tears spilled from her eyes. "I found out when she was born two days ago."

My eyes immediately moved from her face down to her stomach. "But it's too early."

She nodded. "She's in the NICU and will be for a few weeks, but the doctors say she's doing good." She handed me her phone. "Here she is. Sienna Blake Ward."

I took the phone from her hand and stared at my baby girl on the screen. Tubes and wires surrounded her little body, but she was the most precious thing I'd ever seen. "She's beautiful," I whispered in awe. "And you named her after my parents."

"I hope that's okay. We can change it if it's not, but I couldn't bear the thought of her not having a name if something happened," she said and choked on a sob.

"Fuck, Avery, you're killing me. I can't even hold you right now. Are you okay? How was the delivery?"

"They had to put me under general anesthesia and deliver her by an emergency c-section. I didn't even get to see her until hours after she was born, but your grandfather made sure she wasn't alone."

"What about Riley and Braxton?"

"Riley's arm is broken and Braxton has a concussion. He had to spend the night in the hospital but he was released yesterday morning."

I suddenly remembered why the kids were with me in the first place. "Shit, baby, how's your mom?"

"She's going to have a long recovery, but I keep trying to remind myself that she is going to recover. Her hip was broken as well as her pelvis. She's been in a lot of pain, and now she's pissed because she can't help me with this whole situation."

"Did they get the person who ran over her?" I asked.

Avery shook her head. "No, and the last I heard, they don't know who hit you either."

"How is that possible? The grocery store should have surveillance cameras and there had to be plenty of witnesses for my wreck."

"I don't know. Copper said he would handle all of that for us," she said and paused. "Have you seen him yet?"

"No. Why?"

"He's been a blessing through everything over the last two days, but he's also been a mess," she said carefully.

"What do you mean?" Copper always had his shit together. Just like Phoenix, he seemed to know what was going on before it happened.

"When you fell, he tried to catch you. He told me his fingers barely brushed your shirt. Bronze said he didn't hesitate to jump in after you. Actually, none of your brothers thought twice about jumping in to get you. But you can tell it's weighing heavily on Copper," she explained.

"He doesn't have anything to feel guilty about," I said, more to myself than to her. "I'll tell him that when I see him."

"Ms. Parker, I need to take you back to your room now," a nurse said from the doorway.

"Give us just another minute," I said with a charming smile.

"Of course," she said and stepped back into the hall.

I turned to Avery and told her what I should have said to her months before. "I love you, Avery Grace. I love you, your children, and our child."

"I love you, too, Kellan. We all do."

"I don't want you to go," I confessed and didn't give a single fuck at how that made me sound.

She smiled shyly. "I don't want to go either,

but you need to rest, and Copper and Layla will be here with Riley and Braxton any minute."

"Can they come visit me?" I asked hopefully. I had been repeatedly reassured that the children were okay, but I wanted to see them for myself.

Avery shook her head. "No, they can't. The hospital policy doesn't allow children in the ICU. Trust me; they've asked every nurse and doctor they've met in this hospital if they could come visit you."

"Tell them I love them and that I can't wait to see them."

"I will," she said and then her eyes widened. "I almost forgot. Um, Riley told Copper she now hates mermaids because that's what caused you to wreck. Do you have any idea what she's talking about?"

My brows furrowed and I shook my head. "I don't have a clue what she could be talking about, but the last thing I remember is the teacher helping them into my truck. How in the hell would a mermaid cause me to have a wreck?"

Avery shrugged. "I don't know. I was planning to ask her about it when Copper brings her to visit, but I thought I'd ask you first."

"Well, let me know what she says."

"I will," she promised and leaned forward to

kiss my hand.

I brought her fingers to my lips and kissed the back of her hand in return. "I love you, Avery. Thank you for making me a father and giving me a beautiful baby girl."

Her cheeks flushed and she looked down at her lap. "I love you, too."

"Oh, send Copper up when he gets here," I said as she was being wheeled away.

"I'm here," Copper said. I watched as he took Avery's hand and spoke to her for a few moments before he entered the room. "Fuck, brother, it's good to see you awake and talking. You scared the ever-loving shit out of us."

He reached out and I thought he was going to shake my hand, but to my utter surprise, Prez pulled me in for the gentlest of bear hugs. "Thanks for saving my ass, Prez."

"Don't thank me. I let you fall."

"Fuck that. I thought I was fine. Neither one of us knew I was going to faint. And they way it was told to me, you jumped into that cold ass water to get me, not knowing how deep that water was."

Copper waved his hand dismissively. "Me and a few of the brothers jumped off that bridge a few times when we were in high school. We knew how deep it was."

"Seriously, Prez, you pulled us all out of that wreck and got us to the hospital. May not have been the way you intended, but it all turned out the same. Thank you."

"Aw, are you fuckers gonna cry without me?" Bronze asked as he made his way into the room.

Copper slapped the back of his head. "Who let you in here?"

Bronze looked over his shoulder and turned back with a sly grin on his face. "That pretty little nurse over there."

"Please don't fuck over the people who are keeping me alive," I said.

"That means don't fuck the people keeping him alive," Copper added.

Bronze scoffed and feigned offense. "I'm hurt."

"You're going to be if you don't shut your mouth and keep your dick in your pants," Copper grumbled.

I laughed and then groaned in pain. "Look what you did. Out, Bronze."

Bronze got to his feet. "Yeah, yeah, brother." He reached out and shook my hand. "Glad you're on the mend, man. He's been a cranky asshole since we fished you out of the water."

CHAPTER THIRTY-FOUR

Avery

I survived the following few days solely because of the women from Kellan's club. Leigh and Layla helped me with everything, and I do mean everything—from helping care for my children to helping me take a shower. River and Kennedy made sure everything was okay with Kellan, Sienna, and my mother when I wasn't at the hospital to hover over them. Much to my chagrin, I couldn't be at the hospital as much as I wanted.

Once I was discharged from the hospital,

I was torn between leaving and staying. Mom, Kellan, and Sienna were all still there and would be for some time while Riley and Braxton were at home. Leigh offered to drive me to the hospital whenever I wanted to visit. When Riley and Braxton were home from school, Layla offered to stay with them. However, that option didn't work out as planned because they wanted to visit Nana, Kellan, and Baby Sienna as often as they could. Ultimately, I visited for a few hours in the morning, came home to rest, and went back with the kids for a few hours in the afternoon.

After a week in the hospital, the doctors finally said Kellan was ready to be discharged. "I want to make sure I've been very clear about this; you are ready to be discharged from the hospital, but that does not in any way mean you are ready to resume your regular activities. Will you have someone available to help you for at least the first few days?"

"Yes, he does. He will be staying with me," I answered before Kellan could utter a single word.

"Avery, I'll be fine at my place. When Coal isn't there, one of the brothers can come by if I need anything," he countered.

I blamed the pregnancy hormones for what

happened next. Without preamble, I unleashed an angry tirade. "I can't run all over town checking on everyone. I need my people in one place, and until that happens, I refuse to have them in more than two places. So, you will be with me," I demanded.

Kellan cupped my cheek and never took his eyes off of mine when he said, "Looks like I'm staying with her, Doc."

"I think that's a wise choice," the doctor joked. "I'll get started on your orders and we should have you ready to go within an hour or two."

"Thanks," Kellan replied but kept his attention focused on me.

"I'm sorry," I blurted. "I'm exhausted, and I had no idea how much different it would be to recover from a c-section than a vaginal delivery."

He nodded and gave me a knowing look. "And what else?"

"What do you mean 'what else?' I'm stressed, Kellan. I'm worried about you, Mom, and Sienna. Christmas is just around the corner, and I don't have presents for anyone. I'm trying not to even think about the fact that our little girl will spend her first Christmas in the hospital," I explained quickly.

"Yeah, and what else? I know you're keeping something from me. You have a tell," he stated.

"A tell?"

"Yes, you avert your eyes and run your teeth over your bottom lip when you're trying to avoid a topic. So, just get it over with and tell me."

I sighed in exasperation. I should have known I wouldn't be able to avoid it forever, but I just didn't want to add to everything else we had on our plates. "After Ian died, the officers in his district put together a small fundraiser for the kids for Christmas last year and the year before. I received a call from Ian's best friend and coworker, Mark, to tell me that they weren't doing it this year since I moved away from Croftridge and have moved on with my life. And it's not about the money, it really isn't. I just didn't like how he said it. I mean, regardless of what's going on in my life, Riley and Braxton are still Ian's children."

Kellan's face hardened. "Let me get this straight. Because of your relationship with me, they decided not to do the charity fundraiser for your kids?"

I didn't know how to answer him. He was correct, but I didn't want to add fuel to the fire that was clearly burning behind his eyes. "He didn't use those words exactly."

"When did this happen?"

"I'm not sure. A week or two before the accidents?"

He nodded and reached for his phone. After typing what appeared to be a lengthy message, he put it away with a satisfied grin.

"What did you do?" I asked.

"Rectified a situation," he said cryptically. "Is there more?"

"I don't know. I guess he hurt my feelings, too. Mark and Ian had been best friends since high school. When Ian died, Mark helped me and the kids through some really tough times. Even after we moved, he came to visit and spent the weekend with us every few weeks."

"When was the last time he came to visit?" Kellan asked in a tone I hadn't heard from him before.

"The weekend before the kids went on vacation with my parents," I said carefully. "He was supposed to come up the weekend after they got back, but I ended up in the hospital. We haven't rescheduled his visit yet."

"You won't be rescheduling."

"What?"

"You will not have a man spend the weekend

with you in your house, especially if I'm not around," he said and stared at me in a way that dared me to challenge him.

"He's a family friend," I explained.

"Let me tell you something. Men do not spend that much time with a woman they think of as a friend."

"I see. Would you like to piss on my leg while you're at it?" I asked and stuck my leg out.

"Sweetness, I will pull my dick out every time you ask," he said with a cocky smile. "Listen, I'm not saying you can't be friends with him or that he can't come visit. I'm saying I'm going to be there when he does."

"Oh, good grief. Point made. You can stop now."

"As you wish," he grinned and changed the subject. "I want to go see your mom and Sienna before we leave."

"Mom would love to see you, and there's no way in hell I would leave this building without my baby being the last stop."

***

Mom was released from the hospital two weeks after Kellan and just in time for Christmas.

It took a little convincing, but I finally got her and Dad to agree to stay at my house through the holidays. Like I told Kellan, I wanted to keep all of my people in as few places as possible so we could all help each other. Mom could hardly walk two feet with a lot of assistance, I was on the typical restrictions after having a c-section, and Kellan had strict physical restrictions that would gradually lessen over the following four to six months.

Sienna was doing well and steadily getting stronger every day. She had gained some weight and was starting to look less like a sick preemie and more like an extra-small healthy baby.

I knew she was where she needed to be, but it killed me every time I had to leave the hospital without her. It wasn't something I ever thought would happen to me, and I had a new appreciation for all the mothers who'd had to leave their babies in the hospital.

I was also having a tough time with her spending her first Christmas in the NICU, but Kellan reminded me that she wouldn't remember any of it anyway. Mom also pointed out that at least she was here to have Christmas with us, regardless of where it was. They both had valid points, and I was still disappointed, but I tried to make the best of it.

"Are you going somewhere?" Kellan asked when I came down the stairs dressed in something other than yoga pants and a T-shirt.

I nodded. "Yes, Leigh said she would help me do some Christmas shopping for Riley and Braxton before they get out of school. She should be here any minute."

Kellan smiled broadly. "Well, you two have fun and don't overdo it."

"I won't," I promised.

Right on cue, the doorbell rang. I picked up my purse, opened the front door, and froze at the sight before me. Copper was standing on my front porch with Layla by his side and a sea of leather behind them. I caught a quick glimpse of Leigh off to the side before I blurted, "What are you doing here?"

Leigh stepped away from the crowd and waved. "We're helping with your Christmas shopping."

I whirled around to find Kellan walking up behind me. "Surprise, baby," he said softly.

"What did you do?" I demanded.

"I merely suggested the club focus on a particular family or two instead of doing a charity run and donating the money raised to an organization."

"And you picked my family?" I asked even though I already knew the answer.

"Just because you and I are together and have a child doesn't mean I'm going to stop doing things for Riley and Braxton. My reasons may have changed, but I still want to make sure they're taken care of. And I figured this was the only way you'd accept," Kellan said softly.

"But—" I started.

"But, nothing. Remember when you said it wasn't about money? Same principle applies here. This isn't about money. This is about your children never missing out on anything because of me."

I could tell from the look in his eyes that he needed to do it. We'd spent a lot of time talking about our feelings regarding Ian's death. I knew he was still carrying a lot of guilt, and probably always would be, just like I would carry the grief of losing my husband and my children's father. It was a part of who we were and we agreed to be supportive of each other's feelings.

"Okay," I agreed and turned to face the motorcycle club standing in front of my house. "Please, come in."

Copper grinned. "We won't be long. We just

need to know where you'd like us to put the presents that were too big to wrap."

"What did you get that was too big to wrap?" I asked in surprise.

"We tried to get everything on the list Riley gave us," Copper said.

"Except for the living creatures. We didn't buy any pets," Layla added.

"Thank you," I whispered and tried to keep my emotions under control. Kellan gently placed his hand on my shoulder and squeezed. "I'll go open the garage door and you can put the big stuff in there. I think there's a tarp laying around somewhere to keep everything covered."

I watched as they carried in present after present and placed them under the Christmas tree. Then, they filled a corner of my garage with two bicycles, two Power Wheels, a dollhouse that was taller than Riley, and a train table with an intricate set of tracks already setup.

"We went ahead and put the bigger stuff together for you. We thought it might be difficult for you two since you're both still recovering," Copper explained.

I couldn't help myself. I wrapped my arms as far around the big man as they would go and hugged him. "Thank you so very much."

Every muscle in his body tensed and he kept his arms held straight out to each side. "Uh..."

"You can hug her back, Prez," Kellan said from behind me.

With Kellan's okay, Copper returned my embrace. "We were happy to help. The Old Ladies love organizing these kinds of events. Speaking of, I believe they have another surprise for you inside."

I could tell he was uncomfortable with my gratitude. Even though I felt like I owed him more than a few simple words, I let it go and went back inside to see what else they had in store.

"Surprise!" all the women shouted in unison.

"What's all this?" I asked as I glanced around my kitchen.

"We didn't get a chance to give you a baby shower before you had the baby, so we're doing it now," Leigh said excitedly.

And that's when I did cry. Because I had little to nothing ready for Sienna. I hadn't planned on having any more children after Braxton, so I didn't keep any of the baby gear I'd used with both him and Riley.

"If you keep crying, you can't have any cake," Layla joked.

I wiped my eyes and smiled. "Thank you. I can't even begin to express how much this means to me."

"That's how this works. We're a family, not by blood, but by choice. When one of us needs help, we step in and help," Leigh stated as if it was law, and I guess it was in their world.

CHAPTER THIRTY-FIVE

Savior

While the women were occupying the kitchen and dining room for Avery's surprise baby shower, the brothers and I had an impromptu meeting in the living room. "Any updates on either accident?" I asked.

"Nothing solid," Copper said and shook his head. "Spazz was able to match the vehicle description to footage from the drug store's surveillance footage. He even got a clear shot of the license plate, but the tags were stolen. We couldn't get a clear image of the driver, but the vehicle was a black Chevrolet Silverado."

My eyes widened before I could mask it. "That mean something to you?" Bronze asked.

"I used to drive a black Chevrolet Silverado," I mumbled as I fought to keep my mind from going back to the night of the wreck.

"Understood," Copper said.

"What about the vehicle that hit me and the kids?" I asked.

Copper rubbed his chin. "Well, according to the police reports and witness statements, the only vehicle mentioned is a black Dodge Ram, and that's your truck. Or was."

"You're telling me no one saw the other vehicle?" I asked in total disbelief. I was in the middle of school traffic when we were hit. There's no way everyone around us missed the other car."

"That's what I thought, too. So, I called in a favor or two. It took a little longer than I would've liked, but I managed to get a list of the witnesses as well as the list of kids that were picked up right after you picked up Riley and Braxton. We'll start working the list this evening and see if we can get some more information. Now, if you know how to keep Ranger from going door-to-door with his shotgun, I'm all ears."

I chuckled and shook my head. "You're on your own with that one, Prez."

"Copper," Layla called from the kitchen. "It's time to pick up the kids."

"Thanks, Locks," he replied with a smile and turned to me. "You want to ride with me to get the munchkins?"

"Hell, yes. I haven't been anywhere other than the hospital since I got out," I said and quickly got to my feet. Avery and I were still on driving restrictions and I was starting to get a little cabin fever. I knew all I had to do was ask, and someone from the club would take me or her wherever we needed to go. But, they were already doing so much that neither one of us wanted to ask. Plus, between taking care of ourselves, the kids, her mom, and going to see Sienna, we were too tired to do much else.

They say most accidents happen close to the home. At the time, I hadn't realized just how close we were to Avery's house when we were hit. I hadn't even been back by the place where it happened. I don't know if it was a coincidence or if passing by had something to do with it, but as soon as I saw the bridge, I remembered.

"Did either one of you learn anything fun today?"

"I did!" Riley said excitedly and raised her hand in the air. "We learned that a starfish's mouth is on the bottom. Isn't that gross?"

"Why is that gross?"

"Because mermaids put them on their boobies!" she said in horror.

I couldn't hold in my laughter. "What are they teaching you at that school?"

"They teach us all kinds of—"

Riley's words faded as I glanced in my rearview mirror and my eyes landed on the truck barreling toward us. It was going to hit us if I didn't do something, but my options were limited due to all the traffic. I laid on the horn to alert the car in front of me and jerked the wheel to swerve out of the way. I watched in horror as the truck moved closer and made contact with my rear quarter panel. The truck started to spin and then we were hit again causing the truck to roll.

"It was a truck," I blurted, still in a daze from the sudden memory.

"What?" Copper barked.

"It was a truck that hit us. I remember. It was a black Dodge Ram," I said and shared the details of what I recalled. "It was almost like the maneuver police officers sometimes use when they're trying to stop a vehicle they're chasing.

He hit me and made me spin out; then, he rammed me again which made us flip."

"He? You saw who it was?" Copper asked excitedly.

I shook my head. "No, I didn't mean anything by that. It could've been a man or a woman."

"But you're sure it was a black Dodge Ram?"

"One hundred percent," I affirmed. "That would also explain the police reports and witness statements, as well as why there was no visible paint from the other vehicle on my truck."

"When we get back to Avery's, we need to call down to the station and have this added to the reports so they can start looking for the truck that hit you."

"I don't know why, Prez, but I think we should keep this new information to ourselves for right now. Let's see what Spazz can find first before we tell anyone else."

"What are you thinking, Savior?"

I shook my head. "I honestly don't know. It's just a feeling I have." Something wasn't sitting right with me. Even though a truck that looked exactly like mine hit me, at least one witness should have said the wreck involved two black trucks, not just one. And I was completely ignoring the other detail about a black Silverado being responsible for Claire's injuries.

Copper let it drop as he pulled into the school's car line, but I continued to play the accident over and over in my mind. I could clearly see the truck coming up behind us, but I couldn't remember any details about the person behind the wheel nor could I recall any distinctive features about the truck.

"You'll make yourself crazy if you keep doing that," Copper interjected.

"Doing what?"

"Trying to force yourself to remember something. If I had to guess, I'd say you're sitting over there trying to make yourself remember who was driving," he said knowingly. "Fact of it is, you probably didn't see who was driving. Once you noticed what was happening, your mind would've focused on getting you and the kids out of harm's way."

I sighed in frustration. "Yeah, you're probably right. But, damn it, now I want to know who was responsible more than ever."

"We'll find out who it was. It may take a little longer than you or I'd like, but we'll find the son of a bitch, and then we'll make him pay."

I hoped he was right.

"Kellan! Mr. President!" Riley squealed. "You

surprised us!"

"We did! How are you doing today, princess?" Copper asked.

"Great! We had a holiday party today with cupcakes and lots of candy. Today was our last day of school before holiday break," she shared.

Braxton climbed in next. Once he was situated, a teacher placed a large box in his lap and quickly closed the door.

"What is that?" I asked.

"Mrs. Tolbert said someone needed to take home Sir Stingsley. I raised my hand and she picked me!" Braxton said with a broad smile on his face.

"Aren't you a lucky boy? What kind of pet is Sir Kingsley?"

"Not Sir Kingsley," Riley corrected. "Sir Stingsley."

"He's a scorpion!" Braxton exclaimed.

Suddenly, an uneasy feeling washed over me. "Does your mother know about this?"

Braxton nodded his head exaggeratedly. "Yes, she does. I asked her and she said yes."

I highly doubted that. Braxton and Riley both had a bad habit of asking for stuff at the most inopportune time, resulting in Avery agreeing to something without realizing it or remembering it. In any event, the teacher should have spoken with an adult directly before sending a four-year-old home with a scorpion. "Does Sir Stingsley live in the box?"

"No, he lives in a glass box, but Mrs. Tolbert put it in this box because some of the other teachers are scared of him. And she put his food in the box, too. The other teachers don't like that either."

"I don't even want to know," I mumbled as Copper laughed.

"Do you want me to go back to the school?" he asked.

"You can't take him back!" Braxton cried. "No one else's mom said they could bring him home. And if no one takes care of him, he'll die!"

"Fuck," I cursed. I didn't know what to do. I knew there was no way in hell Avery agreed to allow a scorpion with scary food to spend Christmas break at her house, but Braxton was adamant that she said yes.

"If it turns out she didn't agree to this, Sir Stingsley can hang out at the clubhouse with Slither and Squeeze. Bronze won't mind feeding it whatever it eats," Copper said quietly.

"You sure? Because I'm almost one-hundred-percent certain Avery didn't consciously agree to this."

And I was proven to be correct moments after we walked through the front door. "Mommy, tell Kellan and President that you said I could bring the class pet home for Christmas," Braxton demanded.

Avery's forehead wrinkled. "I don't remember agreeing to that."

"Uh-huh. You said 'yes, fine, whatever,' when I asked you."

"What was I doing when you asked me?"

"You were in the bathroom putting those sucky things on your boobies."

Avery's face turned bright red and I could tell things were about to go south fast. "Braxton, go upstairs and play while I talk to your mom."

Avery whirled around to face me. I held my hands up in a placating manner. "Hear me out, sweetness. I didn't think you'd be okay with this, but when I mentioned going back to the school, Braxton got really upset. Copper said Sir Stingsley could stay at the clubhouse with the snakes. Bronze can feed him and take care of him during the break."

She exhaled slowly. "Okay, can you take it over there now? I cannot handle having a scorpion in my house. I just can't."

I laughed, as did a few of the brothers. "Yes, we'll take him over right now. Do you think Braxton would want to tag along and see the snakes?"

"I'm sure he would love th—"

Avery was cut off by Riley's panicked scream. It didn't even occur to me that I was supposed to be taking it easy. I bolted for the stairs, taking two or three at a time, and ran as fast as I could to Riley's room only to find it empty. "Riley!" I bellowed.

"Help! Get it out!" she screamed repeatedly.

I found her in Braxton's room, screaming and running in circles while she wildly swatted at her hair. I caught her and lifted her flailing body into my arms. She was screaming and crying and I couldn't understand a word she was saying, but then my eyes landed on the dark mass in her hair and I knew what the problem was.

"Riley," I said sternly. "Be still so I can help you."

"What is going on?" Avery demanded as she entered the room and reached for Riley.

"Don't," I warned.

"Why no—? Oh fuck! It's in her hair!" Avery screamed which caused Riley to start screaming and thrashing all over again.

"Please!" Riley sobbed. "Get it out!"

"Avery! Sit down and hold her," I ordered. I didn't intend to sound as harsh as I did, but I couldn't get it out of her hair until they both calmed down. "If you two will stop screaming and be still for just a minute, he'll let go of her hair. Just be still and be quiet for a few seconds, okay?"

Avery sat quietly while she tried to hold Riley yet keep her at a distance. Any other time I would have laughed at how ridiculous they looked. "You're going to feel my hand moving your hair so I can get him. I promise I won't let him crawl on you. And then he's going to spend Christmas break at the clubhouse."

I continued to talk to Riley, and Avery, while I waited for the little bastard to open his pincers. Finally, he dropped into my hand and I quickly put him in his box. "He's out. You're okay, princess."

"I'm sorry, Riley," Braxton cried. "I just wanted to show you."

I reached down to pick up Braxton while Avery was trying to calm Riley. Just as I had him in my arms, a sharp pain shot through my stomach that had me dropping to my knees.

"Kellan!" Avery gasped. "Copper! We need

help!"

Copper appeared seconds later and took in the scene. "How about you two kiddos head downstairs for a minute. I hear there's some cupcakes in the kitchen."

"Can we, Mommy?" they asked in unison.

"Yes," Avery answered immediately.

Copper was already helping me to my feet when River entered the room. "I'm okay," I said even though I didn't know if that was true.

"What happened?" Copper asked.

"I think I overdid it running up the stairs and then picking Braxton up. It didn't even occur to me that I wasn't supposed to lift him. I just need a minute. Once the pain goes away, I'll be fine."

"Let me check your abdomen and make sure everything looks like it should," River suggested.

"Okay," I agreed and yanked my shirt over my head. River stepped forward and pointed to Braxton's bed. "Lay down on your back."

I eyed the tiny bed and looked back to her. "You have got to be kidding. How about the floor?"

"That'll work." Once I was stretched out on the floor, she ran her hands over my stomach and carefully pressed around my incision and over my liver causing me to grimace. "Does that hurt?"

"It doesn't hurt, but it doesn't feel great either," I admitted.

"So, it's tender?"

"Yes, but that's nothing new."

She nodded and got to her feet. "I think you're fine, but if anything feels off, you should call the doctor," she said seriously.

"I'll make sure that he does," Avery vowed.

I also got to my feet and pulled my shirt back on. "Let's go back downstairs. I'm sure we scared the hell out of everyone just now."

"Please, get that thing out of my house," Avery said desperately.

"I'll take care of it," Copper promised and picked up the box containing Sir Stingsley and his scary food.

"Thank you!" Avery exclaimed before following River downstairs.

"Listen, brother, I know you're chomping at the bit to track down who was responsible for the wreck, but try to put it on the backburner for right now and enjoy Christmas with your family."

"I don't know if I can, but I'll try," I replied.

CHAPTER THIRTY-SIX

Avery

As expected, our Christmas was very different than any other year, but it was wonderful in its own way. Kellan's grandfather drove up to Devil Springs Christmas morning to spend the day with us. With my parents already staying at my house, we both had all of our family under one roof, with the exception of the newest member.

After watching Riley and Braxton open hundreds of gifts and wondering where in the hell I was going to put them, we had lunch and headed to the hospital to visit Sienna. I knew my mother was heartbroken that she couldn't go, but she hid it well, and my dad opted to stay home with her in case she needed anything. She was able to get up and down to the bathroom with her walker, but that was the extent of her mobility.

Mack offered to drive us in his truck. I couldn't wait to be able to drive again. I hated having to rely on other people to take care of basic needs. It wouldn't have been an issue if Kellan was able to drive, but with both of us on restricted activity, we didn't have a choice but to rely on others for a few weeks.

The NICU only allowed two people to visit at a time, so Kellan and I went back first. We found our little girl resting quietly with what looked like a handmade Santa's hat on her head and a matching stocking covering her body. "Oh, how cute!" I squealed and immediately reached for my phone to take several pictures.

"Where did that come from?" I wondered out loud.

"One of our volunteers makes them for the babies. She makes pink and blue ones for the rest of the year, but she brings in the Christmas ones on the first day of December every year," one of the nurses shared.

"Please thank her for me. This was such a wonderful surprise. How's our girl this morning?"

She frowned. "I don't have Sienna today, but let me get her nurse for you."

A few minutes later, our favorite nurse, Karen, came over with an update. "Miss Sienna is doing great. She's steadily gaining weight and her lab work looks good. She's still requiring some oxygen support, but that's completely normal. Later this week, we'll start trying to feed her some of the breast milk you saved and see how she does. All in all, she's on track to go home in the next few weeks."

I exhaled a sigh of relief. Every time we asked for an update, I subconsciously held my breath and waited for bad news. "Thank you," I breathed. "I can't wait to bring her home, but I want her to be ready."

"We won't send her home before we're sure she's ready," Karen promised. "I'll leave you two to visit, but call me if you need anything."

Kellan chuckled. "Isn't it funny how she's so small, yet she looks like she's grown so much?"

"I know. I was a little scared to hold her the first time because she was so small. Neither Riley nor Braxton were little babies and she seemed so fragile compared to them," I confessed.

"She's definitely a strong girl. Isn't that right, peanut?"

"My dad calls me that," I said softly.

"I know. I've heard him and I like it. Is it okay if I call her that?" he asked sincerely, causing my heart to swoon.

"I love you," I said and kissed his cheek.

"I love you, too, lil' mama," he replied and pulled me close.

We stayed for a little longer before rotating out so everyone had a chance to visit with Sienna. Mack was happy to take Riley back, and Braxton wanted to go with Kellan. He'd become quite attached to Kellan over the last few weeks, which had me slightly concerned. Both Riley and Braxton had already been through a significant loss at a young age, and I didn't want them going through something like that again if things didn't work out between Kellan and me. But, Kellan was going to be a part of our lives in some way or another because he was Sienna's father, and I truly didn't think he was the kind of person who would snub my children if our relationship failed.

"What are you thinking about so hard over there?" Kellan rumbled from beside me causing me to startle.

"Just how much my kids adore you," I hedged.

He cocked his head to the side for a moment before a knowing look washed over his face. "We've got to get to the clubhouse, but we'll talk about this later," he said.

Crap. He was far too good at reading my body language.

***

We arrived at the clubhouse for Christmas dinner. According to Savior, it was something they had been doing every year since the club started. I wasn't used to eating Christmas dinner somewhere other than my own house, but I was extremely thrilled not to have to cook for once.

When we walked inside, I gasped in surprise. "Mom! What are you doing here?"

She smiled. "When we finally got you out of the house, a few of these fine young men came over to help transport me here so we could enjoy Christmas dinner together."

I turned to face Kellan's friends. "Thank you."

"Don't thank us. It was all him," Bronze said

and pointed to Batta.

Batta shrugged. "While they were discussing the best way to get her in the truck, I just picked her up and put her in the seat. Did the same thing when we got here."

Mom smiled broadly. "He sure did."

"Mom," I groaned.

"What? You can't tell me that man's size isn't impressive," she retorted.

Batta rocked back on his heels and stuck his thumbs through his belt loops. "It definitely is," he said and it was obvious he was referring to the size of something else.

"Knock it off, boys; it's Christmas," Leigh ordered. "And it's time to eat."

"Jenna!" Riley squealed and ran toward a little girl standing behind Batta. "Mommy! Mommy! It's Jenna!"

"Riley!" the little girl yelled with just as much enthusiasm.

"Mommy, can we go play?"

"Maybe after we eat," I said hesitantly. We'd been to the clubhouse a few times before, but I wasn't sure if it was okay to let my kids run freely through the place. For one thing, I didn't want them walking in on anything I wasn't planning on explaining to them until they were much older.

Kellan leaned in close, "They can play anywhere in here and be fine."

"Yes," I said with more confidence. "As long as you stay in this room and it's okay with Jenna's parents," I said with a smile.

"It's fine," Batta said and ruffled her hair.

"Oh, I didn't realize she was yours."

"She's not. She's Kennedy's niece. Actually, they live right down the street from you," Batta told me.

"Now that you mention it, I think Riley told me that one time. I know she's been wanting to play with her outside of school, but I didn't realize she was Kennedy's niece. We'll definitely have to plan something after the holidays."

"I'm sure Jenna would love that."

CHAPTER THIRTY-SEVEN

Savior

I was finally able to drive just in time for New Year's Eve, and I had a big surprise planned for Avery. We'd been through a lot in the few months we'd been together, but we'd never been on a date. That was about to change.

It took some careful planning to keep from spoiling the surprise, but I managed to find babysitters for the kids, make arrangements for the evening, and even bought a new truck without Avery knowing. The only thing I hadn't figured out was how to get her dressed and ready without telling her why. Thankfully, Claire took care of that for me.

Avery came downstairs in a pair of ripped jeans and a fitted black Blackwings MC T-shirt one of the Old Ladies had given her for Christmas. Her long, auburn hair perfectly framed her delicate face, and her green eyes held a sparkle I'd never seen before. When she looked at me and smiled, she took my breath away.

"I'm almost ready to go," she said and shoved a few things into her purse. "We shouldn't be too late," she told her parents.

"It's okay, honey," Claire said. "Enjoy your evening. You deserve it."

After giving everyone hugs and kisses, she walked outside expecting to see one of our various chauffeurs waiting patiently in the driveway. "Whose truck is that?"

"Mine," I said. "I bought it yesterday after the doctor gave me the okay to increase my activity, including driving."

"Why didn't you tell me?"

"Because I wanted to surprise you," I said and opened the door for her. Once we were both inside, I held up a blindfold. "I have another surprise."

"We're not going to the clubhouse?" she

asked and eyed the blindfold curiously.

"No, but that's all I'm telling you. Your parents know what the plans are, so don't worry about that. Now, close your eyes, pretty girl."

She did as I asked and closed her eyes while I slipped the blindfold over her head. I followed up by placing a quick kiss on her lips.

After about fifteen minutes on the road, she finally asked, "How long is it going to take for us to get wherever we're going?"

"Now, if I told you that, you might have an idea of where we're going. Nice try though," I laughed.

"I hope I'm dressed okay. I thought we were going to the clubhouse not somewhere else."

"Trust me, Avery, what you're wearing is perfect. Stop worrying, baby. We'll be there soon."

After an hour and a half on the road, I finally turned onto the street that led to our destination for the evening. I hadn't visited in almost a decade, but Gramps assured me that the place was clean and everything was in working order.

I parked the truck in the gravel driveway and went around to open Avery's door for her. "Before you take the blindfold off, I want you to know that even though it might not look like much, this place is very special to me. I've never brought anyone here, but when I was trying to come up with the perfect plans for tonight, I couldn't think of any place I'd rather take you."

"Why were you trying so hard to come up with perfect plans?" she asked.

"Because you and I have a child together and we've never even been on a date. I couldn't let that be once I realized it."

She gave me a beautiful smile. "Well, let me see where we are."

I inhaled deeply and helped her out of the truck before removing her blindfold. "This was my parents' place. Come on, let me show you the best part," I said and pulled her along behind me.

Instead of going through the small house, we followed the wraparound porch to the other side of the house where it connected to large deck that led to the covered dock housing Gramps's boat. The area was lit by small twinkle lights that were hanging from the porch railings. My mother had hung them the first year they had the place, and Gramps made sure to replace them whenever a strand went out.

"Kellan," Avery gasped. "It's beautiful."

"Mom loved it here. We lived in Croftridge,

but we spent our weekends and most of the summer here. After I lost them, I came with Gramps whenever he stopped by to check on things, but once I was old enough to stay home alone, I stopped coming and haven't been back since."

She walked over to me and wrapped her arms around my waist while burying her face against my chest. "Thank you for sharing this with me."

I kissed the top of her head. "Are you hungry?"

"I could eat."

When she saw the table set for two, she turned to me with squinty eyes. "How did you do that? You just said you hadn't been back."

"I can't give away my sources, but I had some help," I confessed and ushered her to the table.

Since neither one of us could drink alcohol—because of her breastfeeding and my liver injury—I opened a bottle of sparkling grape juice to fill our champagne flutes. Avery laughed, "I'll have to remember to get some of this for Riley the next time there's an occasion. She will love drinking out of a fancy glass."

After dinner, I got a fire going in the outdoor fireplace and turned off the twinkle lights before

Avery and I curled up in the giant outdoor bed swing my dad made for mom. Avery snuggled closer and asked, "Why'd you turn off the lights?"

"Roll to your back and look up."

She did and gasped. "Wow! I've never seen so many stars."

"You could see even more without the fire, but it's too cold for that tonight and neither one of us can afford to get sick."

"No, this is perfect."

We cuddled together under the blanket by the fire and silently admired the stars. Before long, we were both fast asleep.

A loud boom startled me, as well as Avery, from sleep. "What was that?" she gasped and dug her fingers into my skin.

"Fireworks," I said and pointed to the sky as another loud boom echoed over the lake before the sky was filled with a starburst of color. "The country club across the lake puts on the best fireworks display for New Year's and Fourth of July. It's one of the reasons I wanted to come out here tonight. I thought you would enjoy it."

I was right. For the next half an hour, Avery oohed and aahed each time the sky was illuminated with a different explosion of color. When the grand finale started, she pulled out her phone and started recording it. I laughed, "I guarantee you'll never watch that video after you finish recording it."

"So," she retorted. "I'm still going to record it."

When it was over, she snuggled back down into the blanket with me. "Thank you for tonight," she said softly and pressed her lips to mine.

I hugged her closer and kissed her back. "I love you, Avery Grace."

I felt her smile against my lips when she said, "I love you, too, Kellan."

"I love Riley and Braxton, too. I cared about their well-being before, but I love both of those kids just as much as I love Sienna."

"I know you do," she assured me.

"You sure about that? We didn't get a chance to talk about it, but it seemed like you were having some doubts."

"More like concerns. My kids adore you. If this doesn't work out between us, it will be more than just me that gets hurt," she confessed.

"You have to know I would never do anything to intentionally hurt them. If something happens between us, I would still want to be a part of their lives."

She smiled softly. "You're a good man."

"And you're a good mother. Now, let's go inside, sweetness," I said and got up to put out the fire.

"Are we staying here tonight?" she asked.

"That was the plan, but we don't have to. It's up to you," I told her.

"Is it bad that I just want to sleep?"

I laughed. "Hell no, it's not bad. I just want to sleep, too."

CHAPTER THIRTY-EIGHT

Avery

When I woke, the sun was just starting to light the sky. I rolled to my side and placed my hand on Kellan's cheek. With his face relaxed while he slept, he appeared so much younger than twenty-six.

I smiled to myself as I got out of bed and made my way to the kitchen hoping to find something I could cook to surprise Kellan with breakfast in bed. When I flipped the lights on in the kitchen, my smile disappeared and I froze at the sight before me.

"Mark," I gasped. "What're you doing here?"

Mark was sitting in one of the kitchen chairs looking worse than I'd ever seen him with his disheveled hair and wrinkled clothes. Even his usually clean-shaven face was covered with a few days' worth of growth. But the most alarming observation was his hand resting on the table tightly curled around a gun.

"I came to see you," he slurred.

"Are you drunk?" I asked.

His palm landed hard on the table causing a loud slap to fill the room. "Does it fucking matter, Avery?" he snarled.

"N-no, I suppose it doesn't," I said calmly while my eyes darted around the room looking for anything that could help.

He leaned back in the chair and rubbed his chin with his gun. "Do you know what it's like to have feelings for someone and have to watch them be with someone else?"

I shook my head. "No, I don't."

"Of course, you don't!" he snapped. "You and your whore pussy get whatever man you want!"

"Mark! What in the hell is wrong with you?"

It felt like my heart stopped for several beats when he pointed his gun directly at my chest and said, "You are."

"What?" I breathed.

"You are!" he screamed and got to his feet. "First Ian and now the motherfucker who killed him!"

"I-I don't understand," I stammered.

"Bitch, please. Don't try and act stupid. You knew I wanted you. Even Ian knew I wanted you," he growled and took a step forward.

I held my hands up in surrender. "Mark, please. I swear I didn't know. But now that I do, let's talk about this," I pleaded. I needed to keep him talking and give him time to sober up.

"There's nothing for us to talk about. I had it all set up perfectly and that son of a bitch in there ruined everything!" he yelled and pointed to the bedroom where Kellan was hopefully still sleeping.

"You had what set up?" I asked. He wasn't making any sense and the more he talked, the more he confused me.

He stared at me with an arched brow. "Tell me, Avery, why did Ian leave you?"

I couldn't hide the look of surprise on my face. No one knew about that other than my parents and Kellan, or so I thought. "How did you know?"

He laughed cruelly. "Because I'm the one

who convinced him to leave you after I told him you'd been having an affair with another officer."

"You did what?" I screamed as red-hot rage began to flow through my veins.

"It was perfect! He was going to put in for a transfer and then I could have you all to myself. But then that motherfucker in there killed him and I had to spend almost a year coddling you and your brats! Just when I was about to make my move, you up and moved to Devil Springs without any warning. One day it was just, 'Oh, fuck you, Mark, I'm moving,' and then you were gone. Then, after all the time I spent convincing you to get rid of your kids for the summer so you would be lonely and depressed when I approached, you go and start fucking the bastard that killed Ian!" he roared.

I was so shocked by the words coming out of his mouth that I hadn't realized he had moved closer to me. Pain erupted in my cheek when his hand made contact with my face. "You turned me into a monster!" he bellowed followed by another fist to my face that had me falling to the floor.

"I'm sorry!" I cried. "Please stop, Mark! I'm sorry!"

"You aren't yet, but you're gonna be! I'm a fucking police officer, Avery! If that truck had gone over the bridge like it was supposed to, I would be a murderer because of you!" he yelled as he towered over me.

Lowering his voice, he pointed his gun at my face and took aim. "I will be a murderer because of you."

The deafening report of a single gunshot echoed through the small cabin. And something warm and sticky splattered across my face and chest. I couldn't hear anything, but I could feel the vibrations of footsteps moving across the floor. All the while, I kept my eyes squeezed closed and remained curled into a ball on the floor.

When hands landed on me, I started screaming and blindly swinging my fists. The hands moved and firmly gripped my wrists to hold them down. "No!" I screamed and tried to get free. Something soft pressed against the shell of my ear and I heard, "It's me. I got you."

My entire body sagged in relief as I dissolved into a fit of tears. "Kellan!" I cried as I clung to him. "H-he, he," I stammered.

"I know, baby. Keep your eyes closed," he said before he wiped something over my face. "Okay, keep them closed while I help you stand."

I did as he said and let him lead me out of

the kitchen. When we came to a stop, he wiped over my face again with a wet cloth. "Open," he said very close to my ear. He stepped back and I read his lips more than I heard the words when he said, "Let's go outside."

My entire body was trembling, but I managed to walk outside while clinging to his arm. He helped me sit in one of the patio chairs and squatted down in front of me. "I have to call this in," he said and visibly swallowed. "I'm probably going to be arrested, but the club will handle it. Don't try to interfere. Just wait for Phoenix to get here and do what he says."

I nodded as tears streamed down my face.

"I need the words, baby."

"I'll do what he says. I love you, Kellan," I cried and pulled him against me.

He held me for a few short moments before he pulled away and pulled out his phone.

CHAPTER THIRTY-NINE

Savior

"Phoenix Black."

"It's Savior. I'm at my parents' lake house and I just killed a police officer," I said and swallowed the bile rising in my throat. "I need you to call Copper and come get Avery. I'm calling it in now."

"Give me five before you call it in. I'm on my way," he said and disconnected the call.

I breathed a small sigh of relief knowing Phoenix was on his way. I turned my attention back to Avery. "If anyone asks, you called

Phoenix from my phone when you saw Mark in the kitchen."

She nodded quickly and squared her shoulders. "I called Phoenix. Got it," she said with steely determination in her eyes.

It was only then that I noticed the unevenness of her face. She flinched when I used the bottom of my shirt to carefully wipe the blood covering her cheek and I saw red all over again. "Did he hit you?"

She sniffled and whispered, "Twice."

"Fuck," I cursed and took a closer look at her.

"It's okay. I didn't even notice it until just now."

"When Phoenix gets here, ask him to call Patch. He's a doctor in the club. Are you hurt anywhere else?"

She shook her head. "No," she choked out and covered her mouth. "Not physically."

I wrapped my arms around her and held her while she cried. I heard him confess to trying to kill her children and me. I also heard him admit to being the reason her husband walked out on her, and I couldn't help but wonder what else he was responsible for.

"Avery," I rasped. "I can't wait any longer to

call."

"I know," she said against my shirt.

I didn't let her go while I dialed 9-1-1 and held my phone to my ear.

"9-1-1, what's your emergency?"

"Someone broke into my house and attacked my woman. I shot him. He's dead and we're outside," I said and gave her the address.

"Officers are en route. Is anyone injured?"

"Yes, my woman's cheek might be broken."

"And the intruder you shot. Are they—?"

"I am one-hundred-percent certain he's dead," I interrupted.

"Okay, sir, if you'll stay on the line with me until the officers arrive on scene—"

"No need. We're no longer in danger. Please let the officers know my weapon is inside the house on the kitchen counter. We're on the back porch and completely unarmed," I added before disconnecting the call.

A small amount of tension left Avery's body when the rumble of several bikes in the distance broke the silence of the early morning, but I didn't let go of her until Phoenix rounded the corner with Carbon and Shaker.

"What happened?" he asked without preamble.

"He broke into the house and attacked Avery in the kitchen. He was Ian Parker's best friend and co-worker. Apparently, he's had an obsession with Avery for several years. He also confessed to being the one who hit me and the kids," I said quickly.

"Where'd you shoot him?"

"One shot to the head. From the front. Put my gun on the counter and got Avery out of there as fast as I could." When I heard the sirens, I added, "Avery called you from my phone."

"Give her your phone. Her bloody prints need to be on it," Phoenix said calmly.

I nodded and passed my phone to Avery. "Can you have Patch or someone look at her face? I think her cheek might be broken."

Phoenix's eyes hardened and he nodded sharply. "If you're not around to do it, I'll make sure it's looked at, but Savior, I don't think you have anything to worry about. This seems pretty cut and dry to me."

"But he's a police officer," I argued.

"So?" Phoenix countered. "He wasn't in uniform or on duty."

"Whew! That's going to be a bitch to clean up," Ranger said as he suddenly materialized. I should have known he'd come with the crew.

His face softened when he saw Avery. "How're you doing, sweetheart?" he asked and held out a bandana for her.

She took it and started carefully wiping the edges of her face. "I'm not sure," she said shakily.

"You're going to have one hell of a shiner there. Look here at the camera but don't smile," he instructed.

Avery turned to Ranger with a blank stare on her face. "Why?" she asked.

"Evidence," Ranger said right as the police arrived.

"Nobody move, and put your hands in the air!"

"Do they not realize we have to move to put our hands in the air?" Carbon grumbled.

"Relax, rookie," Phoenix called out. "Where's Chuck?"

"Fucking hell, Phoenix," an older man said and stepped forward. "What happened?"

"Can you call off the guns?" Phoenix asked, though it wasn't a question.

"Shit, sorry. Holster your weapons," he said to his officers.

Phoenix motioned for me to step forward. "This is one of my members, Kellan Ward. He can tell you what happened. Kellan, Chuck is the Sheriff of Croftridge County."

I cleared my throat and told the Sheriff exactly what happened. Well, almost exactly. I left out the part where Mark said he was a police officer, but I made sure to tell them he was the driver of the other vehicle involved in my wreck and that he clearly said he was going to kill Avery.

The Sheriff listened attentively. When I finished, he looked to Phoenix and asked, "How'd you get here before us?"

"Avery called me screaming and crying. Had my guy ping the phone for the location. He called it in while we headed out to see what was going on," Phoenix explained.

"Anybody been inside?"

"Just Avery and Kellan, and I don't think they've been back in since they came out," Phoenix answered and I nodded in agreement.

"Sheriff," the rookie called from the back door. "We need you to come inside."

"Excuse me," the Sheriff said and followed the officer inside.

"I guess they've identified the body," Ranger observed.

"Avery," Shaker said. "Let me help you over to the ambulance so they can take a look at your cheek."

She turned her worried eyes to me. "Everything's okay, baby. Go with Shaker and at least let them give you an ice pack."

She reluctantly got up and walked with Shaker over to the ambulance parked on the street. I kept my eyes on her until she disappeared into the back of the ambulance.

The Sheriff pushed through the back door and came right over to where we were standing. "Do you know the man you shot?" he asked abruptly.

"No, I've never seen him before today," I answered honestly.

"He's a State Trooper," the Sheriff said. "I'm going to need you to come down to the station."

"That's fine," Phoenix said. "We'll meet you and his lawyer there."

"He's not under arrest," Chuck explained. "But I know who he is, and we need to keep this under wraps until we know what really happened."

Avery suddenly appeared right in front of Chuck. "I'll tell you what really happened. That man had an unhealthy obsession with me that started way before Kellan entered the picture. He used his position as a police officer to stalk me and interfere with my personal life. He meddled in my marriage, my family relationships, and when he still didn't get the results he wanted, he tried to kill Kellan and my children by causing the truck they were in to go off a bridge. Yes, Kellan is the man who fell asleep at the wheel and crashed into Ian's cruiser, but that has absolutely nothing to do with this situation. Having said that, Mark could've had something to do with the hit-and-run involving my mother. So, if by 'keep this under wraps,' you mean protecting a bad cop simply because he wore a badge, then, I'm sorry, but we won't be cooperating with that," Avery stated vehemently.

Chuck shook his head. "No, ma'am, that's not at all what I was suggesting. I believe in honesty and integrity in all areas of life, but I've been Sheriff for many years now and I'm well aware of how the media likes to spin things. This story has all the necessary elements to become a giant clusterfuck in a matter of hours. Surely, you can understand that," he explained.

Avery nodded. "Yes, I know all too well how easily the media can get carried away. Obviously, Kellan does, too."

"I'll tell you what. I've already heard his explanation. Let me hear yours and we'll see about getting you two out of here while we finish up," the Sheriff suggested.

Avery proceeded to tell him everything that happened from the moment she woke up to the moment the police arrived. Her ability to recall so many details during a traumatic event was beyond impressive.

Chuck looked up from his notepad and nodded. "Got it," he said and glanced over his notes. "I don't see any reason why either one of you need to stay. Just don't leave town until we've officially cleared you both."

"We can't stay here!" Avery blurted. "We live in Devil Springs! Our baby is in the NICU. I have to take more breast milk to the hospital today," she said and pointed to her chest causing the Sheriff's cheeks to flush.

She turned to Phoenix with her hands on her hips. "Can they do that? Can they make us stay here if we aren't under arrest? Because I'm telling the lot of you right now, someone will be taking my breast milk to my baby today and every single day that I'm stuck here!"

Phoenix smiled. "You're going to fit in nicely around here. As for you question, the answer is no; they can't make you stay in town if you aren't under arrest."

Phoenix turned to Chuck and glared. Chuck held his hands up in surrender. "Sorry, it's an old habit I've yet to break. Let me just verify your contact information and you're both free to go. Though, we will be putting your firearm into evidence. I assume it's registered to you."

"It is," I confirmed. I expected as much, which was why I left it on the kitchen counter. That, and I didn't want a new cop with a twitchy trigger finger filling my body full of holes if it was on or near me when they arrived.

After confirming our information, I took Avery's hand and started for my truck when Phoenix stopped me. "Go to the Croftridge clubhouse and let Avery take a shower before you drive back to Devil Springs. Annabelle's bringing a change of clothes over for her."

"Thanks, Prez," I said and shook his hand.

He immediately pulled me in for a man hug. "Ranger and I will hang around here and make sure everything goes smoothly. Carbon and Shaker will follow you back to the clubhouse. You did good. Now, go take care of your woman."

He didn't need to tell me twice. I helped her into the truck and got us to the clubhouse as fast as I could.

CHAPTER FORTY

Avery

After showering and changing into some clean clothes, Kellan and I got right back into his truck and started heading back to Devil Springs. I couldn't stop replaying Mark's words over and over in my head, each time sparking a new combination of feelings I wasn't sure how to process.

"Do you want to talk about it?" Kellan asked.

"Do you?" I returned.

"I think we should. He had a lot of things to say. What do you think about what he said?"

"I honestly don't know what to make of it. I had no idea he had feelings for me. He was Ian's best friend, for fuck's sake. My kids called him Uncle Mark. Why would he pretend to be our friend for years if he really wasn't? That just doesn't make any sense to me."

"It doesn't make any sense to you because you think rationally," Kellan said simply. "Something was wrong with Mark that prevented him from thinking like a sane person."

"Yeah, I guess you're right," I agreed.

"Come on, Avery; get it out. Don't hold it in and let it fester."

I inhaled deeply and let it out. "I'm fucking pissed. How dare that self-centered son of a bitch try to kill you and my children! Did he really think I'd want to jump into a relationship with him after suffering a loss like that? And what if he had killed the three of you? What was he going to do about Sienna? Kill her, too? Every time I think about those words coming out of his mouth, I wish I'd had my eyes open when you blew his head off," I fumed.

"Good, baby. Keep going," Kellan encouraged.

"And I'm upset about what he told Ian. Did Ian die thinking I was unfaithful to him? I just can't bear the thought of that," I cried. "I never cheated on him. From the day I met him, I never looked at another man while we were together. I didn't even touch another man until I met you," I confessed.

Kellan inhaled sharply. "The first time we were together was the first time you'd been with anyone since him?"

"Yes."

"Fuck, Avery. I'm sorry. I didn't know. If I had I would—"

"Don't apologize," I interrupted. "I needed it to be that way. I wouldn't have been able to handle sweet and gentle. Not then."

"I'm still sorry for treating you the way I did. It doesn't excuse my behavior, but I was struggling with a lot and I had no idea the answer to my problems was right in front of me."

"I just can't believe this happened. I thought we'd finally found a place where we could be happy together and then Mark goes and fucks it all up," I blurted.

Kellan jerked the wheel to the side and pulled off the road bringing the truck to a sudden stop. "What in the hell is that supposed to mean, Avery?"

"What?" I asked, completely confused by his reaction.

"What. Do. You. Mean? You don't think we can be happy together because of Mark?" he demanded.

"I just meant things had finally smoothed out for us and now we have all this bullshit to deal with. I'm sure you don't want to hang around and watch me go through the loss of Ian, again, as well as the betrayal and hurt Mark caused."

"I told you I would never ask you to forget him. I meant that. I know you loved him. I know that just because he died, your love for him didn't. He's the father of two of your children. He will always be a part of your life. I accepted that the day I realized you were Avery Parker. Regardless of what did or didn't happen between you and Ian will not change my stance on that. Do I want his picture hanging in our bedroom? No. The kids' rooms? Sure, he's their dad. If your wedding anniversary rolls around and you want to spend it in bed with a box of tissues, that's fine, too. But whatever it is you're going through, don't hide it from me."

I unbuckled my seat belt and launched myself across the truck into his arms. "I love you, Kellan," I said before I smashed my mouth against his.

His hands threaded through my hair and he

returned my kiss with just as much intensity. I didn't care that we were on the side of the road. I didn't care that only a few hours ago I'd been covered in the blood of a man I once thought was a friend. I needed him and I couldn't wait any longer.

Raising my hips, I pushed the yoga pants I was wearing down my legs and kicked them across the truck while I undid his jeans and reached inside. "Avery," he mumbled against my lips, but I didn't acknowledge him. Instead, I pointed his hard cock where I needed it and sank down as far as I could go, groaning when I was completely filled with him.

His hands left my hair and firmly gripped my hips. "Fuck, baby. Move," he rasped against my lips.

Following his command, I began to move, reveling in the pleasure created with each pass of my hips.

Kellan shoved my T-shirt and bra up to bare my breasts, but I froze when he took one nipple into his mouth. I was breastfeeding and any kind of nipple stimulation was going to have my milk dripping all over us.

He landed a sharp, stinging slap to my ass followed by, "Don't stop."

"But I—"

"Ride my fucking cock, Avery, while I suck on your sweet tits," he growled and squeezed my ass.

When I still didn't move, he looked up and his eyes softened. "Your body is providing nourishment and immunity for our child. Everything about it is amazing to me. Now, let me enjoy it."

Without giving me a chance to argue, he went back to sucking on my nipple and used his grip on my hips to guide my movements until I forgot about my insecurities and got lost in him.

He switched to my other nipple and sucked hard. "Fuck, baby, you gotta come. I'm not going to last much longer."

"I don't want to. It feels so good," I moaned.

I felt him grin against my skin. "Yes, you do, bad girl. You want me to spank that ass again?" he rumbled and slapped each cheek. "Fucking come, Avery. Squeeze my cock with that tight pussy."

And that did it. The tension coiling suddenly released and pleasure exploded from within. "Yes, yes, yes," I chanted.

"Fuck," Kellan groaned and slammed my hips down while he thrust into me several times before stilling.

I collapsed against his chest, sweaty and gasping for breath but completely sated.

"You okay?" he asked.

"Yeah. Are you? Did I hurt you?"

His big body shook when he laughed. "No, but I wouldn't have given a shit if you did. That was worth it."

We held each other in silence for a few more minutes before I started to climb off of him. And that's when I realized what we did, or didn't do. "Shit," I cursed at the sticky mess between my legs. "We didn't use a condom."

"Were we supposed to?" he asked.

"I'm not on any kind of birth control and I don't want to get pregnant."

"Right now or ever?" he asked seriously.

I gaped at him. "What?"

"Do you mean you don't want to get pregnant right now or ever again?"

"Well," I started and chose my words carefully. "I hadn't planned on having any more children after Braxton, so I wasn't really planning on having any after Sienna, but it's not something I've given a lot of thought to."

"Give it some thought. I want more kids," he said. "With you."

My breathing increased and my heart started to pound against my chest. "You what?" I squeaked.

"I want to have more babies with you. I've always wanted to have a large family," he said quietly.

And suddenly I understood. He only had his grandfather after his parents died. Having a large family would have prevented some of the loneliness I'm sure he felt.

"Kellan—" I started.

"I shouldn't have brought it up after everything that just happened. Put it on the backburner to think about. If it's about money, I have plenty of it. If you're worried about the physical aspects of pregnancy and birth, maybe we could adopt," he suggested.

I exhaled slowly and tried to stave off the panic attack that was working its way onto the scene. I could think about it. Later. Much Later.

CHAPTER FORTY-ONE

Savior

When Avery and I arrived at her house, I was supposed to change clothes and go straight to the clubhouse for Church; but, after one look at her face, I knew I couldn't leave her to share the story with her parents by herself.

"Happy New Year!" Frank greeted as soon as we stepped through the front door. "Did you two have a good time?"

Avery shook her head and burst into tears. Frank wrapped his arms around his daughter and glared at me over her head.

"What happened?" Claire asked from her perch on the sofa.

I looked around the room. "Where are the kids?"

"Upstairs," Frank and Claire answered in unison.

"An intruder broke into the cabin early this morning and attacked Avery," I said carefully.

Claire gasped while Frank immediately pushed Avery back to look her over. His eyes hardened and his jaw clenched when he saw Avery's bruised and swollen face. "Has a doctor looked at this?"

"Yes," I answered since Avery was still sobbing in her father's arms. "Two paramedics and a physician looked at it."

"And where in the hell were you when this happened?"

"Daddy," Avery cried. "H-he, he," she started but couldn't get the words out.

"I was asleep at first, but the yelling woke me. I knew something wasn't right, so I grabbed my gun from the nightstand and walked around the outside of the house to come in from a different angle. I didn't see him hit her, but he was going to kill her, so I shot him."

"Oh, my baby," Claire cried. "Bring her to me," she ordered Frank, who immediately complied. He helped Avery to the couch where she practically fell into her mother's open arms.

"It was Mark," she wailed.

"What?" Claire asked.

"It was Ian's friend, Mark," I clarified. "Apparently, he's had a long-standing obsession with Avery. He admitted to being the one who hit me and the kids," I explained.

"Did you kill him?" Frank asked.

I nodded sharply. "Yes, sir."

He stood from the couch and took purposeful steps in my direction. When he reached me, he pulled me in for a hug and lightly slapped my back several times. "Thank you for saving my girl," he said, and I could hear the emotion in his voice.

"I'd do anything for her, sir," I told him honestly.

"Just so you know, when you want permission, you've got it," Frank said quietly and stepped back.

I couldn't hold back my grin. "Thank you, sir."

"So, what happens now?" Claire asked.

"I actually need to go the clubhouse and talk

to Copper and the club's lawyer. I haven't been charged with a crime and shouldn't be, but he wants her to know what's going on in case any problems arise," I explained.

"Because he was a police officer," Frank said knowingly.

I nodded. "And because of my history with Ian," I said quietly.

"But that doesn't—"

"I know," I interrupted and jerked my chin toward the stairs where Riley and Braxton were doing a poor job of trying to hide while eavesdropping.

"Riley," Claire scolded. "What did Nana tell you about being a busybody?"

"You said no one likes a Nosy Nelly," Riley pouted.

"And what else?"

"And that getting Braxton to listen for me is still being a Nosy Nelly."

"Well, at least you do listen when you're supposed to," Claire huffed. "Go to your room until we call you to come downstairs. You, too, Braxton."

I covered my mouth to try and stifle my laugh. Riley was a clever child, and she was going to be a handful when she got older.

"Thanks, Mom," Avery said and wiped the tears from her face.

"Oh, honey. Are you okay? And I don't mean your face. I mean in here," Claire said and tapped Avery's chest.

"I don't know," she sniffed. "I couldn't believe all the things he was saying to me. He told Ian I was having an affair with another officer. He said that's the reason Ian left me. He wanted to split us up so he could be with me. Then, he said such awful things about Kellan and the kids. He tried to kill my children, Mom! They loved him. They even called him Uncle Mark, and he tried to kill them! How could he do that?"

Claire shook her head. "Something must've been wrong with him. Something he was able to keep hidden from everyone. But you can't dwell on that. The fact is you may never know why he did the things he did, and you can't go back and undo them. But you can take comfort in the knowledge that he's gone and can't hurt your family anymore."

"He can if Kellan gets in trouble for shooting him," Avery countered.

"That's not going to happen," I reassured her. "But I do need to get to the clubhouse to make absolutely certain it doesn't. When I'm finished,

I'll come back to pick you up and we can go see Sienna."

***

When I walked into the clubhouse, Layla was in the common room. She looked up and pointed to Church. I lifted my chin in thanks. I pushed through the door and said, "Happy Fucking New Year," to Copper and Bronze before I dropped into an empty chair.

"You okay, brother?" Copper asked.

I shrugged. "Yeah. Not my first kill, probably won't be my last." When Copper blinked at me several times with a blank expression on his face, it occurred to me that I should've chosen my words more carefully. "I wasn't talking about Ian. I killed the guy who attacked Keegan."

Copper nodded. "I know. I was just seeing what else you would say if I made you uncomfortable."

"Really, Prez?" I asked, somewhat pissed off by his tactics.

"Think of it as my way of making sure you were really okay. You don't have to like it, but it works, so I use it," he explained.

"Got it. For future reference, I don't have a

problem taking the life of a man who was about to kill one of my friends or family members. This motherfucker had his gun trained on Avery, after he hit her, twice. He tried to kill me and her kids. I don't have a single ounce of regret about killing him."

"Good. Phoenix called a few minutes ago with some information. Apparently, Mark Pruitt was terminated from his job as highway patrolman for 'not following department policies.' Not sure what that means, but Byte is going to try to find out."

"When was he fired?" I asked.

"Two weeks ago. Why?"

"The police report for my wreck and the witness statements didn't make any sense. I'm wondering if he altered them to help cover his tracks. And if he did, did he mess with the reports for Claire's accident as well?"

Copper rubbed his chin. "Seems like a good possibility to me. I'll mention it to Phoenix so Byte will have something more specific to look for. Spazz has been looking through Mark's home computer to see if he has anything of interest stored on it."

"He'd be a fucking idiot if he did," I said.

"Or overly cocky, which it sounds like he

was," Bronze added.

"How's Avery?" Copper asked.

"She's hanging in there right now, but I don't think the weight of it all has had time to fully hit her yet. Someone she thought was a trusted family friend was betraying her for years. That's going to have some kind of effect on her."

"Yeah, you're right. Let me know if there's anything I can do to help," Copper offered.

"Thanks, Prez."

A knock sounded at the door before it was pushed open and Spazz entered the room with his laptop. "I think I may have found something."

"You think?" Copper asked.

Spazz placed his laptop on the table and started to explain. "He doesn't have much saved on his machine, but he does have a lot of pictures and videos saved to a cloud. I haven't been through them all, but there's a shit ton of pictures of Avery. At first, I thought the videos were just porn clips he'd downloaded, but then I noticed the dates on them. The first one is from a few months ago and they're all exactly one week apart. Again, I haven't watched all of them, but I did watch a few minutes of the first one and, well, you can see for yourself."

Mark appeared on the screen with a sinister

grin on his face. He stepped to the side and revealed a woman standing with her back to the camera. A woman with long, auburn hair. "Take off your clothes, Avery," Mark instructed.

"The fuck?" I roared.

Spazz held his hand up. "Just wait."

"Fuck that!" I said and pushed away from the table. No way in hell was I going to watch whatever the hell was playing on his screen.

"It's not her," Copper said.

My eyes darted back to the screen and I couldn't hide my shock at what I saw. The woman was facing the camera completely naked, and it most definitely wasn't Avery. "Holy shit!"

"Isn't that your ex-wife?" Bronze asked.

"Yep, that's Kelly," I said in disbelief. "What in the hell is she doing?"

"Looks like she's about to fuck the dirty cop," Bronze stated.

"Shhh," Spazz hissed.

"How did it feel when your boyfriend used your pussy as a get-out-of-jail free card?" Mark sneered.

Kelly's lips curled up in a devious grin. "It was my idea," she purred.

"Was it now?" he asked as he walked toward her. "Bend over, bitch. Let's see why your boyfriend keeps you around."

When Mark thrust into her and started calling her Avery, I'd seen enough. "Turn it off," I barked.

Spazz stopped the video and stared at the three of us expectantly. "What?" Copper finally asked.

Spazz sighed. "He said, 'Let's see why your boyfriend keeps you around.' He also mentioned her boyfriend using her as a 'get-out-of-jail free card.' So, I started looking through the traffic stops Mark Pruitt made around the time of the first video, and Todd Russo was one of them."

"Todd 'we-took-your-gym' Russo?" Bronze asked.

"That'd be the one," Spazz confirmed.

"Was he ticketed?" Copper asked.

"He was arrested for DUI and possession of cocaine," Spazz told us.

"What're you getting at?" I asked.

"I'm not sure yet, but I don't think it's a coincidence that Todd's name is tied to Kelly and Mark. Oh, one other thing, the stolen tags on the truck belong to Todd's uncle."

"How did you figure that out?" I asked.

Spazz grinned. "One of the first things I did was check Mark's browser history. I found an obituary for Todd's grandfather that listed the surviving relatives."

"I know this is fun for you, but put the pieces together for us before I beat it out of you," Copper grumbled.

"I haven't found any proof, but I'm guessing Mark knew who Todd was and tried to blackmail him. I don't know how Kelly plays into it, other than the obvious, but my guess is they had something to do with Claire's accident."

"That fucking cunt," I fumed. Kelly had always been the very essence of a spoiled brat—throwing an all-out tantrum when she didn't get her way—but if she had anything to do with hurting Claire, I was going to make damn sure she paid for it.

"Hold on. Who is Todd?" Copper snapped.

"It's more of who his uncle is. Luca Peccati," Spazz announced proudly.

"As in those Peccatis?" Copper asked in surprise.

Spazz nodded. "As in those Peccatis."

"Fuck," Copper cursed. "What do we know about Luca Peccati?"

"Not much," Spazz admitted. "He's the oldest son of the late Luca Peccati, Sr. He has a home in Cedar Valley, as well as several others around the country. He's a wealthy businessman with his hand in several pots. He tries to keep a low profile, but ends up in the news every now and then with organized crime accusations. Thus far, they've never been able to make anything stick."

"Get me his contact info," Copper ordered.

I looked back and forth between Copper and Bronze as Spazz's fingers moved across the keyboard.

Copper shrugged and answered my unasked question. "The only way we'll find out anything is by talking to him. If he doesn't know that his nephew has been working with a dirty cop and pissing off motorcycle clubs, bringing it to his attention will be seen as a courtesy."

"And, if he did know?" I asked.

"If he did know, then we're about to have trouble with the mafia, and I'd rather know sooner than later."

CHAPTER FORTY-TWO

Avery

After Kellan left to go to the clubhouse, I excused myself and went upstairs to take another shower. Even though I knew I was clean, I still felt like I was covered in Mark's blood.

I turned the shower on as hot as I could stand it and stepped under the spray. As soon as the hot water hit my shoulders, the tears poured from my eyes. How could I have been so blind to what was going on with Mark? And Ian. How could he just leave without talking to me? How could he believe Mark without any proof?

I wanted to scream at the injustice of it all. But I couldn't do that without scaring my children and alarming my parents. So, I did what all mothers do at some point or another and held it all in for the sake of my family.

While I washed my hair and scrubbed my skin, I thought back to the night Ian left. Over and over, I replayed our conversation from that night trying to remember if he said anything I may have missed. I couldn't bear the thought of him leaving this world thinking I was unfaithful to him.

"Mommy?" Riley called, effectively interrupting my thoughts and scaring the shit out of me.

"Yes?" I croaked and cleared my throat.

"Nana told me to come check on you. She said you'd been in the shower for a long time. Are you okay?" she asked.

Upon hearing her words, I noticed the water had run cold and my body was shivering. "Thanks for checking on me. Tell Nana I'm fine and I'm getting out now."

"Okay, Mommy," she replied and closed the door. Then she yelled, "She's fine and getting out now, Nana!"

I quickly dried myself off and wrapped my hair in a towel before diving under the covers of my bed to try and get warm. Within minutes, I fell asleep.

I woke to my father gently shaking my shoulder. "Avery, you need to get dressed and come downstairs."

"Why? What's wrong?" I asked.

"There is a police officer here to speak with you."

My forehead wrinkled in confusion. "How long have I been asleep?"

"I'm guessing around four hours, and that's not counting the hour you were in the shower," he said.

My mouth dropped open in surprise. I hadn't meant to sleep that long. Actually, I hadn't meant to fall asleep at all. "Oh, okay. Give me a minute to get dressed and comb my hair, and I'll be right down."

He nodded and closed the door behind him. I quickly got up and pulled on a long-sleeved T-shirt and a pair of yoga pants. My hair was a lost cause, so I ran a brush through it and pulled it back into a messy bun. After a quick swish with mouthwash, I made my way downstairs.

"Sorry to keep you waiting," I said to the

officer. "If this has to do with this morning, could we speak in the kitchen or outside so my children don't overhear our conversation?"

"Of course, Ms. Parker, whichever you'd be more comfortable with," the man I recognized as the Sheriff said.

"Kitchen it is. Would you care for a cup of coffee?" I asked and gestured for him to follow me.

"Please."

Once I had the coffee started, I joined the Sheriff at my kitchen table. "So, what brought you all the way to Devil Springs?"

"I have a few questions about Mark Pruitt I was hoping you could answer."

"Well, I didn't know him very well, so I'm not sure how much help I'll be," I said sharply.

He cocked his head to the side. "He wasn't a close friend of your family?"

"I thought he was, but he obviously wasn't. Close friends don't attack you and threaten to kill you. And they damn sure don't try to kill your boyfriend and your children," I spat.

"I have to agree with you there," he said and cleared his throat. "So, you didn't know Mark Pruitt had an obsession with you?"

"No, sir. Not until this morning."

"How long had you known Mark?"

I didn't even have to think about it. "For almost ten years. I met him the same night I met my late husband, Ian. Mark was Ian's best friend, so he was always around. He was Ian's best man at our wedding and he gave the eulogy at Ian's funeral. He was like a member of our family. Or so I thought."

When the coffee pot chimed, I rose from the table and poured a cup for each of us. I placed his cup on the table in front of him and reached into the fridge for the creamer before taking my seat. I was thankful to have something to do with my hands—even it was just to wrap them around my mug.

"After your husband died, how often did you see or speak to Mark?"

"At first, I saw him every day and spoke to him several times a day. He was a big help to me and the kids. After a month or so, he would call or stop by to check in once a week. When I moved to Devil Springs, he came to visit maybe one weekend a month until the beginning of the summer. I didn't notice it at the time because I was sick and ended up being admitted to the hospital several times, but that's when the phone calls from him stopped, too," I shared.

The Sheriff cleared his throat and shifted in his chair. "We did a search of Mark's house earlier today and we found enough evidence to support everything you and your boyfriend told us this morning."

"What kind of evidence?" I asked even though I wasn't sure I wanted to know.

"We found pictures of you that had been taken through a zoom lens. We found video recordings of Mark calling other women Avery while he had sexual intercourse with them. He had detailed accounts of your daily activities, as well as those of your parents, your children, and Mr. Ward. We found a black Dodge Ram with visible body damage in a detached garage on his property. And we found some other things that don't have anything to do with your case that we need to look into further."

"You didn't have to come all the way out here to tell me that," I blurted, still in shock at some of the things he'd just told me.

"Well, I wanted to tell you personally that we won't be filing any charges against you or Mr. Ward, but I also wanted to give you this," he said and pulled a folded envelope from the pocket on the front of his shirt.

"I'm not sure how this wound up in Mark's

hands, but I wanted to make sure it ended in yours," he said and pushed the envelope across the table.

"What is it?" I asked as I stared at the piece of paper like it was coated with a light dusting of Anthrax.

"Something you should read in private," he said and got to his feet. "I should get going. Thank you for the coffee."

"Of course," I stammered and walked him to the front door.

He held out his hand and I shook it. "Take care, Ms. Parker."

"What did he want?" my mom asked as soon as the door was closed.

"I'll tell you in a minute," I said and hurried back to the kitchen. Snatching the letter off the table, I headed upstairs and closed myself in my closet.

After inhaling deeply and slowly blowing it out, I carefully unfolded the envelope and pulled out the letter inside.

Avery,

I know you're hurt and confused. And if I know you, mad as hell, too. I'm sorry, love. I had to do it to protect you and the kids. Something is going on with Mark. I stopped by his house last week to borrow his leaf blower, but he wasn't home. I let myself into his garage to grab it and found a wall covered with pictures of you. I was so shocked, I just left. Hundreds of pictures, Avery. Some recent and some from years ago. I was fucking pissed, but I knew I needed to handle it carefully. A few days later, he told me you were having an affair with another officer. He suggested I leave you and request a transfer. So, I let him think that's what I was doing until I figure out what in the hell to do about him. He needs help, but my main priority is making sure you're safe. I love you, Avery. I know you didn't cheat, but I needed your reactions to seem real, because I knew he was watching you. I'm sorry for the pain I've caused you the last few days, but I did it for our family. You, Riley, and Braxton are everything to me. I held out as long as I could, but you deserved to know the truth. Stay strong and take care of our kids. This will all be over soon. I love you with every beat of my heart.

Ian

My eyes landed on the date in the top corner of the letter. The day Ian died. Then my eyes fell to the strange mark that looked like the pen slid off the paper while he was signing his name.

Then, I noticed the drop of blood in the bottom corner and it hit me like a battering ram. Ian was parked on the side of the road writing this letter when Kellan crashed into him.

It was Mark's fault. All of it was Mark's fault. I was so full of rage that I wanted to scream until my throat was raw. I wanted to put his head back together so I could be the one to blow it apart. And I wanted to watch it explode and relish in the blood coating my skin.

Anger. Rage. Fury. Those words didn't even begin to describe the emotion consuming me. I felt like I was going to burst if I didn't find a way to let it out.

CHAPTER FORTY-THREE

SAVIOR

As soon as I walked through the front door, I knew something was wrong. "What happened?" I asked Claire.

"A police officer came by to speak with Avery. She went upstairs as soon as he left and hasn't been back downstairs," she confessed. "Frank went to the house to get me a change of clothes, and I didn't want to upset the kids if she's not okay. Can you go up and check on her?"

I was already headed toward the stairs when she asked. "Avery!" I called as I pushed into the bedroom. After checking the bedroom and bathroom, I went down the hall to check the kids' rooms, but she wasn't there either.

"Avery!" I called a little louder.

"Check her closet," Claire yelled from downstairs.

I jerked the closet door open, but Avery was nowhere in sight. I checked the only other room upstairs and found it empty as well. Jogging down the stairs, I made a quick pass through each room before checking the garage. "Her car's gone," I said to Claire.

"What?" Claire gasped. "I would've heard her leave."

"Where do you think she went?" I demanded.

"I honestly don't know. Let me try her cell phone," Claire suggested and held the phone to her ear only to shake her head moments later. "Straight to voicemail."

"Fuck," I cursed. "Why would she leave and not tell anyone where she was going?"

"I'm guessing something the Sheriff said upset her. Can you call and ask him what he told her?"

"Yes," I said and pointed at Claire. "Yes, I can."

Before calling the Sheriff, I called Spazz and

asked him to try and locate Avery's phone. Then, I called Phoenix to get the Sheriff's number.

"I'll give you his number if you want to talk to him yourself, but I can save you a phone call because I know what he told her."

"I don't care who tells me; I just need to know so I can try to find her."

"He told her what they found when they searched Mark's house, which was basically what Spazz found plus more photos and detailed accounts of her activity. They also found the truck that hit you in a garage on the property." Phoenix paused and cleared his throat. "And he found a handwritten letter Ian wrote to Avery. Chuck said he only looked at the names on the letter and the date before he closed it up, but he was planning on giving it to her."

"What was the date?" I asked even though I already knew.

"The day he died," Phoenix said carefully.

"Fuck," I breathed. "I'm heading that way now."

"There's only one place in Croftridge she'd go," Phoenix said. "I'll send Ranger out to check the cemetery. No sense in driving all the way to Croftridge if she's not here."

"Yeah, I guess you're right."

The moment we ended the call, my phone vibrated in my hand with a number that made my heart stop every time it flashed on the screen.

"Hello?" I answered hesitantly and silently prayed it wasn't bad news.

"Kellan, this is Karen from the NICU. Sienna is just fine, but, um, Avery's here and she's visibly upset. She also has some significant bruising on her face. She assured me she was fine, but she's not. Obviously, we have upset parents in here from time to time, but something about this is different," she said, her voice full of genuine concern.

"Thank you for calling. I'll be right there," I said and exhaled in relief.

"She's with Sienna!" I called over my shoulder. "I'm going to get her."

"Oh, thank goodness," Claire exclaimed.

When I arrived at the hospital, I all but sprinted up to the NICU. I had no idea what I was walking into, but it didn't matter. I couldn't let Avery deal with whatever it was by herself.

I pressed the button and waited for someone to allow me to enter. Karen was waiting by the sink where I started thoroughly washing my hands and arms. "She's been crying since she got here. She wouldn't say anything other than,

'I just need to hold my little girl.' I helped her and Sienna get situated. Thinking she would calm down after a few minutes, I placed a box of tissues and a bottle of water beside her. When she didn't, I decided to call you."

"Thank you, Karen. I'm glad you did," I said sincerely and made my way over to my girls.

Avery and Sienna were tucked away in the far corner of the NICU next to Sienna's designated spot. With our daughter cradled in her arms, Avery gazed down at her while she slowly rocked the chair and tears streamed down her face.

With quiet steps, I slowly approached them. When I was a few feet away, I heard Avery's soft voice. "I love you so much and I love your daddy, too. I swear I do," she whispered.

"Avery," I rasped as I closed the distance between us.

Her face crumpled and she squeezed her eyes closed forcing more tears to spill down her cheeks. I knew she needed to talk about whatever was in that letter, but she didn't need to do it in the NICU with our baby in her arms.

"How's our girl today?" I asked, hoping to distract her with a subject change.

She inhaled deeply through her nose. "Karen said she's been doing good. She had her eyes open for a little bit when I first got here."

I cleared the emotion from my throat. "She does now," I whispered, afraid she would close them if my voice was too loud.

Avery smiled slightly. "She knows her daddy is here."

"Hi, peanut," I said softly and carefully ran my hand over the top of her tiny head. Her little fists opened and closed, and she made the cutest smacking sound with her mouth. Then, her eyes closed and she let out a loud fart.

Avery's eyes sprung open in surprise. "That was her," she insisted.

"Sure, blame the baby, Avery," I teased.

"No, seriously. It was her."

I couldn't hold back my laughter. "If you say so."

Avery gaped at me for a brief moment before she started laughing, too. I loved hearing her laugh. And it seemed like Sienna did, too. Her little eyes opened again while she tried to wiggle her tiny body.

"I don't think she's happy about you blaming your flatulence on her," I teased.

Avery opened her mouth to argue right as Sienna let another one rip. Avery looked down at Sienna and chuckled. "You are not helping, little lady."

We spent the next ten minutes cooing and laughing as our tiny baby continued to randomly fart like a grown man. When Karen came over, we knew it was time for shift change, so we chose that as a good time to leave.

Avery didn't say a word until we reached the parking lot. "Do you think my car will be okay here overnight? I don't want to drive home if I don't have to."

"I'll have one of the brothers come by and get it."

"Thank you. I'm just so tired," she admitted.

Once we were in the car, I asked, "Do you want to talk about it before we go home?"

"No, I don't want to, but I probably should."

"If it helps, I know everything except what was in the letter."

"How?" she asked in surprise.

"I called Phoenix to get the Sheriff's number when we couldn't find you. He filled me in on Chuck's visit," I explained.

Avery nodded and reached into her purse. Without a word, she handed me the envelope. "Read it."

"Are you sure? It's okay if you don't want me to read it."

"I'm sure. Go ahead," she encouraged and tipped her head toward the paper in my hand.

I carefully read the last words her husband had for her, and I noticed the drop of blood in the bottom corner of the letter. Suddenly, I knew why he was parked on the side of the highway that night.

"Was Mark one of the officers that responded to the accident?"

I pinched the bridge of my nose and tried to remember. "I honestly don't know. There was one and then, all of a sudden, there were at least twelve. I was in shock, Avery, and I don't remember a lot of that night."

"He had to have been to have this letter. He told me he wasn't there, that one of the other officers called and told him it was Ian so he wouldn't have to see his friend like that. But he had this letter, so he had to be there."

"You're right," I agreed.

"It's his fault, you know. All of it is his fault."

"What do you mean?"

"If Mark hadn't been insane, Ian wouldn't have left to protect me and the kids, he wouldn't have been parked on the side of the highway, and you wouldn't have crashed into him," she paused and hiccupped on a sob. "And we wouldn't have Sienna. I feel so fucking guilty. How can I be happy about my child that exists because my husband died? I don't know how to handle those feelings, Kellan. I feel like a horrible person because I love you and I love her. What am I supposed to do?"

I pulled her against my chest and buried my face in her hair. "We'll get through this," I vowed. Come hell or highwater, we would get through it.

CHAPTER FORTY-FOUR

AVERY

When we got back to the house, everyone was in the living room waiting for us. "Mommy! I learned a new magic trick. Can I show you?" Riley asked excitedly.

"Oh, Riley, I don't think you should show your mom right now," my father interjected.

"But I want to," Riley whined.

"It's fine, Dad. Show me your magic trick."

"Avery, I really don—"

"It's all right," I interrupted.

He sighed and waved his hands dismissively.

"Okay, have at it, Riley."

"Come into the kitchen and prepare to be mesmermazed!" she said.

Kellan and I followed her into the kitchen. She climbed onto a stool at the kitchen counter in front of a bottle of water. "Now, I'm going to place this quarter under the bottle of water and make it disappear. Are you ready?"

"I think so."

She carefully placed the quarter on the counter and set the bottle of water on top of it. Then, she covered it with a kitchen towel. "Abra-cabra-dabra-zoom!" she declared and removed the kitchen towel.

"It's gone! See!" she squealed and pointed to the bottle.

I leaned over the bottle to look for the coin when she reached out and squeezed the uncapped bottle, soaking my hair and face with water.

"Gotcha!" she laughed.

I stood in my kitchen, dripping water all over the floor, unsure of how to react. Kellan, on the other hand, had no problem guffawing loud enough for the entire neighborhood to hear.

"Sorry, peanut," my dad chuckled. "I tried to warn you."

I wiped my face with the handy kitchen towel and looked at my daughter who was laughing so hard her face was turning red. "Where'd you learn that magic trick, little miss?"

"Papa taught it to me."

I whipped my head back to my dad who was pointing to the living room. "Blame your mother. She did it to me."

I couldn't help but laugh. For as long as I could remember, my parents had always played random pranks on each other.

"Mommy," Braxton said softly as he came into the kitchen. "My tummy hurts."

I picked him up and set him on the counter. "Did it just start hurting?" I asked as I automatically ran my hand over his forehead. "Oh, baby, you feel hot. Let me get the thermometer."

"I'll get it," Kellan offered. "Where is it?"

"It's in the medicine cabinet in the kids' bathroom. It's white and looks like an electric shaver."

"He hasn't said anything about not feeling well all day," my dad said with a concerned look on his face.

Braxton leaned forward and laid his head against my chest. "It's okay, baby," I soothed and gently rubbed his back. My little guy loved to cuddle with me when he was sick, and though I never wanted him to be sick, I thoroughly enjoyed the cuddles when he was.

Kellan returned to the kitchen and held up the thermometer. "Is this it? Because it was the only thing that even remotely fit your description."

"That's it. Thank you." I took the thermometer, turned it on, and ran it over Braxton's forehead.

"Oh, one hundred and two point six. You are running a fever. Let's get you some medicine for that," I said and tried to keep my tone light.

"Kellan," Braxton said weakly and reached out for him.

"Oh, honey, Kellan can't hold you yet."

"Yes, I can. I just can't lift him, but he can climb in my lap," Kellan said as he pulled out a kitchen chair and took a seat.

I placed Braxton on the floor and he made a beeline for Kellan while I went to get the children's fever reducer. When I returned, Braxton was resting against Kellan's chest with flushed cheeks while he stared off into space. Suddenly, Braxton sat straight up with a look of panic on his face. I knew that look, but there was nothing I could do to stop what was about to happen.

I didn't even have time to utter a warning before Braxton opened his mouth and spewed vomit in a way that would make little demon-possessed girls envious. It went everywhere—the kitchen island, the floor, Kellan's arm, chest, and lap.

To my complete surprise, he didn't even flinch. No, he reached up and wiped Braxton's mouth with his bare hand before cradling him against a clean part of his shirt. "You're okay, little man. That was a lot, but you're okay," Kellan soothed as Braxton cried.

As if things weren't bad enough, Riley jumped down from the stool and ran through the kitchen. I assumed the living room was her intended destination, but she never made it. Instead, her feet came out from under her when she hit the slime spewed from her brother and landed flat on her back in the middle of it. Amazingly, Kellan reached out and managed to get his hand under her head before it collided with the hard floor. And then the screaming started.

"Is it too cold to take you all outside and spray you off with the hose?" I asked before I reached down and plucked my daughter from the mess in the floor.

"Let's get you out of these dirty clothes and

into the bath," I said and pulled her shirt over her head.

She shrieked in outrage and slapped her hands over her chest. "They can't see my business! They're boys!"

"They're not looking, honey. I promise," I said and carefully carried her out of the kitchen to the bathroom down the hall. "I'll be right back," I yelled.

"We can handle it, peanut," my dad replied.

"Riley, I know you don't like them, but I need you to take a shower this time so I can go take care of your brother. I'll help you and we can get it done and over with."

"I don't care, Mommy. Just get this yucky stuff off of me, please."

I wanted to laugh, but I couldn't let this wonderful opportunity pass. I started the water and turned to my vomit-coated daughter with a serious face. "Do you understand why I tell you not to run in the house now?"

"Yes," she cried. "Please help me get my pants off."

Thankfully, Riley was so disgusted by her current state that she didn't make a big fuss about the shower. Any other time, it would have been easier to extract a tooth from her than get her to take a shower. She was a bath girl, hands down.

Once we were finished, I wrapped her in a fluffy towel and sent her to her room to put on her pajamas. I tossed her dirty clothes into the washing machine and made my way back to the kitchen.

"Careful; the floor's wet," Kellan said and pointed to the mop propped in the corner.

"Thank you. Where's Brax?"

"Your dad took him upstairs to get a bath started," Kellan said and stopped abruptly like there was more he wanted to say but didn't.

"You can toss your clothes in the washer with Riley's. I'll start it when I add Braxton's," I said and grabbed the medicine from the counter.

When I got to the bathroom upstairs, my dad was visibly flustered and Braxton was in the bathtub crying for Kellan. "What's going on?"

"I want Kellan!" Braxton demanded and slapped his hands in the water.

"Hey, now, little mister. You might be sick, but you can still mind your manners," I scolded and felt like an ass when he cried even harder.

"He wanted Kellan to give him a bath, but Kellan wasn't sure if you were okay with that," my dad said quietly.

"Why wouldn't I be?"

My dad gave me a pointed look. "Avery, he's a man and these aren't his kids. Think about it from his perspective for just a moment."

"Oh," I said as realization dawned. "I, um," I stammered. I trusted Kellan with my children, implicitly, but my emotions were all over the place and I couldn't find the right words to express my feelings, so I settled for, "Will you send him up?"

"Of course. Do you want me to put Braxton's clothes in the wash?"

"Yes, please. And will you start the load for me? Riley's and Kellan's clothes are already in there."

"What about yours?"

I looked down and realized I had some of the nastiness on my shirt, too. "I'll watch him while you grab another shirt."

Braxton settled down as soon as Kellan appeared in the bathroom. I quickly washed him off and got him out of the tub and into pajamas. He managed to take his medicine, followed by a few sips of apple juice and keep it down.

"Mommy, can I sleep with Nana and Papa?" Riley asked from the door.

"Did you already ask Nana and Papa?"

"Yes, and they said it was okay."

"As long as it's okay with them, it's okay with me."

"Thank you," she beamed. "Goodnight, Mommy, Kellan, and sick brother. I'm blowing kisses because I don't want germs," she announced and kissed her palm three times before turning it to the side and blowing. "Love you." She disappeared down the hall before any of us could respond.

"All right, little man, let's get you into bed," I said and scooped my sick baby into my arms.

"I wanna sleep in your room," Braxton said quietly.

"I think that can be arranged," I said and headed to my bedroom.

Placing him in the center of my bed, I crawled in beside him thinking he would roll toward me to cuddle while he fell asleep. Instead, he slapped his palm down on the other side of the bed and said, "Kellan can sleep here."

Kellan's eyes widened. "Oh, um, I, uh..."

"It's okay," I mouthed.

"You sure?" he mouthed back.

I nodded at the same time Braxton patted the bed again. Kellan scooted in behind Braxton, who immediately fisted my shirt as well as

Kellan's and pulled. We scooted closer and he kept pulling until we were essentially cocooning him between us. Braxton yawned and closed his eyes. "Night night, Mommy and Daddy."

Kellan's mouth dropped open in shock while I burst into tears.

CHAPTER FORTY-FIVE

Savior

I placed my hand on Avery's upper arm. "It's okay. He's tired and sick. It was just a little slip."

She shook her head. "He doesn't even remember Ian. Riley barely does," she whispered.

"I'm sorry," I replied softly. There wasn't anything I could say or do to make things better, not immediately anyway. I waited a few minutes to be sure Braxton was asleep before carefully sliding out of the bed. "I'm going to go," I said, unsure if I meant downstairs or back to the home

I shared with Coal. At her nod, I placed a kiss on her forehead and closed the door behind me.

The silence downstairs let me know that Frank, Claire, and Riley had already gone to bed. Feeling like an intruder, I grabbed my keys and locked the front door on my way out.

I couldn't imagine what she was going through, but she knew I loved her kids like they were my own. I knew they weren't mine biologically, and like I'd already told her, I would never try to replace their father; but, that didn't mean I couldn't fill that role in their lives.

When I walked through the front door, I was met with the barrel of a gun. "The fuck?" I asked.

Coal shrugged and put the gun on the coffee table. "Didn't know it was you. You haven't been here in weeks."

"Sorry, man. I guess I should've called."

"What're you doing here? I figured you'd be with Avery after what went down this morning."

I dropped into the recliner and sighed. "So did I. She's not handling things well. Then, Braxton got sick and insisted I climb into bed with him and Avery." I paused and pinched the bridge of my nose. "He called me Daddy as he was falling asleep."

"Oh, shit. What did Avery say?"

"Nothing. She burst into tears. Again."

"Fuck, man."

"Yeah, I didn't want to leave, but I got the feeling she wanted me to. I'm not sure what I'm supposed to do," I admitted.

"Call Harper," Coal suggested. "You know she'd be happy to help. Do you think Avery would talk to her?"

"I don't know, but there's only one way to find out."

I pulled out my phone and tapped Carbon's name.

The asshole answered with, "If you're in more shit, it's not my turn."

"Thanks, fucker. I'm actually calling to talk to your wife if she has a minute."

His tone instantly changed. "She's not okay, is she?"

"No, she's not. And I don't know how to help her, but I thought Harper would."

"Let me get her for you, brother."

A few moments later, Harper's concerned voice filled my ear. "Savior, what's going on?"

I didn't know how much, if any, she knew, so I told her everything, starting with the night Ian died and ending with Braxton calling me 'Daddy.'

"I know it's not how you normally operate, but

I wanted to know if you'd be willing to come to Devil Springs and talk to her. I don't think she'll go for it unless it's sprung on her, you know?"

"I completely understand. I can't force her to talk, but I'll give it my best shot."

"Thank you, Harper. I really appreciate it."

"You're welcome. When do you want me to come up?"

"As soon as possible," I blurted.

Harper chuckled. "Okay, how about tomorrow?"

I breathed a sigh of relief. "Tomorrow's great. Let me know when you're on your way and I'll see if I can get her to the clubhouse."

"Sounds good. I'll see you tomorrow," she said and ended the call.

I had just leaned back in the recliner and closed my eyes when I heard a thump come from one of the bedrooms. My eyes shot to Coal. "Do you have a guest?" I asked quietly.

When he glanced toward the bedrooms, his jaw clenched. "Yes."

I studied him for a brief moment. "You okay?"

"Just tired. I'm going to head to bed."

"All right. Night, brother."

"Night."

I walked into my bedroom and glanced

around the room, taking in the bare walls and meager possessions. It felt strange being in my room, almost like I didn't belong there. Avery's house was warm and inviting and felt like home to me. I hadn't really felt like I had a home since I lost my parents, and I missed the comfort and peace it provided.

I sighed and sat down on my bed while I stared at the phone in my hand. I wanted to call her, to text her, to make sure she was okay, to check on Braxton. Fuck! I'd been gone for a few hours and I was pining for her like a lovesick puppy.

After finally falling asleep, I woke covered in sweat and gasping for breath. The nightmare was different this time. Instead of crashing my truck into Ian's cruiser, I crashed into Avery and the kids.

My bedroom burst open and Coal started sweeping the room with the light on his gun. "It's okay, man. Nightmare," I said and wiped the sweat from my brow as I studied him. His muscles were tensed and he was on high alert. "You all right?"

"Yep," he clipped and left the room.

Something was going on with him, but Coal was extremely levelheaded. I knew he'd ask for help if he needed it; otherwise, he'd talk about it when he was ready.

I made the mistake of looking at the clock and cursed. It was already five o'clock in the morning, which meant there was no point in going back to sleep. But, it also meant I didn't have shit to do after showering and getting dressed. After having a cup of coffee, I decided to head to the clubhouse because it seemed like someone was always awake no matter what time it was.

I was right. When I walked through the front door around six o'clock, Tiny, Splint, and Spazz were in the common room eating breakfast. "Hey, look what the cat dragged in," Tiny said.

"Morning, brothers," I said and jerked my chin toward the food. "Any of that left?"

Leigh emerged from the kitchen with Splint's father, Dean, right behind here. "There's plenty left," she said with a smile. "Help yourself."

"Thank you," I replied and loaded my plate with food. Leigh's cooking was not something I ever wanted to miss out on.

"What're you doing here so early?" Splint asked.

"Couldn't sleep and I got tired of staring at the walls in my bedroom," I said with a shrug.

"Your bedroom? You weren't with Avery?" Spazz asked.

"Not last night," I said tersely, hoping they would let it drop. I didn't feel comfortable talking about what was going on with Avery since it had more to do with her than me.

"How's Sienna?" Splint asked.

I smiled like the proud father I was. "She's getting bigger every day. If everything keeps going the way it has, she should be able to come home in a few weeks."

"That's awesome, man. I'm glad to hear she's doing well."

We continued to shoot the shit until everyone but Spazz had to leave for work. "Have you been able to find anything new?"

He shook his head. "No, but it's not for lack of trying. Byte's been hitting dead ends, too. It just means we need to dig a little deeper."

"I just want whoever is responsible for hurting Claire to pay for what they did. Claire being hit is the reason I picked up the kids that day, and that led to Sienna being born weeks before she was ready. We all could've died that day."

"But you didn't, brother. Remember that," Spazz said and clapped me on the shoulder right as Copper arrived.

"Church in an hour," he barked and headed for his office.

"Sounds like he got in touch with Luca," Spazz mumbled.

Spazz was right. Copper had been in contact with Luca Peccati and arranged a meeting at a restaurant in Cedar Valley at noon.

"Judge and Batta will attend the meeting with me, but I want the rest of you in Cedar Valley and on standby. I'm not anticipating any trouble, but it's always better to be prepared for anything," Copper continued.

Fuck! Harper was supposed to be coming up to talk to Avery. I was already having trouble figuring out how I was going to get her to the clubhouse without an explanation, and that was before I found out I wouldn't be able to be there.

"You all right, brother?" Judge asked and clapped me on the shoulder.

Suddenly, an idea came to me. "Do you think your mom would be willing to help me out with something?" I asked and quickly explained my plan.

Judge grinned. "I'll give her a call. I'm sure she'd be happy to help. And, you just saved your own ass by asking. If Mom found out Harper was in town and she didn't see her, Mom would've been all over your ass like shit on Velcro."

"Me? What about Harper?"

Judge laughed. "Harper can do no wrong in my mother's eyes. She's the daughter Mom never had, and she's the baby of our blended little family."

"Noted. Thanks, man."

A few minutes later, Judge let me know that Leigh agreed to pick Avery up and bring her to the clubhouse for lunch. I hoped Avery wouldn't be pissed at me, but more than anything, I hoped Harper would be able to help her.

We rolled into Cedar Valley thirty minutes before the scheduled meeting. Since I still couldn't ride, I rode in the SUV Grant was driving. He seemed okay when we first left Devil Springs, but the closer we got to Cedar Valley, the jumpier he became.

"You good, man?" I asked before we got out of the car.

"Yeah, I guess I'm a little nervous. I've never been to anything like this, and I don't know what to expect," he admitted.

"Nothing to worry about. They're just going to talk. No one's going to start shooting in broad daylight."

We followed the group into a small diner that was roughly a block or so from where Copper was meeting Luca. "You guys order something to eat and wait here. If things go downhill, I'll send a signal to Bronze. If that does happen, follow his orders and be mindful of the general public. The main goal is to get out of there as quickly and safely as possible; we can worry about retaliation later if it even comes to that." With that, Copper, Judge, and Batta walked out the front door and climbed on their bikes.

CHAPTER FORTY-SIX

Avery

I tossed and turned all night. When my mind finally stopped running in overdrive long enough for me to fall asleep, my thoughts haunted my dreams. Thankfully, Braxton only woke up once and that was because his pajamas were soaking wet after his fever broke.

"Mommy, where's Kellan?" Braxton asked when he woke.

"I'm not sure. How is your tummy?" I asked.

"Good," he said and wrinkled his forehead. After a moment, he announced, "I'm hungry."

"Okay, let's try some toast for breakfast."

"Can it be cinnamon toast? Please."

"Sure, sweetie. Let's go see if Riley, Nana, and Papa are up."

I wasn't surprised to find my dad and Riley in the kitchen. Dad had always been an early riser and Riley loved mornings. While Braxton was distracted by my father, I quickly peeked outside to see if Kellan's truck was in the driveway, and my stomach sank when I saw that it wasn't.

"He left last night, peanut," he said quietly. "Did something happen between you two after we went to bed?"

I shook my head. "Nothing that was his fault."

"A lot happened yesterday. No one would blame you if you needed some time to process everything."

"Thanks, Dad," I said and started making breakfast for the kids.

A few hours later, the doorbell rang and I was surprised to see Leigh standing on my porch. "Sorry to stop by unannounced, but I need some help preparing a big meal at the clubhouse. Layla was supposed to help me, but she woke up sick this morning. Any chance you're free?"

"Uh," I mumbled and glanced over my

shoulder. "The kids are here, so—"

"Your mother and I can watch the kids for a few hours," my father interrupted. "Leigh's been such a big help to all of us. I'm sure you're itching to repay the favor."

I was. I would've felt awful if I'd had to tell her I couldn't help. "I just need to put on my shoes and grab my purse," I told Leigh.

When we arrived at the clubhouse, I was surprised to see the parking lot empty. The few times I'd been there with Kellan, there were several bikes and a few cars parked out front. "Is anyone here?"

"Yeah," Leigh replied quickly. "The clubhouse is never completely empty."

I wasn't sure I believed her when we walked inside and it was so quiet you could hear a pin drop. Leigh continued on through the clubhouse as if everything was as it should be.

"Avery, you remember my niece, Harper?" she asked as we entered the kitchen.

"Hi," Harper waved.

I smiled and nodded. "Of course, I do. What brings you to Devil Springs?"

She gave me a small smile and cut her eyes to Leigh. "Avery," Leigh started and clasped her hands together. "I sort of lied to you, and for that

I'm sorry. Layla is sick, and I could use some help, but that's not the reason I asked you to come to the clubhouse with me today."

Her confession caught me by surprise, but I knew Leigh wasn't the kind of person to do anything with malicious intent. "Okay, well, why did you ask me to come with you?"

"Savior called last night and asked if I would come to Devil Springs to talk with you. I'm not sure if he told you that I'm a licensed clinical therapist. I'm more than happy to help, but I know he sprung this on you, so I completely understand if you're not interested," Harper explained.

"Crap!" Leigh exclaimed. "We're out of butter, and it looks like we're running low on milk, too. I need to run to the grocery store real quick. I'll be right back," she said and darted out the door.

Harper giggled and shook her head. "Smooth, Aunt Leigh," she called before turning her attention to me. "Please know that anything you say to me will be kept one-hundred-percent confidential."

"Why did you become a therapist?" I asked. I wasn't about to deny my need for some professional counseling, but I wanted to know a little more about her before I decided to open up about myself.

"I was kidnapped when I was a child. It took my brother a couple of months to find me and rescue me. During the time I was gone, my last living parent died. Needless to say, I was a traumatized child, and I soon realized there weren't enough people out there trained to help other kids like me."

"Well, shit," I sighed. "I was expecting a generic reason like, 'I want to help people.' I wasn't expecting you to be so honest."

"Ah," she said knowingly. "You weren't going to share if I didn't." When my mouth dropped open in surprise, she smiled. "I work with teenagers. They're much more difficult to crack than you are."

"Yeah, I bet they are," I laughed nervously. "Um, what do you already know?"

"When Savior called last night, he gave me a rundown of the major events that have happened over the last few years, starting with the death of your husband. Now, as a woman, I would probably be pissed if my man called a woman I didn't know very well and shared everything about my past with her. But, on his behalf, he sounded so lost on the phone last night, and I truly believe he only has your best interest at heart."

I smiled at the way she was trying to protect Kellan. "I know," I said. "He's a good man, and I know he wouldn't share the intimate details of our lives without a reason."

"He is a good man, and I'm glad to finally see him happy," she said and shrugged. "I mean, no pressure or anything."

I laughed. Harper was easy to get along with, and surprisingly, I felt comfortable talking to her. I just didn't know how to start.

An awkward silence fell between us for a few moments, but she didn't let it last long. "So, there's a few ways to get this ball rolling. If you know where you want to begin, by all means, start talking. But, if you need me to ask a few questions to get us to where we need to be, I can do that, too."

"How do you know where we need to be?" I asked, genuinely curious.

"Trust me; we'll both know when we get there."

I nodded and thought about what I wanted to talk about; but, I had no idea where to begin, so I told her just that.

"Let's start with last night. What happened that had Savior calling and asking me to come to Devil Springs?"

"I thought he already told you everything," I hedged.

"He did, but I want to hear it from you."

"My husband and I had separated, and he died before I found out why he left. Yesterday, the police found a letter Ian had written to me on the night he died. He knew something was going on with his friend and he left to protect me and the kids. Then, last night, my son got sick and wanted Kellan to lay in the bed with him. And Braxton called him 'Daddy' before he fell asleep," I shared and looked down at my clasped hands.

"And then what happened?"

I smiled sadly. "I think Kellan knew it was too much for me. He tried to dismiss it by saying Braxton was just tired, but as soon as Braxton was asleep, he left the room. I assumed he went downstairs, but he wasn't there when I got up this morning and I just...I don't know, I wasn't ready to talk about it."

"Why not?" Harper gently prompted.

I balled my hands into tightly clenched fists. "Because I'm fucking pissed!" I blurted, then clarified, "Not at my son."

I took a moment to breathe through it and gather my thoughts. Or I tried to. "Don't think about it. Tell me what you're feeling right now," Harper insisted.

"I feel selfish right now. Why can't I grieve for my husband like a normal widow? Every time I think I've found a little bit of peace, and dare I say happiness, in my life, something comes along and rips my heart out all over again. I don't want to forget Ian and I would never try to replace him, but it was a hell of a lot easier to move forward with my life when I was mad at him. Then, yesterday I found out he was the noble man I loved all along. I understand why he did it the way he did, but I think he should've fucking told me! What in the hell am I supposed to do now? Be in love with my dead husband as well as Kellan? I'm so damn angry I just want to scream at the top of my lungs! Why me? Why did this have to happen to me the way that it did? I want to know why?!" I sucked in a huge lungful of air at the end of my rant.

"Do it," Harper said simply.

"Do what?"

"Scream." When I looked at her like she'd lost her damn mind, she said it again. "No one's here. Scream your frustration to the heavens." She waited a few seconds and got to her feet. "Okay, I'll go first."

And she did. The little woman let out a ferocious roar toward the ceiling. She kept going until she ran out of breath and coughed. "Your turn."

"Fuck it," I shrugged and inhaled deeply. "WHHHHYYYY?" I screamed followed by a deep, animalistic noise I didn't know I was capable of producing.

"Again!" Harper encouraged and clapped her hands together loudly.

I was in the zone so I did as she said without question. "Fucking WHHHHYYYY?! Mark, you motherfucking bastard!! You did this to all of us! You might as well have killed him yourself! I hate you! I hope Satan is fucking your ass with a red-hot fire poker right this very second!!"

I inhaled deeply and dropped into my chair. It was only then I realized I'd been standing.

"Good!" Harper said excitedly. "Feel better?"

"A little," I admitted.

Harper nodded. "That's a good answer. If you'd said 'much' or 'completely,' I would've known you were lying. This isn't something that can be mended by one session of screaming. But continually working through your feelings will get you to a place of acceptance. And that's what I want to help you do. Now, I can't come to Devil

Springs every week and I know you can't make it to Croftridge every week; but if you're willing, we could do some counseling sessions via video chat."

"I'm willing to try anything at this point," I confessed.

"Good. I'll do whatever I can to help," she said and glanced at her phone. "We still have some time before my aunt comes back. Earlier you asked if you were supposed to be in love with your dead husband as well as Savior. Let's talk about that."

I focused my eyes on the table. "Uh, I don't really know what to say about that."

"Let me ask you this. Why do you see it as a problem?"

"Well, uh, I, um," I stammered. "Because you can't be in love with two people at the same time."

She leaned forward and propped her chin up with her fist. "Why is that?"

I blinked at her in confusion. "Because it's wrong. It's a form of cheating."

"And there it is," she said with a Cheshire-like grin. "The source of your guilt."

"What?"

"You feel like you're cheating on Ian with

Savior, which is why it was easier for you to handle when you were angry with Ian. Did you think that he might have left you for another woman?"

My hand flew up to cover my mouth as I slowly nodded. I didn't want to believe it, and I didn't have any proof, but what woman wouldn't think her husband was cheating on her if he came home from work one day and told her he was leaving without any explanation? "I didn't know for sure, but it did cross my mind more than once."

"And that was enough for you to justify your relationship with Savior. But, that all went out the window when you learned the truth about Ian, leaving you to feel like you'd betrayed your marriage."

I stared at her in complete and utter shock. The feelings coursing through me that I had been unable to identify suddenly had names and descriptions.

"Do you and Savior talk about Ian?" she asked carefully.

I nodded and cleared my throat. "We do occasionally. He told me he would never ask me or the kids to forget about him. He's been unbelievably understanding of the entire situation and even encouraged me to have pictures in the kids' rooms."

She smiled fondly. "That sounds like Savior and his big ole heart. Okay, I have a suggestion for you two. It may seem strange, but hear me out. I think you and Savior should go talk to Ian, together. Tell him about your relationship, tell him about the baby, and tell him how you both feel about the situation. You don't have to hide your relationship from Ian and you don't have to hide your love for Ian from Savior. Savior can love you in a way Ian can't right now, and his heart is big enough to love you, your children, and Ian."

"Damn, you're good," I blurted causing her to smile.

She waved her hand dismissively. "I don't know about all that, but I hope I was able to help. Now this last part is my personal opinion and that's mainly because I don't have a professional opinion to offer on this particular topic. About your son calling Savior 'daddy,' I don't think you should address it unless it happens again. At that point—and you're probably not going to like this—I think you should let the two of them discuss what they're comfortable with. Savior may not like it or Braxton may have simply made a mistake. In other words, don't stress over it right now. You've got enough on your plate as it is."

"Well, I definitely agree with you there."

CHAPTER FORTY-SEVEN

SAVIOR

I was almost finished with my lunch when Copper, Judge, and Batta walked into the diner. Copper handed the waitress a wad of cash and said, "This should be more than enough to cover the tab. Keep whatever's left." Directing his attention to the rest of us, he barked, "Outside," before spinning on his heel and heading to the parking lot.

I swallowed my last bite of food, washed it down with a huge gulp of sweet tea, and rushed to get my ass outside to find out what in the hell was going on. They were back much sooner than any of us expected.

In the far corner of the parking lot, we huddled around the SUV for an impromptu Church. "After briefly speaking with Luca and two of his associates, he felt it would be better to discuss the details somewhere with more privacy. I completely agreed with him until he suggested we continue our meeting at his estate. He understood my concern and assured me he was not looking for trouble with our club. As a show of good faith, he agreed to allow us to keep our weapons, but we can't take our cell phones and will have to consent to being searched for a wire. Coal, Spazz, and Grant will stay back in case shit does go south. Y'all head to the Croftridge clubhouse. Phoenix is expecting you. As for everyone else, let's roll."

"Prez," I called out. "I rode in the SUV with Grant."

"Shit. You take the SUV. Grant, you're gonna have to ride bitch with Coal."

Coal grimaced, but Grant didn't utter a word. When I watched him climb on the back of Coal's bike backwards, I laughed so hard my side started to hurt. Coal pulled out of the lot behind Spazz and Grant gave us a one-finger salute.

On the drive to Luca's estate, I thought about calling Avery. I didn't want to interrupt if she was in the middle of talking to Harper, but I wanted to check on Braxton and make sure she was okay. I convinced myself that Claire would have called me if something was really wrong. Instead, I called the hospital to check on Sienna and breathed a sigh of relief when the nurse told me she was fine.

Ten minutes after I ended the call, we pulled through the gates and followed the long, tree-lined drive to the sprawling, brick mansion situated amid a perfectly landscaped lawn that looked completely out-of-place in the middle of what should be a forest.

I followed my brothers to the front door, feeling extremely thankful that Copper knew what in the hell he was doing. Had I been in charge, I would've looked like a fumbling idiot. Instead of ringing the doorbell or knocking on the front door, Copper stood tall and stared at the door as if he was willing it to open. Moments later, we were greeted by Luca's butler and shown to a conference room in the east wing of the house.

"Mr. Peccati will be in momentarily," he said

and began pouring glasses of water for each of us.

I eyed the glass placed in front of me suspiciously. He could easily poison us all in one fell swoop. I wanted to laugh when every other brother in the room did the same thing.

Five men entered the room; one sat at the head of the table with a man to his left and one to his right while the other two remained by the door. "Allow me to introduce myself. I'm Luca Peccati. These are my business associates, Piero and Cristofano."

After Copper introduced those of us who didn't attend the earlier meeting, Luca began, "I hope I haven't caused you any inconvenience in requesting we discuss matters in a more private location. You understand how these things can be."

Copper nodded in agreement. "We do."

"Allow me to save you some time. If my information is correct, my nephew and his girlfriend have wronged a member of your club and his family. As I understand it, this is the same as having wronged a member of your own family, no?"

"That is correct," Copper said, seemingly unsurprised by Luca's knowledge of the situation.

"And you want to know if I was aware of their

misdeeds?" Luca asked with an arched brow.

Copper leaned back in his chair and crossed his arms over his chest. He pinned Luca with a glacial stare but didn't utter a word.

Luca nodded to himself. "As I suspected. I can assure you and your associates, Mr. Black, that I was not aware of Todd's activities, and for that, I do apologize. My sister's stepson has been…difficult for our family. I have tolerated his behavior out of respect and love for her. But, his most recent behavior is inexcusable."

Luca glanced at Piero, then Cristofano, and exhaled slowly. "Gentleman, if you'll accompany me to the basement."

"Excuse me?" Copper asked.

Luca held out his hands. "I wish to make things right with you and your men. I cannot do so in this area of my home."

Copper gave a slight jerk of his chin and stood. The rest of us got to our feet and silently followed five mafia men to the basement.

It took everything I had to hide my reaction when my eyes landed on the two bodies in the basement. Todd Russo was hanging from the ceiling by his wrists and Kelly was tied to a chair with a gag in her mouth.

"My associates and I have already questioned

them. They were very forthcoming with their answers, but you're welcome to ask any questions you may have."

Copper glanced back to me. I cleared my throat and glared at Kelly. "I want to know why."

Piero untied Kelly's gag and she immediately began screaming demands. "Get me out of here, Kellan! I'm going to have all of your asses when I tell my father about what you've done!"

Kelly continued with her bullshit until Piero silenced her by slamming the handle of his gun into the side of her head. "Perhaps it'd be better if you told them," he suggested to Luca.

Luca nodded. "Ms. Vayer became involved with Mark Pruitt after my nephew was arrested by him for driving under the influence and possession of illegal drugs. The three of them came up with a plan to steal money from me, as well as Mr. Ward. Essentially, Kelly stole one of my license plates in hopes to implicate me in the death of Kellan Ward, and in turn, blackmail me to clear my name. Upon Kellan's death, Kelly would have collected your life insurance money and the remainder of your trust fund, as she is listed as the beneficiary."

I snorted derisively. "That dumb cunt. I changed that shit the day we separated."

"Yes, well, clearly she didn't think of that," Luca said in disgust.

"But why did they target Claire?" I asked.

Luca grimaced. "I'm afraid this part will be unpleasant to hear. To ensure she received all of your money, Kelly needed to be the sole beneficiary. She mistook Mrs. Cameron for Mrs. Parker."

I heard every word he said, but it took a moment or two for it to fully register in my head. "You mean she was trying to kill my unborn child!" I roared.

Batta's hand landed on one shoulder while Judge's landed on the other. "Easy, brother. Rein it in."

"And Todd's role in all of this?" Copper asked while I fumed.

Luca almost snarled at the mention of his nephew. "He's a lazy little shit who thinks he's entitled to the finer things in life simply because his father married a Peccati. I had already reached my limit of patience with him, but he will no longer be a part of this family because he broke the most valued rule—he betrayed us. He plotted against me, he conspired with a police officer, and he almost started a war with you and your club by attempting to kill one of your members." He shook his head. "Greed has been the downfall of many men."

Kelly regained consciousness and started screaming behind her gag that had thankfully been replaced.

Luca clapped his hands together. "Well, no sense in dragging this out longer than necessary. I do apologize, but out of respect for my sister, Todd must be dealt with by me. I hope you understand," he said and fired one round into Todd's forehead while he kept his eyes trained on Copper.

Luca held the gun out to Copper. "But, you may do with her as you wish."

Copper's eyes flicked to mine and I nodded once. Luca held the gun out to me. "I prefer you to use this one. It will be disposed of with the bodies."

I took the gun and let the rage I had been holding back consume me. "I never hated you. Until today. You tried to kill the woman I love and my unborn child for what? Purses and shoes? Yeah, burn in hell, cunt," I said and squeezed the trigger hitting her in the chest. I didn't want her death to be immediate. I wanted her to spend her last few moments knowing she was paying the ultimate price for her selfishness.

CHAPTER FORTY-EIGHT

Avery

After my session with Harper was over, I stayed at the clubhouse for a few more hours to help her and Leigh prepare a few freezer meals before Leigh drove me home. She apologized again for deceiving me, but I assured her I understood. And I did.

When I got out of Leigh's car, I walked into my garage and sent a text to my parents letting them know I was going to see Sienna before I came inside. I knew Riley and Braxton would want to go visit as well, but I tried to limit the amount of times I allowed them to visit because their excitement could be overwhelming at times.

I was happy to see Karen was assigned to Sienna for the day. We worried much less about our little girl when she was in Karen's care. "How's my girl today?" I asked after washing my hands.

"She's doing good. We decreased her oxygen again. So far, she's not had any issues." She filled me in on a few other details and the plan for the week while she helped us get settled in the rocking chair. "Let me know if you need anything."

"I will. Thank you," I said and focused my attention on the little bundle in my arms. I rocked slowly and let my thoughts go down whatever path they chose while I cradled her against my chest.

"Mommy is not going to play the 'what-if' game any more," I said quietly. "I can't change the past, so there's no point in trying to guess what the future would've been. Things happened, and they happened for a reason. And you wouldn't be here if they hadn't happened. So, Mommy is making you a promise right here and now. I'm not going to play that game again, and I'm going to work on accepting the things that happened and finding a way to be happy. But no matter what, I will always love you and your daddy will, too."

After my visit with Sienna, I headed back to my house. I needed to get dinner started for my parents and the kids and I had tons of laundry to do before they went back to school.

"Mommy, where's Kellan?" Braxton asked when we all sat down to dinner.

"He had to do something with Copper today," I lied.

"He's going to miss dinner," Riley cried.

"I'll put something in the fridge for him," I assured her.

"But he's always here for dinner," Braxton pouted.

"Listen, kids, I know you've gotten used to Kellan being around, but he's getting better and will be going back to work soon, so he's going to—"

I was cut off when Kellan entered the kitchen. "Sorry I'm late," he said and kissed the top of my head. "Smells delicious," he almost whispered.

I glanced from the bowl of steamed broccoli in my hand back to him in confusion. "It does?"

He shook his head and winked. "No, but you do."

I felt my cheeks heat and I quickly glanced around the table to see if anyone had heard him. If they did, no one commented, including myself. Instead, I continued plating food and passing bowls.

The rest of dinner was stilted. My parents tried to keep a conversation going, but they finally gave up and we finished the meal in silence. Mom and Dad ushered the kids into the living room while Kellan and I cleared the table and started on the dishes.

I placed a stack of dishes in the sink and collided with Kellan's firm body when I went to take a step back. His hands came around my waist and he buried his face in the crook of my neck. "How are the kids?" he rasped against my skin.

"Good. Riley's ready to get her cast removed, Braxton seems to be fine, and Sienna is doing well."

He gently kissed my skin, causing shivers to run down my spine. "I know we need to talk, but I don't want to tonight. I've had a long day, and I just want to spend some time with Riley and Braxton before crawling into bed with you."

Something in his voice had me slowly turning in his arms and studying his face. Somehow, he looked wound up and exhausted, all at the same time, but the weariness in his eyes was what concerned me. "Did something happen?"

"Yes, but it's nothing to worry about," he said and softly kissed my lips. "We can talk about everything tomorrow."

I placed my hand on his cheek. "Are you sure you're okay?"

"Mommy!" Riley interrupted. "Are you coming to watch the movie with us?"

"I'll be there in just a minute," I promised. "Sorry," I said quietly, "I promised the kids we could have a movie night after dinner."

Kellan's face relaxed a little and his lips turned up in a soft smile. "That sounds perfect. Come on, sweetness; leave the dishes for tomorrow."

As much as I hated waking up to a dirty kitchen, watching a movie with Kellan's arms wrapped around me was too good to pass up. My parents were already situated on the couch while Riley and Braxton were excitedly waiting on the love seat, which left the oversized chair for us. Two seconds after Kellan sat down and pulled me into his lap, Riley shouted, "Hit the lights, Braxton; it's time to enjoy the show!"

I woke to my body being moved. "Come on, Avery, let's go upstairs," Kellan whispered.

I slowly sat up and rubbed my eyes. "Where is everyone?" I asked, followed by a yawn.

"Your dad helped your mom to bed and then he carried the kids up to their rooms."

I got to my feet and glanced at the clock, surprised to see that is was only eleven o'clock. Kellan silently took my hand and led me upstairs. I climbed into bed without bothering to wash my face or brush my teeth, and Kellan did the same after stripping out of his clothes.

When he got into bed, he rolled me so I was facing him and crushed his lips to mine. He wasn't gentle and it reminded me of the first time he kissed me—full of aggression and need. "Fuck, Avery," he mumbled against my skin. "I need you."

"Okay," I said quickly and started pulling my shirt over my head while he divested me of my pants and panties. I didn't want to talk or think. I wanted to get lost in his body as much as he wanted to get lost in mine.

He suddenly stilled and squeezed his eyes shut. "I can't be gentle. Not tonight. So if you want me to go, I will." He paused and visibly swallowed. "I never want to hurt you," he whispered.

I wrapped my hand around the back of his

neck and pulled his lips down to mine. "I don't want you to be gentle."

He kissed along my jawline until he reached my ear. Taking the lobe between his teeth, he bit down and said, "Good," as he unexpectedly pushed inside of me causing my back to arch.

He kept his face buried in my neck as he thrust in and out at a firm and steady pace. I dug my fingers into his back and clung to him, relishing the feel of his muscles moving under my hands while listening to the soft grunts and gasps he released with each stroke.

"Fucking come, Avery," he groaned.

I was close, but he sounded like he was closer, so I reached between us and started rubbing my clit while he continued his punishing rhythm. Moments later, I was using his shoulder to stifle the sounds of pure pleasure that refused to be contained.

We usually found our releases at the same time or he reached his climax seconds after I did, but not this time. He continued at the same pace for long minutes before his thrusts became faster and harder. Then, his rhythm faltered, and his body stilled while he released inside of me.

He didn't move, didn't say a word, didn't press

a kiss to any part of my body. Just when I was about to ask him if he was okay, I felt his body tremble, ever so slightly, followed by a shaky breath. After a few seconds of internally panicking over what to do, I finally did the only thing I could—I wrapped my arms around his shoulders and gave him my silent support. Whatever happened during his day had thoroughly shaken him.

"I'm sorry," he croaked.

"You don't have anything to be sorry for," I said. "You don't have to hide your emotions from me."

"I know," he replied. "Let's get cleaned up and go to sleep. We can talk tomorrow."

I cleared my throat and followed him to the bathroom. "I think we should talk now. You're clearly upset about something and we'll have all kinds of interruptions tomorrow."

"Yeah, I guess you're right," he said quietly and walked back to the bed. Once I joined him, he asked, "Did you talk to Harper today?"

"I did. And while I want to be pissed at you for arranging that without my knowledge, I understand why you did it that way. Plus, she was very helpful, so I feel like I can't be mad," I admitted.

"I knew she would be; that's why I called her.

Do you want to tell me what you talked about?"

"Yeah, I do, particularly because one suggestion she made involves you," I said and told him what Harper said about going to see Ian.

"I've already been to see him, but I'll go with you if that's what you want."

"You what? When?" I asked in disbelief.

"When I realized Grace from the bar was really Avery Parker. I left your house, grabbed some whiskey from the clubhouse, and went to his grave to apologize."

I sat there staring at him at a complete loss for words. "I, you, um," I stammered.

"You don't have to say anything. I just wanted you to know that I understand."

"You're a good man," I told him for the hundredth time. And he was. He was kind, caring, honest, noble—just to name a few.

He bowed his head. "I'm not a good man. Especially not after what I did today."

"What was that?" I asked cautiously.

He kept his eyes focused on the sheets and shook his head. "I can't tell you. It's not that I don't want to, but it's club business, and in this instance, it's better if you don't know any details."

I couldn't contain my gasp. What could

he have possibly done that he couldn't tell me about? "Was it something illegal?" I asked.

He rolled to his back and pinched the bridge of his nose. "Let me ask you this. If you found out the person who ran over your mother was actually trying to run over you in an attempt to kill Sienna and said person was right in front of you, what would you do?"

"I'd kill them!" I said without giving it a single thought.

He reached over and took my hand in his, giving it a soft squeeze. "So would I," he whispered.

I slapped my hands on the bed and sat straight up. "What?"

"Shhh!" he scolded and urged me to lay back down. "It was a hypothetical question."

"No the hell it wasn't. I'm not stupid, Kellan. Now, who the fuck tried to kill me and my unborn child and almost killed my mother by mistake?" I demanded. His so-called hypothetical question was far too detailed to be anything other than the truth.

"Don't ask me, because I won't answer, but if you think about it for just a minute, I'm sure you can figure this out," he said and gave me a pointed look.

I relaxed back into the bed and closed my eyes while I started going through names of who he could possibly be referring to, but couldn't come up with anyone.

"Who's the one person who wanted you and Sienna out of the way?" he prompted.

Once again, I slapped my palms down and pushed to a sitting position. "Kelly!" I exclaimed. "How did you find out?"

He shook his head and grimaced. "Sorry, sweetness."

"Is that what you were doing today?"

"Baby, I can't answer anything you ask. Just know that I made sure those responsible for hurting our family will never be able to do it again."

"Those? As in more than just her?"

"I love you and the kids, Avery. I would do anything to protect you. Anything. And that's what it was—making sure our family was safe, not for vengeance. Part of keeping you safe is not sharing any information that could put you in any kind of jeopardy."

"But what about you? Doesn't it put you in jeopardy?" I asked.

"It's a risk I'm willing to take," he said and pulled me against his chest.

CHAPTER FORTY-NINE

AVERY

I woke up alone and tried to ignore the sinking feeling in my gut while I got out of bed. I knew Kellan and I still had some issues to work out, but I thought we'd made some progress the night before.

I tried to mask my disappointment with a fake smile and went downstairs to make breakfast for my family. "Morning, Mommy," Riley said excitedly.

"Good Morning. What's all over your face?"

Riley smiled proudly and shook her head. "I

can't tell you. It's a secret."

"Breakfast is ready," Braxton mumbled sleepily.

I walked into the kitchen to find nothing less than a feast on the table. "Morning, sweetness. The kids and I made breakfast," Kellan smiled.

"Surprise!" Riley shouted.

"Oh, well, thank you. This is a nice surprise."

"We have another surprise for you," my dad said as he and my mother walked into the kitchen.

"You can walk!" I blurted.

"I'm getting there," she said with a smile.

"That's wonderful!" I beamed.

"All right, everyone, dig in," Kellan announced.

The kids inhaled their breakfast and ran off to play. Both of them still had toys they'd yet to open from Christmas.

"Any plans for today?" my mother asked knowingly.

Kellan wiped his mouth with a napkin as he nodded his head. "Yes, Avery and I need to take care of something after we see Sienna. Do you mind watching the kids for a few hours this afternoon?"

Mom smiled. "Of course not. It's not like I'm

going anywhere."

"You will be soon. I can't believe you walked into the kitchen this morning," I said and tried to hide the hint of sadness in my voice. I hadn't realized how much I missed having my parents close by, but after having them around for the past few months, I didn't want them to go.

"Well, I still have a ways to go before I'm back to my old self," Mom said with a wink. I had the feeling she was up to something, but I couldn't quite put my finger on it.

I got up to start clearing the table, but Kellan took the plate from my hand. "Go ahead and start getting ready. I'll take care of the dishes." It hadn't escaped my notice that he'd already taken care of the dishes from the night before.

"Thank you," I said softly and kissed his cheek.

While I was in the shower, my mind was flooded with thoughts. I had an idea of what we were doing after our visit with Sienna, but a large part of me was trying to ignore the possibility.

A few hours later, when Kellan turned onto an achingly familiar road, I could no longer ignore it. "I probably should have talked to you about this first, but I didn't want you to have time to dread it."

"That was a smart move. Because I would have dreaded it and probably found some way to get out of it, or at least delay it."

"I know, sweetness. But this needs to happen. You and I both know that," he said and gently caressed my cheek. "I'll wait right here and give you some time to yourself."

"Thank you," I whispered. With a deep breath, I got out and walked toward Ian's headstone.

Surprisingly, my nerves and anxiety vanished by the time I reached him. I ran my fingers over the smooth marble and carefully sat down so I could continue to trace his name while I spoke.

"Ian," I breathed. "Why didn't you tell me? Never mind, I know why you didn't. It's been hard for me since you've been gone. I was left with all these unanswered questions and emotions I didn't know how to deal with. And just when I thought I was going to be okay, I found out the truth about Mark. I wanted to be pissed at you. Well, I was pissed at you, but after the initial shock of it all, I was hurt and confused… and I felt guilty. Because I've opened my heart to another man, and I'm sorry, I'm so fucking sorry, but that was so much easier to do when I was mad at you. And then my reason for being mad at you was taken away and reality hit me hard."

"You know I've always believed things happen for a reason, even when they're hard to accept. And somewhere along the way, I forgot about that. But, through the help of some new friends and a lot of soul-searching, I'm starting to see how the pieces are coming together for me and our family."

"I love you, Ian. I loved you with all of my heart when you were here, and I will love you until the day I take my last breath. And I know you would want me and our kids to be happy. I've met someone who loves me and loves our children like they are his own. He protects us and watches over us. He's already put his life on the line once to save our kids and once to save me. He's a good man, and I hope you will give me your blessing to bring him into our family, not as a replacement, but as an extension."

Chills ran up my spine and my skin broke out into goosebumps when I heard the sound of a police siren in the distance followed by a strong gust of wind. I smiled toward the sky. "I'll take that as your blessing."

I gasped when I looked back down. A cardinal was sitting on top of his headstone no more than a foot from where I sat. "Thank you, Ian."

I pushed to my feet and turned to find Kellan walking toward me at a slow pace. "Do you need more time?"

"No, we just finished," I said with a soft smile. I reached for his hand and pulled him closer. "Ian, this is Kellan Ward. Um, I think you two have already met."

Kellan's cheeks flushed as he cleared his throat. "Yeah, I've been here a few times before."

A female cardinal landed on Ian's headstone beside the male who was still sitting there quietly watching us. "Look," Kellan whispered.

"I know. The male showed up right after I asked Ian for his blessing," I said softly. "There's another pair over there, too." Kellan turned to where I pointed and slapped his hand over his mouth. "What's wrong?"

He shook his head. "Nothing," he croaked. "Those are my parents' graves."

Once again, my skin broke out into goosebumps. I turned backed to Ian's headstone. "Message received."

"Avery," Kellan called. When I turned to face him, it was my turn to slap my hand over my mouth. Kellan was down on one knee with a sparkling diamond ring pinched between his fingers.

"I wasn't going to do this here, but I think they want me to," he said and paused for a moment. "I love you, Avery, with every breath of my being. And not because of our past. Because of our future. We were brought together by a power much greater than us. I love you, Riley, Braxton, and Sienna, and I want us to be a family. Forever. Marry me, sweetness."

"Yes! A hundred times yes!"

EPILOGUE

SAVIOR

One Month Later

"Kellan," Riley whispered—which wasn't anything close to a whisper. "We need your help."

"With what? We're supposed to be leaving in just a few minutes," I reminded her and started making my way up the stairs to see what she needed.

"We made a present for Sienna and we want to hang it in her room before she comes home,"

Riley explained.

"Okay," I said and glanced around. "Where's the present?"

She giggled. "In her room."

I followed her to the nursery and came to a complete stop when my eyes landed on a piece of poster board in the middle of the floor. "Isn't it beautiful?" Riley proudly asked.

"I've never seen anything like it," I blurted. "Has your mother seen this?"

"No! It's a surprise for her, too."

I cleared my throat and lied to a child for the first time in my life. "Well, I don't know if I have the right tools to hang it on the wall before we bring Sienna home. But, let's go ahead and show your mom before we leave. I don't want it to get messed up if we leave it on the floor."

"Okay," Riley agreed. "Mommy! Mommy! We got a surprise for you!"

I quickly filled the doorway to intercept Avery. "Sweetness, we'll deal with it later, but they're extremely proud of themselves."

"What did they do?" she whispered.

I knew I couldn't explain and keep a straight face, so I stepped to the side and revealed the picture Riley and Braxton made for Sienna.

"Surprise!" Riley and Braxton shouted.

Avery gasped in horror, but quickly masked it. "Oh, how sweet! You two did this by yourselves?"

"We did!" they both squealed excitedly.

"Oh, thank you!" Avery said and bent down to hug them.

It was all I could do to hold in my laughter. The kids had taken a piece of poster board and created a picture of three flowers with tampons for petals and vibrators for stems.

"Do you like the flower pots, Mommy?" Braxton asked. "That was my idea."

I turned to face the wall and bit down on my cheek to keep from laughing. Because the flower pots were actually unwrapped condoms.

"That was very creative, son," Avery managed to say. "Now, both of you go on downstairs and get your shoes on. We don't want to be late."

As soon as they were downstairs, we both lost it. "What are we going to do? I can't hang that in here!"

"Sure you can. Just say it's an abstract piece," I laughed. "Looks like it's worth a lot of money."

She slapped my arm as realization dawned. "Fuck! They wasted several hundred dollars! I bet my vibrators are ruined."

I pulled her into my arms. "If it makes you

feel any better, I was going to throw those out," I said and kissed the side of her neck. "You don't need them anymore."

"Somehow, I knew you were going to say something like that," she laughed.

"We'll figure this out when we get back. Let's go bring our girl home."

Other Books by Teagan Brooks

Blackwings MC - Croftridge

Dash - Blackwings MC Book 1

Duke - Blackwings MC Book 2

Phoenix - Blackwings MC Book 3

Carbon - Blackwings MC Book 4

Shaker - Blackwings MC Book 5

Badger - Blackwings MC Book 6

Blackwings MC — Devil Springs

Copper - Blackwings MC - Devil Springs Book 1

Judge - Blackwings MC - Devil Springs Book 2

Standalone Novella

Beached

Website

WWW.TEAGANBROOKS.COM

Made in the USA
San Bernardino, CA
18 November 2019